DEACON : THE BLADED

A PARANORMAL VAMPIRE ROMANCE

EVE BALE

Deacon
The Bladed, Book 1

Editor: Beth Hale

Cover designed by MiblArt

www.evebale.com

v3

CONTENTS

Beauty saved the vampire princess from certain death...

A dynastic wedding to a vampire with a lineage
as long as hers?
The plans have been made.
Nurturing the future heir of the Mortlake line?
Set in stone.
Marrying for love and passion?
Not an option.

Vampire Ophelia Mortlake hoped to find a way to slip from the shackles that would chain her to a man she doesn't love. But with her father's seat on the Council in jeopardy, it seems the time for such a miracle has run out. A Bladed has been hired to guard her. There's nowhere to run. More than ever Ophelia realizes just how trapped she is.

As a human member of the Bladed, Deacon Chase never hesitates to put his life on the line in hopes of proving himself to the vampire Council. And in return for his years of service? The vampires reward his sacrifice by having him guard a bratty vampire princess in the days leading up to her wedding.

Then... he looks her in the eyes and knows fate has other plans for them both. Ophelia Mortlake is a caged bird desperate for escape... and every fiber of his being longs to fly free beside her. All that stands in their way is her father. A vampire willing to sacrifice anything to cling to power. Even his own flesh and blood.

This series is a spin-off from the Voracious Vampires of Las Vegas paranormal romance series and is intended for adult audiences.

18+ Contains adult language, sexual situations and mature themes.

CHAPTER ONE

The humans who served as Bladed were good for one thing and one thing only: guarding the feeding rooms from nosey human tourists who viewed rules as nothing more than suggestions.

At least, that was what the vampires had always told Deacon Chase.

But they expected him to play personal guard to a stuck-up vampire princess from the highest enclave above the city? A position which came with a bonus on completion big enough to have him eyeing the supervisor of Bladed recruits, his boss and sometimes friend with suspicion as he waited for the other shoe to drop.

But it was tempting. The bonus. And the challenge too; he couldn't say he wasn't tempted by it. And it would be a change from the tourists sticking cameras in his face or sidling up to him to sneakily take selfies as if he were one of those British guards who for some absurd reason couldn't move.

This wasn't England. It wasn't even America anymore.

Not since the vamps had taken over ownership. Vegas was in the hands of the vamps now, and over the years, people had learned vampires had no hesitation about using force whether or not it was called for.

It'd been one of the first things he'd learned after he'd signed up. That, and the Bladed issued wakizashi short sword could cut through just about anything. Intrigued, he'd stayed—and been the only human in a group of twenty who had.

Deacon was under no illusions about the job. Even if he took it, things wouldn't change for him. Soon, he'd find himself right back where he started. Stuck in the same tiny apartment he'd been in since he'd moved in five years ago. Still earning less. Much less than his vampire counterparts, with no promotion or even the hint of one on the horizon.

But his boss had singled him out for the assignment.

Maybe he'd seen the writing on the wall that he wanted out, and was ready for this year to be his last as a Bladed, since nothing had gone the way he thought it would when he'd come to Vegas in search of a fresh start after the Marines.

At least, outside of Vegas he could work his way up to something better. Here you were nothing unless you had money or you knew someone who did. Being a vampire didn't hurt either.

Pierce was holding something back. Something his boss hadn't wanted to talk about at Bladed headquarters. Narrowing his eyes, Deacon leaned toward him.

"Who's the girl, Pierce? And why does she need a guard, especially up there?"

"Big wedding, haven't you heard? A uniting of dynasties." Pierce slid a black folder across the table, but Deacon ignored it.

"You're fucking shitting me! They realize it's the twenty-first century, right?"

"Keep your voice down." Despite the sternness of his voice, the brief flash of amusement in Pierce's cool gray eyes reassured Deacon that Pierce's supervisory role training up recruits hadn't fully deprived him of his sense of humor. Not yet, at least.

Picking up his beer, Deacon leaned back in the cracked leather booth of the downtown British-style pub that the human contingent of the Bladed liked to spend their downtime in. What little they had of it, that is.

As he took a healthy swig of his lager, his eyes roamed over the pub. Other than an old man nursing a pint of Guinness who looked about to tip off his barstool at the counter, and the bartender who rested his head on a bent elbow and looked close to drifting off, he and Pierce were alone.

The tourists wanted nothing to do with such a worn-down pub where vampires had no interest in visiting. They came to Vegas for the vampires, the gambling, and the clubs—excitement, in short. When the tourists wandered into The Rising Sun Pub, it was to use the bathroom or ask for directions. Not in search of a good time.

"Why me?" he asked, returning his gaze to his boss.

"You've made an impression on the right people. Or wrong." He shrugged. "Who knows, you might like it better than the door work. So, you gonna take a look?"

Pushing his bottle aside, Deacon flipped open the file.

3

He had no recollection of picking up the photograph in it, but suddenly it was in his hand. His eyes locked on the beautiful—no, the word didn't do her justice—redhead who looked to be in her early twenties, all long flowing hair and sensuous curves standing front and center. Fierce arousal spiked as blood went straight to his cock, and in no time whatsoever he was primed and ready to go.

Between the long waves of her red-gold hair, and the expanse of creamy peaches-and-cream skin on show in a pale green slip dress, he wasn't sure where to look first. And that was before he even caught sight of the size of the sparkling diamond on her left hand.

The photographer had caught her leaving a bar, mid-laugh, with her head half-turned to a pale dark-haired woman beside her in a leather dress.

But her eyes…

As his gaze fixed on the green-hazel of her eyes, fringed by long, dark lashes, he saw in them something that had him frowning. Triggered a deeper need than simple lust. A need—his need to protect.

"Who is she?" he murmured, distracted.

"Ophelia Mortlake."

His head snapped up to meet his boss's eyes as he lowered the picture but didn't release his grip on it. So that was the catch then. The reason for the big bonus. He'd be playing personal guard to August Mortlake's daughter, the sole vampire Councilor who'd chosen to make his identity publicly known. "Mortlake, huh?"

"Yep."

"Why me?" Despite himself, Deacon found his eyes

drawn back to the photograph in his hand. Why couldn't he stop looking at her? "I'm human. I'd have thought he'd want only the best for his little girl."

"You're handy with a sword."

"But I'm human," Deacon repeated, louder this time. In case his boss had missed it.

Pierce's snort had Deacon raising his head. "Quit fishing for compliments, Chase. If August Mortlake wants you guarding his daughter, that's what he gets."

"And I don't get a say in this?"

A smile twisted the corner of Pierce's lips. "With a bonus this big and the hungry way you're eyeing the photo, you don't look like a man about to say no. Or am I wrong?"

"But why would a Councilor need a Bladed to guard his daughter?" Deacon asked, pointedly ignoring Pierce's question.

Although Pierce's smile widened, a sure sign he'd noticed Deacon changing the subject, he surprised Deacon by letting it go. "Why don't you ask him?"

"There's something else going on. There has to be more going on than just a simple job guarding a Councilors' daughter. I mean, she's a vamp, right?" At Pierce's nod, he continued. "Surely, she can defend herself."

"She's young."

Fuck.

Deacon's eyes shot back to the photograph in his hand, lifting it closer to his nose. She hadn't looked underage to him, and with the dangerous curves on her—

"Not"—Pierce sounded like he was laughing at him —"that young. Young for a vamp."

"Well, that's a relief." Deacon didn't even attempt to hide how much.

"Hmm, the less said about that, the better. There's a security pass in the file. And make sure you're not rocking a hard-on by the time you get up to the house. I doubt August Mortlake would appreciate it."

"And what makes you say that?" Deacon asked, all innocence. Pierce's clear gray eyes, like those of a sharp-eyed wolf, never missed a thing.

Pierce shook his head. "Might have something to do with her falling out of that sorry excuse for a dress."

Deacon laughed. "I wouldn't exactly call it sorry."

"Hmm. Just... Don't do anything stupid. And get going. Mortlake is expecting you, and you know how vampires feel about waiting. For anything."

Pierce tossed him a pack of mints and Deacon caught it easily. "I don't have my sword, and I'm not dressed for meeting a Councilor."

"Then hope he's in a good mood. Or maybe you could use that famous charm everyone tells me you have." Pierce's voice was so dry, Deacon couldn't help but laugh.

"See, I knew it. You do have a sense of humor hiding under there."

Pierce picked up his beer. "Get the fuck out of here, Chase."

"You shouldn't be here," Ophelia murmured, shooting a glance behind her to where the sound of music drifted from the brightly lit white stone mansion in the distance. "You know how he'll react if he finds you here."

But Selene ignored her. Instead, she grabbed Ophelia's hand, tilting it this way and that as she examined her Tiffany three-carat diamond engagement ring. No one could deny it was beautiful, with a round center stone the size of her thumbnail and surrounded by a cluster of smaller diamonds.

It wouldn't surprise Ophelia if it didn't cost upward of a million dollars.

"So, you're going to go ahead with it then?"

Ophelia shrugged as her sister continued to peer at her ring. "It's not like I have much choice. What are you looking for? Checking to make sure it's real?"

"I wouldn't put it past Byron to try it," Selene muttered, dropping her hand to pick up the bottle of Krug champagne from the immaculate lawn they sat on, their backs pressed against a tree.

Taking a swig from the bottle, she passed it over.

"As if Councilor August Mortlake would let him get away with playing him like a fool. It's real, don't you worry about that," Ophelia said, taking a smaller sip.

She wasn't the biggest fan of champagne, but Selene had been right to bring it with her. If there was a time for her to figure out how much alcohol it took to get a vampire drunk, the time was now.

They sat in silence, gazing out across the manicured lawns to the lake at the bottom of the hill, sparkling with moonlight.

"You should leave," Selene said, her voice quiet.

Ophelia sighed. "You think he'd let me go? You know how big of a deal this is for him."

"I left."

She handed the bottle back to Selene. "Because he let you—because he had plans for me. He'd kill me if I did. You know what he's like."

"Max and I will help you get away."

"He would track me down before I've even left the city. And if they kick him out of the Council... I'd be lucky to survive a day."

"But that has nothing to do with you," Selene said, turning to face her for the first time.

"Of course, it does, you know as well as I do a—"

"Mortlake has always sat on the Council," they both intoned before grinning at each other.

But the smile on Selene's face faded away in mere seconds. Reaching out, she tucked a strand of Ophelia's hair behind her ear with gentle fingers. "You're my little sister, I want the best for you, not to be some little shit's trophy wife or a pawn in the great August Mortlake's game. You deserve to be happy."

"And maybe I will be, you don't know that," she said, forcing cheer into her voice.

Going by Selene's raised eyebrow, she doubted how successful she'd been.

"And anyway, it's not like we even have to see each other if we don't want to. I'm sure we'll have separate wings of whatever mansion we live in, and he will live his own life, and I'll live my own. It's not like I even have to let him touch me for us to have a baby."

"Yes, I can see how excited you are by the prospect

of… how long will your marriage be, exactly?"

Ophelia snatched the bottle out of her sister's hand and downed what felt like half the contents in one gulp.

"I don't want to talk about it," she muttered, lowering the bottle, and wiping at her mouth with the back of her hand.

"Mm, are you sure I can't—"

"I think you've said and done more than enough. Don't you?" an icy voice spoke from behind them.

Ophelia dropped the bottle and scrambled to her feet, desperately trying to smooth the creases, and brush the grass of the back of her Monique Lhuillier black tulle dress. "Father, I—"

Their father glowered down at Selene, who was climbing to her feet at a more leisurely pace.

"*You*," August Mortlake bit out. "You are not welcome here. I believe I made myself clear the last time you saw fit to intrude on my property."

Selene's voice was calm. "Yes, Father."

"You are *not* my daughter," he snapped, taking a threatening step forward.

Ophelia glanced between Selene and their father and gulped. "Father, perhaps we could go inside? I'm sure the guests must wonder what's happened to us."

But her father didn't take his eyes from Selene, and Selene continued to gaze back at him steadily, not at all intimidated by his menacing glower.

"I told you what would happen if you ever stepped foot on my property again," August said, narrowing his eyes.

"It's my sister's bridal shower. I was hardly about to

miss it," Selene said, her voice indifferent.

"You are no longer a part of this family."

Selene's eyes narrowed to slits and she moved forward a step. "That's where you're wrong. Ophelia still is, and will always be, my sister. Nothing you say or do will ever change that."

Ophelia eyed the small space separating them and hesitated about stepping between them. Casting a frantic, desperate glance back at the house, she saw a familiar figure waiting inside the French doors watching events unfold on the lawn.

But, as she'd expected, as soon as her eyes connected on the short, portly figure of their servant Stanley, he stepped back and disappeared from view.

As always, he was absolutely no use to her.

With no help from that quarter, she turned back to find her father... smiling?

That couldn't be good.

"Well, we'll have to see about that now, won't we?" he said, and spinning around, started up the lawn toward the house.

"Ophelia, to the house. Now!"

Left with no other choice but to follow, she started after him, but hesitated and wheeled around to fling herself into Selene's arms.

Selene's arms were around her, holding her in an embrace that didn't feel even close to being long enough to ease the hole her absence had left in her heart. Her breath was warm on her neck, and Ophelia squeezed her eyes shut as they burned with the promise of unshed tears.

Then just as suddenly, Selene released her and stepped back. Her eyes, when Ophelia met them were in the distance, and her lips were a thin line.

"Selene?"

"You should go, sis. We'll speak soon, I promise."

Selene loved her, she knew it with every fiber of her body, and hearing the love in her voice made it a million times harder to leave her. Although her face and body were that of a woman in her twenties, she was nearly eighty and had all but raised her with an overabundance of love and endless patience.

Selene had, without complaint accepted the intrusion of having a squalling baby sister thrust on her by a father disappointed he hadn't had a son.

"Ophelia!" her father snapped.

She jumped. She didn't even know when she'd get a chance to see her again with wedding preparations taking over her life, and her father becoming more and more paranoid by the day.

At least most of her wedding preparations were in the city, and with him busy with Council meetings, and the other things that kept him tied up most nights, she'd be free to meet up with Selene whenever she wanted.

Brightening at the thought, she followed her father up the hill, to where he waited for her in one of the reception rooms filled with French antiques.

"Give me your phone," he said, holding his hand out.

She frowned. "My phone? What do you need it—"

He snapped his fingers, and his face turned white with anger. "Now."

Angling her body away from him so he wouldn't see,

she slipped her cell phone from where she'd tucked it in her bra. Like most of her designer dresses, it didn't come with pockets, so storing it in her bra was the only way she could keep her phone with her.

Taking the phone, he passed it to their servant without looking. "Destroy it. And all the others in the house as well."

"Wait? What!" Her eyes widened as Stanley glided into view and taking the phone from her father's hand, retreated again, tucking the phone from view.

"You are to have nothing more to do with Selene. Not to speak to her at home, nor to see her in the city." His voice was a lash, and she hunched over as she always did when he spoke to her like that, making her feel like she was little more than a child.

"I don't see why—"

"You don't have to see anything," he interrupted. "You just have to do what I demand."

Fear warned her to stay quiet and not cause any trouble. There was a smaller part of her that wanted to argue back, to fight for her sister, to say all the things she felt in her heart but didn't know how to say.

But as always, she stayed silent.

She could never win in an argument with the great and powerful August Mortlake, the Councilor who'd sat on the vampire Council the longest.

How could she when all her life she'd never come even close to making him see things her way? When she was more used to doing what she was told than doing or saying anything that would cause a fuss.

But she could still see Selene if she were quiet; they

might bump into each other in the city. How would Father know if she was careful to let no one see them?

"Yes, Father," she said, her voice soft.

His eyes narrowed and he stepped forward.

"Don't think I don't see your mind whirling. Thinking I'll be busy with the Council and you can do whatever you want, and I won't know."

At her flush, he smiled, looking smug.

"If you think for one second that I'm going to stand by and let anything interfere with this wedding, you're mistaken."

"But Father, I'm marrying Byron like you want. I don't see why I can't see Selene."

Her father stepped forward, his black eyes hard and glinting. "After what she tried to do? I am no fool, Ophelia. You will concentrate your focus and your every attention on the wedding preparations. You will spend time with your fiancé, and any remaining time you have outside of those two pursuits, you will spend them preparing to raise the next Mortlake."

An overwhelming surge of panic rushed over her at the thought of everything changing. In a matter of days, she'd marry Byron, a false, vain vampire who would never care about her. Never love her. And that was before a baby—her and Byron's baby—entered the picture. She hadn't ever held a baby in her life.

It hadn't felt real, even though she'd known all her life this is what her life would look like. But now the moment was here, the thought chilled her.

"Well," a voice drawled from the doorway, "as heart-warming a scene this is, I've been told you have a piece of work for me."

Ophelia spun around at the voice.

And sucked in a breath at the sight of a heavily muscled stranger, a man in black jeans, a long-sleeved black t-shirt rolled up to his elbows, and long blond hair tied back from his tanned face.

Her mouth went dry as she took in his perfection. He was a sun-god. A veritable sun-god. It was the only way to describe him. Perfectly carved cheekbones, a straight sloping nose, full lips curved in the hint of a smile. And that tanned golden skin. She wanted to touch. Her fingers itched to see if it was as warm as it appeared to be.

Until this moment she'd never craved the touch of the sun on her skin as she did right now.

She was staring, she thought as her eyes snapped back up to his face from his forearms. And she wasn't the only one. His unusual amber eyes lazily roamed over her, pausing a beat to linger on the curve of her breasts, and hips before he turned to face her father, giving nothing of his thoughts away.

Her eyes dropped to the distinctive mirrored sunglasses in his hands, and she struggled to force down her panic as she met her father's eyes. The smile that greeted her was the same smile that had been on his face when he tossed Selene out of the house.

"Father, what's going on?"

"As I said, I am no fool. This Bladed will accompany you during all your preparations."

Ophelia could only gape at her father, her mind trying to process what he'd said—what he was telling her.

"You hired a Bladed to watch me," she said, her voice low, stunned.

The Bladed faded into the background. It was the reason they wore black-on-black. It was why they hid their eyes behind dark mirrored shades.

But this Bladed—this perfect specimen of man would never be—could never be a piece of furniture. Not with those thickly-lashed amber eyes she could still feel watching her.

Her father smiled, and cupping a hand around the back of her head, pulled her close to press his lips against her forehead. She fought the need to recoil from his touch.

"Go up to your room. I have some business to discuss with the Bladed," he said, his tone leaving her no room for argument.

Glancing at the man, who continued to watch her as he leaned against the wall with his muscled arms crossing his chest, she sighed.

"Yes, Father," she said, heading toward the door that would take her through the library and into the foyer. It would've been quicker for her to reach the main staircase through the doorway behind her, but that would mean passing far closer to the Bladed with cat-like watchful eyes than she ever wanted to come.

He hadn't brought along the distinctive sword that marked him out as what he was—a well-trained guard under the control of the Council, but that didn't mean he wasn't dangerous.

CHAPTER TWO

*D*eacon stood before the antique cherry wood desk in a library surrounded on all but one wall with floor to ceiling bookcases, and the scent of expensive leather and old books lingering in the air.

He'd been standing in silence for several minutes after following August Mortlake to his office. August sat in his office chair; his eyes trained on Deacon as he stood with his hands folded behind his back, awaiting his instructions.

August was trying to make him uncomfortable. It was a tactic Deacon had come across time and time again during his years in the Marines. And if he hadn't just witnessed August's casual intimidation of his youngest daughter, being stared down by a member of the vampire Council would have resulted in more fear and less disinterest.

"I saw the way you were watching my daughter," August said without warning.

He didn't react to the accusation he heard in the

Councilors' voice. "I have no interest in your daughter." He paused a beat. "Councilor."

August's eyes narrowed. "We'll see about that, won't we?"

Deacon waited for him to continue. August was fishing, and he had no intention of making it easy for the Councilor.

Still, he needed to be careful. Antagonizing a vampire who could snap his neck in a heartbeat was one thing, but pushing said vampire into full blown rage was quite another.

After another pause, August spoke, "Ophelia marries in two weeks. Your orders are clear. You will ensure this wedding goes ahead without a hitch."

"I believe that's what a wedding planner is for."

The ease in which the words rolled off his tongue was enough to have him hiding a wince. Yep, he had a serious problem with August, and it had everything to do with what he'd seen—what he'd heard between the Councilor and his daughter.

August's black eyes hardened as he sat forward in his chair, the leather creaking ominously in the silent room.

"You came recommended," August said. "So highly recommended that your heroics in that delicate matter means separating your head from your shoulders would lead to consequences I neither have the time nor the inclination to deal with."

Deacon's training served him well and his face remained expressionless.

"But, there will come a point when the consequences

will cease to concern me in the least. Have I made myself clear?"

He met August's eyes. "Yes, Councilor."

"Good. You will ensure my daughter has no contact with the woman claiming to be her sister."

Deacon blinked. *Ah!* So, *this* was it then? The reason for his being here.

He'd heard about August disinheriting his oldest daughter. He doubted anyone in Vegas hadn't, not when August Mortlake functioned as the sole public face of the Council.

What she'd done to deserve being cut off and tossed out, he didn't know. All he knew was that the event had happened at the engagement party he'd thrown several years ago.

Did August think the sister had the power to stop the wedding? Surely there were other ways that didn't involve hiring a Bladed to guard Ophelia.

"Yes, Councilor," he said.

"I can see you must wonder why I don't simply kill her?"

"No, Councilor," Deacon said, deadpan. "It is not my role or duty to wonder."

August didn't like that; Deacon saw how much in the tightening of his lips. No, he wanted to control the conversation, wanted to show Deacon he could read him in the same way he'd read Ophelia, but he wasn't about to make it easy for him.

"Get out of my sight," August snapped, his patience with Deacon evidently at an end

"Yes, Councilor." Deacon turned to leave.

"I don't think I need to warn you what will happen if you fail, now do I?" August's voice was silky with both threat and promise.

Deacon didn't respond as he exited the office. If there was ever a question that didn't need answering, it was that one.

Stepping outside, he closed the office door behind him, and finding himself alone in the expansive marble foyer, he let his expressionless mask fall away. He needed to get through the next couple of weeks without killing August, getting himself killed, or ending up in bed with the leggy redhead with the vulnerable eyes upstairs.

If he could manage all three, it'd be a miracle.

Leaning against the wall at the top of the sweeping grand staircase, Ophelia closed her eyes and sighed. Her father thought Selene would convince her to not go through with the wedding. It was the only thing that explained his stopping her from seeing Selene when he hadn't cared about it before.

As much as the thought of jumping into an open-top classic car and roaring into the distance with her hair blowing in the wind appealed to her, it would never happen. Selene was the brave one, the fearless one. Not her.

Selene hadn't even blinked when Father had kicked her out. But Ophelia wasn't like that. If he ever kicked her out, she'd be lucky if she even survived one night on her own.

Suddenly conscious she was no longer alone, her eyes snapped open, and she met the Bladed's eyes. He stood at the top of the staircase, one hand on the banister, and the other clutching his mirrored sunglasses as he watched her.

He stood only a few feet from her. How he'd got as close to her as he had without being aware of his presence made her frown.

"You're not supposed to be up here," she said, in her coldest voice as she straightened from the wall.

His lips curled in a mocking smile. "Because I'm the hired help?"

"No. Because you're here to work for my father, not me, and the less I have to do with my father's creatures, the better." She turned to leave.

"So, I'm not needed tonight?" he asked, following her down the hall.

His steps were silent, but the steady beat of his heart remained as unchanging now as it had when she'd heard Father threatening him a few minutes before.

"Unless you're here to watch me get undressed…" she trailed off, stalking into her bedroom.

"That wasn't on my list of orders." His voice still held that thread of mocking laughter, and Ophelia turned and found him studying her as if she were a curious specimen that he couldn't quite work out.

"No," she said. "You're here for a specific reason, aren't you?"

"So, you were eavesdropping?"

She narrowed her eyes. "I was not eavesdropping."

"Is there another word for listening in to a private conversation?"

"Haven't you heard?" Her voice was bitter now. "There's no such thing as a private conversation in a vampire household."

Turning away from him before he could respond, she strode past her custom-built bed, and into her walk-in closet on the other side of the vast suite. Kicking off her heels, she reached her hands behind her to unzip her dress.

Since her bridal shower was over far sooner than expected, and with her father having apparently sent all her guests home, she had little else to do with herself. It wasn't even midnight yet.

She could go into the city and try to get drunk to distract herself from thinking about the wedding, but it didn't appeal to her. Never mind the fact she'd have to take the Bladed with her.

They'd have to sit in the car, and she'd have to make small talk with him to avoid seeming rude. She hadn't even asked him his name, and listening in to her father's conversation—eavesdropping really, the Bladed hadn't been wrong about that, Father hadn't mentioned his name either.

But whoever this Bladed was, whatever he'd done must have been impressive if he was being recommended to her father.

Sliding the straps of her dress down her arms, she prepared to step out of it when someone cleared their throat. The Bladed. He was still there. He hadn't left.

Spinning around, expecting to see him peering in, she sagged in relief when she found the doorway empty. She was alone in her stark white walk-in closet with its rails filled to bursting with designer clothes, a wall lined with more shoes which made the space akin more to a store than a closet, and a glass case which held her mounds of jewelry. Most of which she never even wore. Someone could have broken in and walked away with half the contents of her closet, and she doubted she would have even noticed.

Swearing under her breath that a stranger who she hadn't even invited in had invaded her private space, she yanked her dress back up. Then she paused, and after a brief second tugged her dress down and stepped out of it. This was her room, her closet and she'd made it clear he wasn't welcome, yet he still didn't seem to get the message.

Glancing at her reflection in the mirror lining one wall of her closet, she eyed the cream silk shift that left little to the imagination and tugged the silver clip from her hair, so it tumbled down her back and settled around her face.

Then she stepped out of her closet. "Oh," she said. "Are you still here?"

He hadn't moved from his position in front of her door.

But as soon as she stepped out of her closet, his eyes turned to her. There was little more than vague disinterest as he scanned her loose hair and silk slip, and Ophelia couldn't help but feel a touch disappointed he didn't show even the slightest bit of interest.

She wasn't vain, but surely, a guy—any normal guy

would show more of a reaction than this Bladed was at a half-naked woman surprising him.

"I need your schedule for the next two weeks," he said, his eyes settling on her face, and not moving from it.

"You can get that from my father."

"I doubt he knows the ins and outs of all your scheduled events and appointments."

She folded her arms across her chest and glared at him. "Since you're his pet, not mine, I'm sure what you get from him will be sufficient."

"Your eyes are more hazel than green when you're angry," he said, leaning toward her. "Like now."

"No, they aren't," she snapped.

Were they? Had no one ever noticed? Surely, Selene would have.

He nodded sagely, as he was imparting great wisdom on her. "Oh, I see. No one's ever told you."

"You're making it up." She needed him to leave so she could go look in the nearest mirror. Instead, he leaned closer. Close enough for her to draw in the scent of his skin, all cedar and warmth, and... beer?

Had he been drinking before meeting her father? What kind of a Bladed would do something that stupid?

And wait a second, was he flirting with her, when he hadn't shown the slightest interest in her near nakedness?

"Ah, so no one's ever noticed, is that it? Am I the first?"

He was talking about her eyes. She knew it. He knew. But hearing him talking about firsts put her in mind of other firsts.

As heat spread over her cheeks, and her nipples hardened, she spun around to hide her reaction from him, intending to retreat into her closet.

"That's interesting." He sounded intrigued, fascinated.

Despite herself, even knowing she shouldn't, she paused. "What?"

"Your eyes."

"Yeah, I know. You already said about my eyes."

"Not that. It's when you're turned on, they turn this incredible shade of—"

Her cheeks burned. "I am *not* turned on," she snapped.

"Emerald jade," he murmured, speaking as if she hadn't interrupted him. "With these fine strands of hazel running through it. I don't' think I've ever seen anything like it before in my life." He spoke as if entranced, as if he were half-dreaming.

Ophelia closed her eyes as the impact of his words hit home. The man was lethal. The things he said and the way he said them... she had no defense against him.

"Ophelia, stop flirting and give the man your diary." Her father's voice rang out to her as clear as if he'd been standing outside her room and she jumped, her face flaming.

Oh god, her father. He'd heard all of it, and worst of all he couldn't have missed her body's response to the Bladed's words.

"Yes, Father," she muttered, and stalking over to her delicate silver and glass desk, conscious of his eyes silently tracking her movements, she yanked open her drawer and scooped out her wedding planner. But when she swung around, his eyes were no longer on her.

He was staring at her bed and his expression was carefully blank. She glanced over and flushed at the sheer number of throw cushions she had on it. It was obscene how many she had.

And it wasn't just her bed. It was everything, she had too much of everything—the Persian silk rugs, delicate antique furniture and the luxe inky-black Parisian drapery covering the double doors leading out onto her balcony. Was all of it necessary? No. Did any of it make her happy? Comfortable yes, but truly happy? Not for a second.

As if feeling her eyes on him, he turned and grinned at her. Boyish and carefree. He'd been toying with her saying the things he'd said about her eyes, trying to get a rise out of her. He hadn't meant a word of it.

She prepared to snap at him, but stopped herself in time. Selene would laugh if she were here. Self-consciousness always seemed to result in her bitchiness to rise to the surface, and without fail, it always sent her sister into peals of laughter.

The sudden sting of loneliness was sharp and unexpected. Catching her unaware. How would she be able to see Selene again with this Bladed guarding her?

With tears threatening, she thrust the diary at him and turned away.

But his hand on her wrist stopped her. Startled she glanced down at the warm weight of his hand, the pads of his fingers rough with the callouses he'd no doubt gained from wielding his sword, and glanced up at him.

His eyes were watchful, and just as he seemed poised to speak, he released her and stepped back.

It was on the tip of her tongue to ask him what he was

doing. What he'd been about to say, but frowning she turned away. They were not friends, would never be friends. Not when she was fully aware his sole purpose for being here was to spy on her for her father.

"You can go now," she said, knowing she was being rude. She'd had enough.

She was tired, lonely, and heartsick. And she wanted the Bladed gone so she could stand under a hot shower and pretend the water running down her face wasn't tears.

"I'll make some notes and return it tomorrow."

Ophelia didn't turn as she continued to the bathroom. "Keep it."

"Aren't you going to ask me my name since we're going to be spending so much time together?" The laughter was back in his voice.

She paused with her hand on the door to her bathroom and turned to face him.

"The Bladed don't have names," she said. "And if they did, I do not need to know it."

His lips twitched, and her eyes dropped, suddenly noticing how full his top lip was. On any other guy, she'd find it attractive—sexy even.

But this was a Bladed—soon to be her keeper. There was nothing about him she found sexy. At least, that was what she told herself.

"Sounds like you were paying attention in school, princess." He smirked, turning to leave, idly twirling her planner in his hand.

Her sadness disappeared under a wave of indignation

that sent heat rushing over her face. "Excuse me!" she spluttered, outraged.

He waved the planner at her. "Deacon. Deacon Chase."

She blinked in confusion. "Deacon?"

"My name. See you tomorrow, princess."

Stepping out, the Bladed closed firmly behind him. He'd had the gall—the sheer gall to make fun of her, to give her a ridiculous nickname when he knew her father was listening.

She glared through the door, hoping he could feel the heat of her anger. "Jackass," she muttered, and stalked into the bathroom, slamming the door shut behind her, her tears forgotten.

CHAPTER THREE

"*Y*ou have to get me out of this, Boss."

"No can do." Pierce's tone was jovial as he continued to scan the file in front of him. "Mortlake requested you by name, and you don't turn down an order from the Council."

"This will not end well. August Mortlake is—"

"If I were you," Pierce interrupted, "I would stop right there."

Though his tone was mild, the warning when he glanced up at him was unmistakable. Deacon heeded it.

"You're saying there's no way out of this? You can't even switch me out with someone else? Surely there'd be volunteers if you spread the word?"

Pierce chuckled. "A position with a hefty bonus and the opportunity to watch Ophelia Mortlake try on dresses? No doubt about it."

Deacon frowned at the thought of someone—of Julian or another Bladed seeing Ophelia in the sheer slip that'd left him hard in record time.

He'd tried not to think about how close they'd been to that enormous bed of hers, a size he'd never seen before and which looked big enough to fit three or four people. But when she'd crossed her arms over her chest which had in turn raised generous breasts barely contained by the silk material…

It'd taken every ounce of self-control to keep his eyes on her face.

"I don't watch her try on dresses, and they wouldn't be…" he trailed off when Pierce raised his eyebrow.

He couldn't say why he'd felt the need to comment on Pierce's throwaway comment, but he sensed he'd revealed a little more of his thoughts than he'd intended.

"Doesn't matter either way. There's no backing out. It's a couple of weeks max, and then you can walk away from the job—from Vegas entirely with enough cash to start over. If that's what you want."

Surprised by Pierce's words, Deacon was silent.

"Did you think I couldn't tell you wanted out?"

"That's not what—" he stopped. Sighed. "I've been in the same position for five years Pierce, no advancement, nothing. I need more—I need to *be* something more than just a door guard on the Strip."

"It'll come. You're making a name for yourself. It's only a matter of time before—"

But Deacon was already shaking his head. "We've had this conversation before. It doesn't matter what I do, whose life I save, I'll only—we'll only ever be human, and human Bladed will never be the same as a vampire. I had more responsibility when I was eighteen in the Marines."

Pushing his file away, Pierce leaned back in his seat

and eyed him carefully. "It's not even been a couple of hours," he said after a long pause. "What has you trying to quit when in all the time I've known you, I've never seen this side of you?"

Instead of answering, he turned to stare at a map of Vegas pinned on the wall.

Pierce had been one of the first human recruits in the Bladed ten years ago when the vampires had taken over ownership of Vegas. He'd proven himself loyal when not all humans had been, and this had been his reward, a tiny office in the basement level of Bladed Headquarters.

Between the desk, Pierce's chair, and his coat hanging on the back of the door, there was nothing else that could reasonably fit inside. It was nothing more than a broom closet, and Pierce had sacrificed too much of his life—ten years of it for it.

In the five years Deacon had served as a Bladed, he hadn't even brushed up against the possibility of a promotion. Was he prepared to wait another five for the promise of a poky freezing cold office? He didn't know.

"I have some concerns about how well the Councilor and I will work together," he said, aiming for diplomacy.

"So, this has nothing to do with Ophelia Mortlake?"

"I don't know what you mean," he lied.

"If she's behaving like a brat, I'm sure you can deal with it in a way without making an enemy of the Councilor."

"As if it were as easy as that," he muttered under his breath.

"What was that?"

Glancing back, Deacon saw Pierce was back to flipping through the paperwork on his desk. He sounded distracted and Deacon was hesitant to repeat himself.

As much as he wanted to trust Pierce, he could only rely on him so far because if it came down to it, Pierce's loyalty lay with the vampire Council and the Bladed, not him.

"Nothing," he said. "I'll see you around." He turned to leave.

"You know you can talk to me, Deacon," Pierce said, sounding a whole lot less distracted than he had a few seconds ago.

Peering over his shoulder, Deacon flashed him a quick grin. "Sure, I can. Later."

The lower floors of the Bladed Headquarters in what had once been a converted hotel on the Strip were quiet as Deacon strode down the narrow hallways. As ever, the lights remained permanently turned on in the building which had its windows sealed.

There weren't many vampires around, less than he'd expect to find during the day as they heading to the gym for a workout. Mostly they still slept during the day, but here they didn't have to since this was a place where the sun couldn't touch them.

The extent the builders had gone to—cementing the windows shut, had showed they weren't messing around in making certain the building was blacked-out to the extreme.

He sighed as his thoughts centered on the real reason he wanted out of his assignment. The reason he could tell no one, least of all his boss.

He'd seen the pain on Ophelia's face, had heard it in

her voice when her icy mask had slipped. She wanted him gone, not because he'd invaded her space, but because she didn't want him to see her pain.

While he hadn't missed her reaction to his comment about her eyes, he hadn't been trying to draw out a response from her.

Her eyes were incredible. Like a stone one of his sister's had pointed out to him once when she'd been into crystals and the like. Jadeite, he recalled. And she had been interested in him. He couldn't help but wonder how much.

But her vulnerability wasn't the only thing about her to surprise him. The photograph Pierce had shown him hadn't done her any justice. If he'd had any idea how beautiful she'd be standing in front of him, he'd have turned Pierce down regardless of the consequences.

He snorted. Who was he kidding; the thought of turning down the assignment had disappeared the second he'd seen her photograph. And the sight of her stepping out of her closet in her silk slip which revealed her slender but curvy form had his cock straining against the front of his pants. He'd never gotten so hard so fast in his life.

Fortunately, his years in the Marines had kicked in and he'd been able to keep his heart rate steady as he'd learned to do in times of stress. So, other than the initial jolt when she'd first emerged, he doubted she'd been able to pick up the extent of his reaction to her. Which was just as well. The last thing he needed was to reveal how strongly she affected him.

Wanting to fuck her was one thing, but this other

thing... this need to save her was dangerous and he had to stamp it out, not when it couldn't lead to anywhere good. He recognized a caged animal when he saw it. The truth of it was always in the eyes.

Emerging from the elevator and onto the main floor, he started for the exit. He needed to grab some food, and then he'd spend the rest of the night going over in detail Ophelia's upcoming wedding events in her planner.

He didn't know if that was how her life usually was—night after night of parties at the biggest clubs and casinos in the city, but to him, it sounded like hell. No privacy. No night to rest and be alone. No spontaneous fun. Everything carefully planned and organized.

He shuddered. Thank fuck this assignment was only two weeks.

At the exit, he hesitated. It was nearly midnight, which meant most, if not all, of the Bladed would be out working, so the training center would be all but empty.

He'd left his workout clothes at home, not expecting to be training today with it being his day off, but he felt sorely in need of some exercise. He'd grab a spare pair of sweats in the changing rooms for those coming straight from guard duty and do some katas on the mat. It might help him burn off some of his excess energy.

Hours after Ophelia had soaked in the bath and washed her hair, she lay dozing in bed, not quite ready to close her eyes, stop her heart, and settle into true rest.

While she'd been in the bath, her father must have

gone out, and his return made it clear where he'd been and what he'd been doing. The heavy scent of blood in the air had her nose twitching as she rose and reached for a towel.

Then her father started shouting, "Stanley! Clean up this mess."

Swinging her legs off the bed, she glanced at her bedroom windows, long since covered with ultra-blackout blinds and the heavy floor to ceiling velvet drapes that served as added protection from even the hint of sunlight. Although twilight was mere minutes away, a deep sense of unease filled her at the thought of still being awake. Ignoring the feeling, she padded on bare feet to her bedroom door.

As she stepped out into the hallway, the rich scent of blood that hung in the air had her stomach cramping in hunger, and her fangs extending at the thought of feeding. But hunger fled at the sight awaiting her as it had the last time she'd seen it.

Her father stood at the top of the stairs with blood soaking through his shirt, molding the material to his body. Blood covered his face and his hair. He looked like he'd survived a massacre, which, considering what he'd done, wasn't far off the mark.

"Ophelia, you should be sleeping," he said, his black eyes lit with a familiar wildness when she continued to stare at him in silence.

"Sire?" Stanley said from the foyer downstairs.

Her father turned to their servant. "There's a mess on the grounds and in the car. Deal with it," he said, before he sauntered in the opposite direction toward his wing with bouncing energetic steps.

Waiting until she heard his bedroom door snicking closed, she started for the stairs. Pausing halfway down, she watched as Stanley disappeared into a coat closet. Seconds later, he emerged with an armful of black sacks.

How long could he keep on doing this? His hair was already more gray than black now, and he hadn't exactly been young when she'd been a child. He had to be in his sixties now going by the lines on his face.

Reaching for the front door, Stanley paused and turned to face her. "Miss, it's time for your rest. The sun is rising."

She knew it, could feel a tingling on her skin—an uncomfortable itch she could never scratch, and a pervasive heaviness in her very bones. Her body warning her with increasing volume she should already be sleeping. Stanley waited for her retreat in silence.

He wouldn't open the door, not while she was still there. While he may be another of her father's creatures, he'd helped raise her and he wouldn't let any harm come to her.

"There's more blood—more bodies than last time," she said, in a whisper, unsure if she were talking to him or herself.

"Mistress?"

Shaking her head, she turned and started back up the stairs.

"Good night, Stanley."

"Good night, Mistress."

Walking slowly up the stairs, she felt his eyes on her back until she closed her bedroom door behind her.

Leaning against it for a moment, her preternatural eyes scanned the cool darkness of her room, pausing on the empty spot on her bedside table. Where her phone used to be.

If Stanley was anything, he was thorough, which meant if her father told him to ensure she didn't have access to a phone in the house, Stanley had made sure there was no cell or landline anywhere.

She closed her eyes.

How she was going to get through the next two weeks without Selene by her side, she had no idea. But somehow, she had to find a way.

CHAPTER FOUR

"*I* thought your father was giving a speech tonight?" Deacon asked.

Ophelia, sitting beside him in the sleek black Mercedes as her driver made his way toward the Strip, kept her gaze pointed out of the window. "He will be, just... later, I guess."

"You guess?"

She turned to scowl at him. "I've never done this before, so please forgive me if I don't know every little thing that's supposed to happen."

"The norm," Deacon said, "is for a bachelorette and bachelor party to be separate. At least they have been in all the ones I've been to. Didn't your wedding planner go through all this with you?"

Flushing in embarrassment, she ripped her gaze away from his and resumed staring out of the window as she continued to twist her engagement ring around her finger. "I'm sure she did. But I... I had a lot on my mind then."

Deacon made no comment. He hadn't been trying to embarrass her, but he'd done it anyway. Best he didn't say anymore.

Studying her, he couldn't shake the feeling that something was wrong with her. Had been since before he'd arrived at the Mortlake mansion in the super exclusive enclaves high above the city where only the wealthiest vampires lived.

He'd had to pass through three gates guarded by Bladed on his drive up. But even on reaching the final check post, the security pass Pierce had given him had been examined just as closely as before, despite it being the same vampire who'd checked him in the night before.

He'd found her dressed and ready to go in a clingy burgundy silk dress, her makeup immaculate, and not a hair out of place as she waited for him in one of the reception rooms.

It'd taken no more than a cursory sweep of the room for him to realize that the delicate antique furniture wouldn't hold his weight, and the room felt just as cold and formal as all the other's. More akin to a museum than a home.

The quiet panic he'd caught glimpses of in her hazel-green eyes had warned him her mind wasn't as calm as she'd first appeared. And there'd been no sign of August, nor any servants, if there were any beside Stanley who'd let him in before disappearing into the bowels of the house.

But that wasn't the only thing he'd noticed in the all too quiet mansion. On the banister, at the bottom of the stairs had been a bloody handprint.

He'd examined her as they left the house, but she hadn't appeared to be injured. But then again, she was a vampire. If she'd been hurt after he'd left last night, she'd had more than enough time to heal herself.

"Ophelia?"

"Yes," she murmured, her gaze still outside, sounding distracted.

"Did something happen last night?"

She glanced at him, and for a split second, he thought she might tell him. But as he watched, a brief flash of vulnerability disappeared behind a veil of icy indifference. If he hadn't seen it, he would have doubted its existence.

Her voice was frigid. "I don't see how that's anything to do with you. You're not even a vampire. I'd have thought you'd know by now not to stick your nose where it doesn't belong."

Deacon nodded, and removing his mirrored glasses from the pocket of his black suit, he slipped them on. "Whatever you wish, Mistress Mortlake."

Her lips tightened at his use of her formal title, but she didn't respond even though he could see she wanted to.

Her gaze returned to the window, and the silence between them was sharp with tension.

At the entrance of the Wynn, Deacon climbed out of the car first, scanning the hotel arrivals dragging suitcases in their wake as they surged past the white stone columns, and in through the glass entrance, as he strapped his sword around his waist. Then turning, he held his hand out to Ophelia.

She stared at his hand in silence, but after a brief hesitation, she placed her hand in his and he tugged her out of the car.

Up close, she smelled exactly how she looked—expensive and rare. Unlike any woman he'd ever met.

He couldn't be sure if it was the creamy softness of her skin or the lush scent of it that made him want to crowd her. Probably a combination of both, he thought as the feminine scent of her, a warm rich vanilla and an elusive flower that was both fruity and woodsy, tickled his nose.

The coldness of her hand surprised him, and even though he knew he was physically blocking her from entering the hotel, he didn't move.

Lowering his head, he spoke directly into her ear. "When was the last time you fed, princess?"

At his words, she yanked her hand from his and stepped around him.

"Not your concern, and stop calling me that," she hissed under her breath.

Even in five-inch heels, she moved fast, and Deacon shook his head, impressed as he caught up to her at the door.

She'd soon learn he wasn't as easy to ditch as that, he thought, as he stuck like glue to her side.

A vampire peeled himself away from where he stood in front of a tall potted plant and approached, clipboard in hand. His glance took in Deacon and the short sword strapped around his waist, before stopping a few feet away. "Mistress?"

"Ophelia," she said. "Ophelia Mortlake."

The vampire nodded. "Yes, of course. You're early—the first arrival."

"I'm assuming you're here to direct me?" Narrowing her gaze at the vampire, she peered down her nose at him as if she doubted his ability.

Deacon raised an eyebrow, grateful his glasses hid the act.

Now, this was the vampire princess he'd been expecting to meet once Pierce had told him who she was.

"Of course, Mistress. The Sunset Terrace is this way," the vampire said, leading her through the lobby.

She was drawing attention. The way she swept through the entrance in a dress that clung to and flowed over her curves, drew both male and female eyes to her.

She gave the impression of being royalty, or famous, and the guests to the hotel, standing about, murmured to each other, pointing and nudging each other as Ophelia brushed past them.

But she didn't react in any noticeable way to the lingering stares she was receiving. Instead, her gaze remained focused on the thin vampire with the clipboard leading the way through the lobby, past the long, marbled check-in counter and toward their private event.

When they reached the terrace for the sunset cocktail party—an outdoor space with lush plants and trees, the scent of exotic flowers heavy in the air, and tables with glasses of blood-spiked champagne dotted here and there, Deacon saw the vampire had been mistaken.

Ophelia was early, but she wasn't the first person there.

41

A woman with long black hair, black kohl-lined eyes, and pale skin rose from a table and approached.

Her tight leather jeans looked painted on, and a hot pink bra was clearly visible through her lace top. She was undeniably beautiful, but more striking than Ophelia's classic beauty.

Deacon studied her in silence. He'd seen her before. And recently.

"Excuse me," the vampire with the clipboard said with a frown. "But this is a private party, and you—"

"Don't care," the woman interrupted, never taking her eyes from Deacon's face.

"But I—"

"You can leave," Deacon interrupted, cutting the man off as the raven-haired woman studied him.

She looked like the woman who'd been in the picture with Ophelia that Pierce had shown him. And after his meeting the previous night, he'd had long enough to stare into August Mortlake's black eyes to spot the resemblance.

This must be the sister. The one August had disinherited.

What had her name been again...?

Sarah... Ste—*No*, Selene. Selene who'd once been a Mortlake, but was one no longer.

After a few seconds of hesitation, the sharp sound of the vampire's footsteps announced his withdrawal from the courtyard.

He could feel Ophelia's eyes on him, but she didn't speak, seemed instead to be waiting for him to say or do something.

"Ah! A guard. So that's what he was talking about. I'm guessing you're under strict orders to keep me away from Ophelia?" Selene asked, looking more amused than anything else.

He didn't respond. Without a word, he retreated a step and turned his gaze outward, so he faced the door the vampire had left.

"Mm," he heard her murmur. "A Bladed not bending over backward for a Councilor? Isn't that interesting, Fifi?"

Fifi?

Deacon's lips twitched, grateful neither woman could see his reaction.

"For the love of... I told you to stop calling me that," Ophelia snapped, sounding exasperated. "It makes me sound like a pampered poodle."

Selene chuffed out a laugh. "Of course, you're pampered, and spoiled, just look at those pretty curls..."

"You just live to drive me crazy, don't you?" Ophelia muttered.

Deacon fought back another smile. It was a relief to know she wasn't alone. That she had someone to laugh with. Living under the same roof as August Mortlake could hardly be a barrel of laughs.

"Don't all big sisters? Anyway, I can't stay long," Selene said, sounding like she was leading Ophelia away. "But I had to see you. Now tell me what's wrong?"

He'd been right. There was something wrong with her, and whatever it was must have had something to do with the blood on the banister? Had it been hers, August's, or someone else's?

"He's started…" In the brief pause which followed, Deacon felt eyes digging into his back. "…doing it again," Ophelia said.

Selene snorted. "As if he ever stopped. You all right?"

Curiosity piqued, he couldn't help but try to work out what it was they were talking about. The only thing he could make out was the sisters were talking about August Mortlake, something neither of them wanted him to know.

"I'd feel better if he hadn't taken my phone," Ophelia said.

"Can't you—"

"He got Stanley to get rid of all the others in the house as well."

Deacon narrowed his eyes at hearing that. He was liking August Mortlake even less and less. How controlling could a person be?

"I could—"

But Ophelia interrupted Selene again, "No, there isn't anywhere I could keep any phone you gave me safe. And if Father found it…"

Selene swore, loudly and colorfully.

Deacon turned his head to look at her, impressed. He hadn't thought a woman raised with the wealth and privilege Selene and Ophelia had would even know how to paint the air blue quite like Selene had.

"Ravenborne Academy," Selene told him. "You'd be surprised at what you pick up in boarding school."

When she turned back to Ophelia, he resumed his close examination of the door.

"I'll be okay, Cee," Ophelia said.

Listening to her, Deacon wasn't sure he believed her. There was a softness to her, a gentleness he couldn't help but notice every time he met her eyes.

"Of course, you will, you're a Mortlake."

"Because being a Mortlake is all that."

"Hey, things will work out. I promise. Now, give me a hug. I'd better get out of here before people start arriving."

Turning around, he watched the sisters embrace.

"How did you even know to get here when you did?" Ophelia asked, her voice muffled against her sister's shoulder.

"When were you ever late for an event, Fi? I'll try and see you again."

"But how when I don't have my phone?"

Selene's face hardened. "Don't worry, we'll figure something out."

"I love you, Cee."

"I love you too, Fifi."

Her mood had plummeted as soon as Selene left.

The only person who knew and cared for her wasn't at her bachelorette party, and although everyone who was anyone in Vegas had accepted their invitation, she'd have been happier if the only person to turn up was Selene.

She had no idea where Byron was, and for that, she couldn't help but be grateful that she didn't have to deal with his presence.

Then there was her father who was due to give a speech in less than an hour, and who hadn't even turned up yet. And when he did, would he have that wild light in his eyes?

Or would he be the charming Councilor periodically trotted in front of the cameras to stem the public outrage when yet another vampire killed a human?

Through it all, as the minutes ticked on, and as she fought to keep her mask of indifference on her face, the Bladed watched her. Even behind his mirrored sunglasses, she felt the intensity of his eyes as he watched her.

He was drawing attention, and she'd already had to dodge countless questions about why she would need a Bladed to guard her. In the end, she'd chickened out and after blurting out she needed fix her makeup, she'd rushed in the bathroom and left him to wait for her outside.

Her father had warned him to stop her from seeing Selene. She couldn't help but overhear, and Father had to have known she was listening to their conversation as well.

But the Bladed—Deacon hadn't. He'd done the opposite, not only getting rid of the vampire with the clipboard, but he'd turned his back to give her and Selene at least an illusion of privacy, even though he couldn't give them the real thing.

Raising a hand to her throbbing temple, she closed her eyes and wished the jazz band performing would stop playing for five minutes.

Deacon had been right to ask her about when she'd

DEACON : THE BLADED

last fed. It'd been too long, and the headache was just another sign she needed to feed and feed soon.

"Move," a woman snapped from just outside the bathroom door.

There was a lengthy silence.

"I told you to move," the woman repeated, her voice rising.

Opening her eyes, she turned to the bathroom door with a frown. She knew that voice.

Where did she...

There was a faint hiss of metal.

Was the Bladed drawing his sword from his sheath? Is that what that sound had been?

In two seconds flat, she was at the bathroom door, yanking it open.

Deacon stood with his back to her as he blocked a small circle of women from entering.

Ophelia didn't know what to say. She'd found it unusual no one had tried to enter the bathroom in the fifteen minutes she'd been inside. But it'd never crossed her mind that Deacon would stop anyone else from encroaching on her privacy.

"Oh, is he with you, Ophelia?"

Watching as Deacon slid his sword back into his sheath, she turned to face the beautiful blonde woman, model thin in a turquoise dress.

A woman who made Ophelia conscious she wasn't as tall, as thin, or as beautiful.

Over the years, she'd had more than her fair of men who'd hopped straight from her bed to Lenore's.

"Lenore. I'm pleased you could make it," she said.

Lenore didn't take her eyes off Deacon. Her deep brown eyes, remained fixed on him.

Ophelia had seen that look on her face before, just before she'd snapped a server's neck for accidentally spilling a drink on her dress.

Deacon had been right to go for his sword.

"I'm sure you are. Why do you have a Bladed guarding you?"

Although Lenore was talking to Ophelia, not once did she take her eyes off Deacon. For just a second, unexpected jealousy stirred.

Lenore was a predator, there were no two ways about it, but she was stunning and there weren't many men who could ever—*would ever*—turn her down. But that was stupid; if the Bladed wanted to hook up with Lenore, so what?

Ophelia shrugged as if it didn't matter. "Father insisted. Did you need the bathroom?"

"Not anymore. But he's human. What's the point? What good is a human Bladed, anyway?"

Lenore's three friends who also seemed to no longer need the bathroom either tittered, their eyes malicious as they soaked up all the bitchiness oozing out of Lenore. God, they were pathetic.

Ophelia forced a smile on her face. Not only had Deacon done nothing to deserve it, but he was also a Bladed and a well-trained one at that.

And although he showed no reaction to Lenore's words, they incensed her as nothing else had done before.

What was is with this Bladed stirring raw emotion to

the surface? And how was he able to do it without his even having to say a word?

"I'm sure Father had his reasons."

"Perhaps he doesn't believe you're capable of protecting yourself?"

She shrugged. "Perhaps. Did you want something?"

"He's pretty," Lenore said her eyes turning hungry as she moved closer toward Deacon and trailed a finger down his arm. "I'm sure I can find a better use for him."

Deacon's blank expression didn't change, but Ophelia had the sense he didn't like Lenore touching him. For all Lenore was one of the most beautiful women in the city, she'd hardly made the best first impression.

"I'm sure you can. But the Bladed are busy, too busy to be warming your bed... if he could find some space in it that is. Perhaps you'd better look elsewhere."

Lenore's eyes snapped to her for the first time. Her lips curling into a sneer, Ophelia prepared herself for more of Lenore's poison.

"Mistress Mortlake?" a voice interrupted.

The vampire with the clipboard stepped forward when he saw he had her attention. "Sorry to disturb you."

"Yes?" she asked.

"Your father has arrived and is requesting your presence."

"Of course." She turned to Lenore. "If you'll excuse me."

Stepping around Lenore, she felt Deacon close behind as he trailed her down the hallway and back to the main room. He didn't speak, and neither did she.

It was only as they re-entered the party where people

stood around chatting to each other and sipping blood-spiked champagne that for the first time since they'd arrived, Ophelia felt Deacon's attention shift from her.

Glancing behind her, she found his head tilted away from her, with one hand hovering near the hilt of his sword.

"Deacon, what is—"

"Ophelia. Where have you been?" her father's voice cut through the sounds of the guests, and the music in the background.

Looking at him, no one would have been able to guess what he'd been doing, and how he'd looked hours ago. There was not even the hint of madness in his eyes as he frowned at her with his perfectly coiffed hair, and smart tailored pants and shirt.

"Powdering my nose, Father," she said, offering her cheek for a kiss when he leaned down to her.

Behind him, her eyes fixed on a vampire approaching she hadn't seen earlier. He'd probably only just arrived, she thought. In his suit and white shirt, a briefcase tucked under his arm, looking newly arrived from work.

Perhaps he was one of her father's attorneys or accountants...

"Father," she said. "I think there's someone who wants to—"

A short black sword, identical to one only the Bladed wielded appeared in the man's hands, blurring in motion as the vampire slashed it at her father's neck. Only her father was no longer there. But she was.

She froze. But her father didn't.

The next moment she was sucking in a sharp breath as

her throat... burned with agony. At the same time a hard grip on her arm was propelling her back.

She hit the ground hard, her hands instinctively clamping around her throat.

Gasping at the sharpness of the pain, she blinked rapidly as she fought back a sudden need to cry. And then Deacon was crouching beside her, clutching a bloody sword in his right hand.

Her gaze drifted behind him. Took in the crowd stood frozen as they stared at her, their faces and clothes painted with blood.

Her blood.

Only the sheer volume of it didn't seem right. The vampire had cut open her throat, but had she really lost that much blood in such a short time?

Then she remembered the blood on Deacon's blade.

There was a body on the floor, and someone's head as well.

The two were no longer attached.

Lenore stood close by, her mouth hanging open as she stared down at Deacon.

"Ophelia?" Deacon asked, drawing her gaze back to him.

Opening her mouth to speak, his eyes dipped to her throat and he shook his head.

"No, don't speak. Let's get you out of here."

Was it that bad then? Her heart pounded harder. It must be bad, much worse going by the look in Deacon's eyes.

After slipping his sword back into its sheath, he bent to lift her.

"They dare…"

Deacon paused, and Ophelia's eyes found her father. His eyes were on the dead vampire, and his face was as blood splattered as those around him.

"They would dare…" he spoke in a low whisper, no less terrifying for its lack of volume. His face was an icy mask, and his black eyes whirled with a fury Ophelia had never seen before.

The crowd edged away from him.

Deacon seemed to be the only one in the room not held transfixed by her father's rage. Scooping her up, he rose. Her hands remained clamped around her throat.

The blade had cut deep, and Deacon, the human Bladed Lenore had mocked in the hallway moments before, had prevented the attempted assassination of her father, saved her life, and killed the person responsible likely before anyone even knew what was happening.

Lenore was probably wondering what would have happened if Deacon had drawn his sword in the hallway. Would she have seen it coming?

"Take her home," her father snapped, and then he was stalking away, the crowd scattering around him.

Deacon didn't slow, or even acknowledge her father's order as he continued through a crowd that silently parted around them.

CHAPTER FIVE

*O*phelia's blood soaked the front of Deacon's shirt as her head sagged against his shoulder. He frowned as a steady flow of blood continued to pour from her wound.

"Ophelia?"

The driver rounded a corner a little sharper than Deacon would have liked, making Ophelia gasp, and he lifted his head to glare at him through the glass separating them.

Ophelia murmured something beneath her breath, and he turned away from the driver to look into her face.

It was pale, bone white even and her blood was a vivid splash of bright color against the paleness.

"Come on, princess," he muttered, covering her hand tightly with his to apply more pressure on her wound.

Her eyes opened, but immediately closed again. "Whaaa…" she slurred.

Relief surged through him she was still conscious, that the sword hadn't cut her vocal cords. Still, it wasn't enough to silence his fears. She'd lost a lot of blood—was still losing more, and there was no sign of it stopping.

She should already be healing. Why isn't she?

Although the attack would have been enough to kill anyone else, she was a vampire. She shouldn't be bleeding to death in his lap. It didn't take him long to work out the reason why.

"You haven't been feeding, have you, princess?" he murmured into her ear.

Though her eyelids flickered, she didn't respond.

"Why is that?" He glanced out of the window as he tried to figure out what his next steps would be.

There was enough traffic on the road that they still had a fair way to go until they'd reached their destination. And with the condition she was in, the last thing he wanted to risk was moving her, or potentially exposing her to more danger. Not that he could think of anywhere safer to take her than where he'd directed the driver. Still, he was having serious doubts she'd still be alive when they got there.

He'd spent a bit of time researching her, and he'd learned she was still young for a vampire. August had turned her soon after her twenty-first birthday over ten years ago, and ten years as a vampire wasn't nearly enough time for her withstand an injury like she'd suffered.

It took time for a vampire to grow into their immortality, which made a strange kind of sense when he thought about it. He'd heard the process could take anything from thirty to fifty years for immortality to 'take'.

He didn't know if Pierce had told any of the other human Bladed, but it wouldn't surprise him if he had. Ignorance was dangerous, Pierce was fond of saying, and he didn't like the idea it might one day kill them.

Brushing strands of bright copper hair from her face, he came to a decision. What he was about to do wasn't something he'd ordinarily ever agree to, especially when he couldn't be sure Ophelia wasn't still a target.

Right now he needed to be sharp, ready to act, and at the top of his game. The last thing he needed was to be weak, and less than his best in case whoever had tried to separate August Mortlake's head from his shoulders turned their attention to his more vulnerable daughter.

Leaving one hand on her neck to stem the bleeding, he pressed his other hand against her cheek. Her skin was icy cold to the touch, and as she lay limp in his arms, he saw the unmistakable tinge of blue around her lips.

He had no choice. If he didn't do something, and soon, he'd lose her.

"Ophelia?"

Silence.

"Ophelia?" he repeated.

Yet more silence.

"Princess!" he snapped, letting her hear the sharp anger in his voice.

Her eyes fluttered open, and she blinked at him tiredly. "Deacon?"

He bent close to her. "You need to feed."

She stared at him, confusion shadowing her face. "I don't…"

"You're not healing. Which means you need to feed."

She shook her head. No, her entire body was shaking. Shivering as if she were cold. "No, I..."

Deacon bent closer. "You are going to die if you don't feed," he spoke slowly. "And since I'm the only one here, I guess I'm going to have to be the volunteer."

Her eyes widened, and she struggled. "I can't feed from you. I can't."

If nothing else, the weakness of her struggles revealed just how bad of a state she was in. There was so little strength in her it required barely any effort to hold her still.

He'd been a Marine, and he worked out enough that he knew his own strength. Still, Ophelia was a vampire. It shouldn't have been this easy for him to stop her struggles. The thought that she could die in his arms had his heart lurching.

"Suck it up, princess. Whatever you feel about me doesn't mean shit right now. Drink, or die. Or does living —does your sister mean so little to you, you'd rather die instead of fight to live?"

She flinched. Dropping her gaze to his throat, she swallowed.

"What if... what if I can't stop?" Her voice was a thread of sound.

Deacon didn't even have to think before he answered her, "you can."

She lowered her head further. "What if I don't want to?"

He almost didn't hear her as he regarded her bent head in silence. There was something going on with her. Was that fear in her voice? Fear about feeding?

Shaking his head, he shoved the thoughts aside. Now wasn't the time for it. Not when she was sagging in his arms again, the fight going out of her. He'd think about it when he didn't have her bleeding to death in his lap.

He caught her chin and raised her head a little, being careful of her wound. Just enough for him to meet her eyes.

"You will." His voice was firm. Absolute.

She blinked at him. Doubt swirling around in her eyes, but she then she nodded.

"Okay," she whispered. "Okay, I'll do it."

Leaning his head back against the seat rest, he tilted his head as she bent her face to his throat.

At the first swipe of her tongue at his pulse point, he clenched his jaw.

When her fangs punctured his skin, desperately he grabbed at the back of her head. Holding her face against his neck, he was powerless to silence his deep groan at the erotic pleasure-pain of her bite. His hands tightened in her hair at the incredible feel of her feeding on him.

His eyes fluttered closed as the pressure of each sucking motion went straight to his cock, growing harder and harder. This. Her. It was unlike anything he'd ever felt before, and he was desperate for it to never stop.

Over the years, Deacon had more than his fair share of women nuzzling his neck during sex. But the feel of Ophelia's tongue lapping at the sensitive hollow of his throat, and the eager hungry sounds she was making had him ready to explode.

When she shifted in his lap, her small hand brushing

against his straining cock, he started fumbling with the buckle of his sword belt, and shoved it away.

His sword hit the floor with a dull thud as her hands slipped under his shirt. He needed to be inside her. Now.

The soft strands of her hair brushing against his throat drew another desperate groan from him, even as his hand left her hair to stroke down the curve of her back. Then her hands were on his belt, as his hand continued down her hip and to the hem of her dress.

Once she released him from his pants, all he would need to do was lift her dress over her hips and he could be inside her in seconds.

His cock twitched at the thought, and even as he was tugging the hem of her skirt up, she suddenly froze.

Blearily, he struggled to remember how to speak, but before he could say a word, she was throwing herself out of his arms. She stared up at him from the floor, her back pressed against the glass partition.

All he could do was blink down at her in confusion, his cock straining in his half-open pants. Then at the feel of something sliding down his neck, he raised his hand to investigate what it could be. Glancing down, saw blood coated his fingers.

"Ophelia?"

Her eyes fixed on his neck. She licked her lips. Then she rose, and before he could do little more than blink, he felt a warm firm stroke of her tongue against his neck, and then she was back against the glass, her arms wrapped around her legs.

"I drank too much," she whispered. "I've weakened you."

He felt fine. A little tired, and in need of a drink, but otherwise he was okay, he thought as his eyes took in the wound on her neck. What had once been a gaping wound was one no longer. In its place was a straight red line going across her neck, fading as he watched.

That a couple of pints of blood, or however much she'd taken could heal such a devastating mortal injury in seconds was nothing short of amazing, and he shook his head at the sight.

When he lifted his gaze, he saw she'd turned away from him. Was pointedly staring out of the car window as if she couldn't bear to look at him.

Suddenly conscious that his pants were half-open and his sword, a weapon he valued more than anything else in his life was lying abandoned at his feet, he was trying to figure out what to say to her. But then the car ground to a stop.

She was out of the door before he could stop her. But she didn't go far.

"Deacon?"

Zipping up his pants, he picked his sword from the floor and followed her out of the car to where she waited for him just outside.

"This doesn't look like my father's house."

"That's because it isn't. Come on."

Ophelia stared at Deacon's back as he drew the curtains closed.

Her father had ordered him to take her home. She'd

heard him say it clear enough, but he'd brought her here, to his place. Somewhere no one would know where she was. A place where even she didn't know where she was.

"You probably want a shower," he said, tossing his sword onto a worn black couch.

Having a shower would mean getting undressed, which would mean being naked in Deacon's apartment.

She didn't move from her spot beside the front door.

On his way through a door leading to his bedroom, he glanced back at her before stopping when he realized she hadn't moved. "I'm not going to hurt you."

"My father told you to take me home. This isn't home."

"This is home. My home," he said, a hint of a smile on his lips.

"That isn't what he meant, and you know it." She turned to leave.

"And where do you think you're going?" he called after her, sounding amused.

Grabbing hold of the door handle, she twisted. "Home. My home. You know, the place my father ordered you to take me."

"Right," he said. "You mean where everyone heard you would be, too weak to fight off another attack? And how do you plan on getting there when I sent the driver home?"

She paused.

She'd noticed him leaning in through the driver's side window before he'd led her into his apartment complex. But at the time she'd been more distracted with what had nearly happened between them in the car to be paying much attention to the driver. It certainly hadn't crossed her mind that this would not be a quick stop on their way back to her home.

"What do you mean?"

"I'm sure it hasn't passed you by someone tried to kill your father, not you."

Turning around, she met his eyes but didn't move from the door. He was right. At least, that was what it'd looked like, but she wasn't ready to concede defeat. Not yet.

"So what?" she asked.

Returning to the lounge, Deacon perched on the edge of the couch and started unlacing his boots, his eyes not leaving her as he spoke.

"Everyone knows where August Mortlake lives. Are you seriously going to tell me the safest place for you to be is his mansion?"

"Like you said, they wanted to hurt my father. Not me. It's his life in danger, not mine."

Toeing off one boot before he moved onto the other, he gave her a look filled with pity. "You can't really believe that, can you?"

"It doesn't matter whether or not anyone comes after me. I think we both know what the chances are of my father swooping in to save me."

His other boot hit the ground with a thud, and despite herself, she jerked at the sound.

"You sure about that? I mean, from where I'm standing, he seems to want this wedding pretty bad."

Ophelia studied him. He was right. Probably about everything, but most definitely about the marriage. Her father wanted—no, he needed this marriage to go ahead with Byron. He needed for Byron to do as he'd agreed on the marriage contract and take the Mortlake name so he could pass it onto their child.

Since he'd cut Selene off, as far as she knew, she and her father were the last Mortlake's in existence. There was no way her father was about to let the Mortlake name die out. Not for anything.

She took her hand off the door. "So, you want me to stay here then? In your apartment?" she asked, taking her eyes off him for the first time to examine it.

It was small. Spotlessly clean from what she could see, but positively tiny. It wouldn't be an exaggeration to say her closet was at least twice the size.

How was it possible for her to have more clothes, more shoes than Deacon had belongings? Guilt stirred in the pit of her stomach. It was obscene how much stuff she had. Deacon must think she was nothing more than a spoilt brat.

Between a black couch, mismatched armchair, coffee table, and a two-seater dining table that looked like it would tip over at the slightest touch, there wasn't a whole lot of surface area to put… things. He had to be at least five-eleven, if not six feet tall. She didn't know how a guy his size lived in a place so small.

He must be forever crashing into things.

"For a few hours, yes. Until it's safe enough for me to take you home," Deacon said, rising from the armchair.

But then he stopped half-standing, and his hand went out to catch at the chair arm. He stayed that way for a beat before he continued to straighten.

Shame poured through her at his weakness. "Look, Deacon, I'm sorry for—"

"No need," he cut in and started for the door leading to his bedroom. "Come on, the shower's this way."

She followed without a word, not knowing what else to say.

Blood coated the front of her dress, and she didn't even want to know what she must look like, but Deacon was right, she would give anything for a shower right now.

"Is it always like that?" he asked, stopping in front of a chest of drawers beside another open doorway.

Considering there was little else in his bedroom except a single bed, a chest of drawers, and a wardrobe, it took no more than a glance to take everything in.

She blinked. "Is what like that?"

"Feeding." He fished out a black t-shirt and sweats and pushed the drawer closed.

Eyeing his usual uniform of black-on-black as a Bladed, she knew it shouldn't have surprised her his drawers were full of yet more black clothes.

"Well, yeah. It's always... kind of intense," she said, trying to project cool indifference about her and Deacon nearly having sex in the back of the car.

She didn't even want to think about what the result of that would have been when her driver reported their actions to Father.

And the pull between them? She wasn't nearly ready to confront her need for him. A need that seemed to grow the more time she spent with him.

Feeding from him had been a mistake, she realized.

She'd never craved—hungered for someone the way she had Deacon, even now thinking about it had her stomach clenching.

The taste of him in her mouth had been… intoxicating, and that was putting things mildly. If she hadn't come to her senses, there was no doubt in her mind they would have had sex. And she was certain, absolutely sure the experience would be just as memorable as feeding from him had been.

Something about the way he'd felt against her, touching her, the firm grip of his hand in her hair, had been just enough to convince her he'd know exactly how to satisfy her in bed.

And while she hadn't had more than a handful of partners, sex had more often than not been a bitter source of disappointment to her. Or rather, the performances of her partners had.

They'd, each one of them proved themselves as men more intrigued by the idea of having sex with a Councilor's daughter, than actually wanting her for herself.

But Deacon. The way he'd touched her. The almost desperate hold he had on her… he'd wanted her. Her, Ophelia. Not just Ophelia Mortlake.

Blinking, she returned her attention to Deacon. And found him staring at her with an intensity that bordered on physical touch. She felt exposed, and for a heart-pounding second, she had the inexplicable sense he was reading more about her than she wanted him to know.

Flushing, she bent her head to the bundle in his hands and reached out to take it.

"Are these for me?"

But he didn't release his grip on the sweats, and after a second, she glanced back up into his face. The look on his face was inscrutable if a little intense. She'd tried to apologize but he'd cut her off. Maybe he didn't think it was good enough.

The Bladed were all about control. All about discipline. She knew that from everything she'd heard her father and Selene say, and from what she'd seen of them herself. They were probably all control freaks. And she'd just made one of them lose control.

"This was your first bite," she guessed.

"Yes."

It was impossible to read him the way it was with other humans. He wasn't putting out any feelers, and it was beyond frustrating not knowing what he was thinking, or what he felt.

In the car, it'd been impossible to miss his obvious interest since the rather large bulge in his pants had more than given him away, but that had been because of her—because of her bite.

"It can't be easy losing control like that," she said, forcing herself to meet his eyes. "You Bladed never lose control for a second, do you?"

He blinked, and finally released the bundle in his arms.

"Typically, no. It takes a certain type of personality to take on the role we Bladed do." His eyes never moved from her face.

They were in his bedroom, she thought. In his shoebox bedroom beside his perfectly made-up bed, and all she could suddenly think about was how good it'd felt sitting in his lap, his hand stroking firmly up and down her back.

She cleared her throat. "So, it can do that to you... sometimes. Being bitten, that is. Make you feel things—or make you do things you wouldn't ordinarily do. It's... er, it's normal."

"Is that what you think?" he asked, stepping toward her. "That I'm angry at you—that I stopped you from apologizing because of the way your bite made me react?"

Her mouth went dry seeing his amber eyes turn liquid gold.

Then her eyes dipped to his neck, to the muscled column of his throat. Her stomach cramped.

God, she craved another taste of him.

She could still taste him in her mouth, and he was standing close enough for the heat coming off his body to warm her. To overheat her senses.

"Ophelia?" His voice was husky with need, tempting. And her eyes shot up to his, the sound of his voice bringing her back to her senses. Swallowing, she gripped the sweats he'd given her tight to her chest and edged back.

The soft smile that ghosted across his face was taunting as if silently mocking her for her retreat. Shaking his head as if he found something funny—as if she'd done something amusing—he stepped around her.

"Shower's through here. I'll grab you a clean towel."

Stepping out of his minuscule bathroom, she heard him before she saw him. With her hair wrapped up in a towel and his black t-shirt swamping her, she cut through his bedroom and headed toward the sounds she was hearing coming from the lounge.

He sat perched on the edge of his armchair, a solid blue-grey rectangle block resting on the coffee table and his black steel sword laying on top of both. Looking up as she stepped through the doorway, his eyes slid down her body, lingering on her bare legs before he lifted his eyes back to her face. It looked like he was sharpening his sword, though, having never seen it done before, she couldn't be sure.

"You find everything all right?" he asked.

Nodding, she crossed over to the couch. She smelled of him now, of cedarwood, man, and the fresh scent of outdoors. But something was missing.

Although his bathroom—the body wash she'd used reminded her of Deacon, there was something about the scent of him that was him and him alone. A scent too intoxicating to come from any bottle.

"Yes. The sweats were too big. I left them on your bed. I didn't think you'd want me going through your drawers, but thanks."

He nodded, his gaze lingering on her bare legs. "I can see that."

"Thanks for the shower. I feel a lot better," she said, her gaze returning to the sword in his hand.

Nodding again, he bent his head back to his task. Holding the hilt of the sword with his right hand, he pressed down on the tip with his other hand, drawing the sword on its flat edge along the stone before repeating the action. The metallic hiss was so hypnotic, for several seconds she watched him in silence.

"You need to feed?"

Her eyes flew to his face, but he didn't return her gaze.

"What? Uh. No… no, I'm good. Thanks," she stuttered.

Deacon nodded.

"What are you doing?" she asked, finally giving in to her curiosity.

"Sharpening my sword. It's never a good idea to use it and neglect cleaning and sharpening it regularly."

Right.

He'd used the sword when he saved her life. There'd been blood coating the blade which he must have wiped off while she'd been in the shower.

"I didn't realize humans could be so fast with the sword," she started. "I don't think I was the only one surprised by it."

Lenore's face flashed into her memory. There'd been fear in her eyes. She must have been thinking about Deacon's hand on the hilt of his sword outside the bathroom.

If he'd wanted to, he could have ended her life then. And Lenore wouldn't have been the only one not to have seen it coming.

"I practice. You want to tell me why you went so long without feeding?"

Deacon's question was unexpected, and she let silence fall between them as she debated what to tell him.

No matter what she said would lead back to her father, and revealing anything about her father and what he was doing would never be a good idea. She could never let herself forget Deacon was a Bladed, and the Bladed served the Council.

At her continued silence, Deacon paused sharpening his sword to gaze up at her.

Right. He was waiting for her to say something.

She opened her mouth.

"I would rather." He stroked the sword against the stone in a smooth move born of long familiarity. "You told me you can't tell me than lie. I've always preferred honesty over lies."

She considered him in silence. "Fair enough. I don't trust you."

He nodded. "Better."

"I know you saved my life, and you didn't stop me from speaking to Selene, but—"

Deacon's cell phone interrupted her, and she glanced at his phone vibrating on the coffee table beside him. But he didn't take his eyes from her. Instead, he seemed to be silently urging her to continue.

She cleared her throat. No matter how she said it, it would sound... beyond rude to tell him what she thought. Especially with his having just saved her life.

"You still think of me as your father's pet?" he asked with a raised eyebrow.

She flushed. Then gave a sharp nod, dropping her gaze to his chin. She wasn't feeling brave enough to meet his eyes.

"It'll do," he said, reaching for his phone. "For now."

Before she could ask him what *that* meant, Deacon was answering his phone.

"Pierce?"

Watching as he rose and started for his bedroom, she tried to keep her eyes on his back, and not where they wanted to be. On the firm globes of his ass.

Since he would know her preternatural hearing would enable her to hear both sides of his conversation, especially in an apartment this small, she knew he wasn't retreating to his bedroom for privacy.

But through his partially open door, when she saw him untuck his shirt from his pants, she blushed and turned away.

Oh, okay. That made sense.

This Pierce sounded like he was Deacon's boss, going by their conversation. Since it wasn't exciting, it didn't take long before a yawn snuck up on her and she raised a hand to muffle the sound.

Shifting so she was curled up on her side on the couch, she closed her eyes as she continued to listen to Deacon fill his taciturn sounding boss in on what'd happened at the Wynn.

Yawning again, she let the sounds of Deacon reassure his boss that she was okay ease her. She hadn't realized how soothing she found the sound of his voice.

It was low, with that ever-present sense a smile lurked close by. And soon it felt like the most natural thing in the world to let herself drift off to sleep.

CHAPTER SIX

*I*f Deacon had been expecting August to cancel the night's event so his daughter could have a night off having nearly died the night before, he'd have been disappointed.

Instead, as he drove through private gated entrance leading up to the white stone Mortlake Estate, the first thing he saw was Ophelia dressed in a knee-length white shift dress made of some silky fabric that clung to the swell of her generous breasts, perched on the top front step. Looking achingly beautiful.

Parking his khaki green Ford Expedition to the side of the imposing columns at the front entrance, he turned the engine off and after grabbing his sheathed sword and sunglasses, climbed out of his car.

"The dress is nice. Suits you, princess."

Glancing down at the dress, she shrugged as if it were nothing before standing as the driver idling in his car outside the garages started toward them. "Tonight's more of a casual thing."

He eyed her closely. He'd expected a glare at the bare minimum about his using her nickname. "I'm assuming your father won't be in attendance then."

Ophelia shrugged again, a delicate lifting of a bare shoulder before she stepped past him and slid inside the car door he held open for her.

"He's busy," she murmured, shifting a little further away from him when he eased into the seat beside her.

He fought back a smile at her move away from him. Suddenly she was acting shy around him and he didn't know why. Was she embarrassed that he'd found her curled up and sleeping like a cat on his two-seater couch after he'd finished changing?

"You're quiet," he said into the growing silence. "Is this a trust thing?"

Turning from the window, she stared at him for a beat before she spoke. "No. No, it's nothing to do with that."

He waited for her to continue.

Eyeing him as if she were weighing him up, finally, she seemed to make her mind up about something. "It can get pretty exhausting doing all of... *this*. Being me. I don't always want..." She trailed off.

"To be Ophelia Mortlake, August Mortlake's daughter?" he guessed.

Nodding, she turned a little to face him, looking a little less hesitant when he didn't mock her, or show anything other than interest for her to continue.

"It's worse when I'm with Byron."

He didn't try to hide his confusion. "Byron?"

A smile curved her lips, drawing his attention to her plum lipstick coated lips. "My fiancé, Byron Hawthorne."

He whistled low. "He sounds like the hero from some gothic romance. Byron Hawthorne, seriously?"

She giggled, and the low husky sound entranced Deacon.

Her first genuine laugh. Scratch that, the first time he'd made her laugh. He liked it. He liked it a lot.

"He's from an old aristocratic line. Almost as old as the Mortlake line, which I'm sure you know all about already."

"I was told what I needed to know. Namely that you're getting married, and August Mortlake wants this marriage more than he wants anything else."

The brief flash of amusement faded from Ophelia's face and Deacon kicked himself for not thinking before he spoke.

She turned to face the driver and started toying with her diamond ring, tugging it until it was nearly free of her finger, before sliding it back on again.

If that didn't tell him how she felt about her upcoming nuptials, her face certainly did. It was nothing less than the cold vampire princess mask he was coming to hate.

"So, tell me about this Hawthorne guy."

A lock of deep gold and copper hair slipped free from her loose updo, and he fought back the need to brush it away from her face, forming fists to stop himself.

"He's the perfect vampire prince."

Deacon waited for her to continue, and when she didn't, he prodded her. "And?"

"That's it. He's the perfect vampire prince. All artfully tousled hair and deep brown soulful eyes. He even has a dimple on his chin. And together we will have a perfect vampire baby after our perfect wedding."

He couldn't help but wince at her bitterness, but before he could comment, the driver was pulling up to another private entrance to one of the mega-mansions about five minutes down the road and up a steep slope of the deserted tree-lined enclave the Mortlake's called home.

Glancing at Ophelia in confusion, she stopped toying with her ring and settled back in her seat, looking perfectly poised.

"Byron decided at the last minute to have the party at his family's house. I think he thought Father would view it as a sign he cared about my safety. Or something."

It sounded like Byron was cut from the same cloth as August, Deacon thought. But at least Ophelia knew it. At least she wasn't going into this marriage blind.

"You realize we could have walked, or do princesses not walk anywhere?" he asked, hoping to draw some of the dark shadows from her eyes.

Ophelia eyed him like he was crazy. "I'm not walking up a hill in these heels, Deacon."

Taking that as an invitation, his eyes slid down her white silk dress, slender legs, and her spiked five-inch strappy sandals.

"Mm," he said, picturing her wearing nothing but those sandals and lingerie in bed. In his bed. He felt his cock stir to attention at the thought.

When the driver came to a stop, and he lifted his eyes back to Ophelia's face, he found her gazing up at what was likely a multimillion dollar mansion with its front doors standing wide open, and a servant hovering at the entrance.

With her gaze fixed on the tall arched doorway of the mansion, she raised her head and squared her shoulders as if she was preparing for battle.

By the time she stepped out of the car, and he was joining her at the entrance, she'd wiped away all trace of vulnerability from her face.

"I take it Byron's upstairs," she said, passing the servants as she entered the mansion, and started up the grand black and white monochrome staircase. Ignoring the hum of conversation and music drifting down the foyer where guests gathered.

"He's otherwise engaged at present, Mistress. Perhaps you might like to wait for him in the ballroom?" a trailing servant suggested helpfully, if not a little desperately.

"No. I don't believe I will," Ophelia said, continuing up the staircase.

"But perhaps…"

"No, I'd rather not." She stalked down the hallway, heading unerringly toward a set of closed double doors. More than a little curious, Deacon slipped his mirrored shades on and followed close behind her.

On reaching the doors, she didn't knock or bother to wait for a servant to open them for her, instead, she flung them open and stepped inside.

The musky scent of sex hit Deacon in the face, announcing well before he entered what had been going on inside.

In the spacious bedroom larger than Ophelia's, the

sight of a naked man, laying entwined with an equally naked woman in a four-poster bed stopped him dead.

The man lifted his head, his dark curly hair in disarray, and turned at the intrusion.

"Ophelia, what are you doing here?" he asked, sounding and looking more bored than annoyed as he wiped at the smear of blood on his lips.

"I was just about to ask you the same thing, Byron."

With a neutral expression on his face, and his eyes hidden behind his glasses, Deacon's gaze moved from Ophelia to her fiancé lying in bed with another woman. She didn't seem even the slightest bit surprised at what she'd found, and Byron did nothing more than grin and reluctantly roll off his partner.

He looked unrepentant, not even bothering to apologize. Deacon hated him at first sight. The only person who appeared even the slightest bit embarrassed was the woman who flushed before raising her sheets a little higher to cover herself.

"Isn't it obvious? I'm hunting for the perfect woman to carry the Mortlake heir," he said, stretching.

Deacon glanced over at Ophelia, waiting to see what she would do, and how she would respond.

"I don't think you've understood quite how it works," she said, drily.

If he hadn't heard her words in the car. If he hadn't seen her vulnerability, a side of her he doubted many people ever saw, he'd have believed the cool disdain on her face was real.

"Then why don't you come over here and show me?"

It took more effort than Deacon thought it would to

hold back his sneer at the sight of Byron's eyes raking over Ophelia's body. The man was lying naked in bed with another woman, when Ophelia would have been enough for any man. Did he seriously believe she'd be interested in joining him in his tainted sheets?

"If I thought for a second you knew the first thing about satisfying a woman, I might consider it. But as I don't…" Now it was her turn to examine Byron, and the slow perusal of his lean muscled chest and pasty skin was more than enough to show her cool disinterest.

Deacon's lips twitched, and perhaps sensing the humor he was trying to keep leashed, Byron's head swung toward him.

"You find something funny, Guard?" He sneered.

Deacon said nothing.

"I'm talking to you, Guard."

"He doesn't have to say a word," Ophelia said, turning to leave. "He reports to my father, and only my father. Now, as you're otherwise engaged, I should go. I'll leave you to it. "

"What do you mean? You just got here."

"And I found you in bed with another woman. I couldn't possibly stay. Not with how devastated I am." Ophelia spun on her heel, heading back down the hallway and Deacon fell in behind her, silently following in her wake.

"Ophelia! Come back here. I know you're just looking for a reason to leave."

But she didn't slow her steps, so neither did he.

They headed back down the wide staircase, out the

front door, and toward the driver who hadn't even had time to park yet.

Opening the door, Deacon waited until she slipped inside before he rounded the car and climbed in the other side.

"You want to tell me what that was about?" he asked once the driver had pulled out of the gates of the Hawthorne estate.

"I don't want to talk about it," she said, staring out of the window.

"He was right," he said. "Byron. You were looking for a reason to leave."

"Is that judgment I hear in your voice, Bladed?"

"It's curiosity. Why didn't you tell your father you didn't want to go out? It wasn't as if you didn't have a good reason not to."

Her laugh was a hard sound, devoid of humor. "How sweet. The truth. Why didn't I think of that?"

She was mocking him, and he shook his head though she couldn't see it.

"There is nothing wrong with a bit of honesty."

Ophelia turned to face him. "There is a great deal wrong with it. And a great deal of pain and hurt that can come from it. For a Bladed, I'd thought you'd know that."

"Ophelia—"

The driver pulled up outside the Mortlake mansion, and Ophelia pushed open her car door before she paused, her gaze on the front door. "You're here to do one thing Bladed. And that one thing is not to offer your opinion on things you know nothing about. You don't know my father, and you don't know me."

Stepping out, she slammed the door shut behind her and started up the front steps, her back a long straight line.

He'd made her laugh moments before. It had been the start of her lowering her guard and he knew it, could sense he'd been making progress with her. And then he'd spoken without thinking first.

For a second, he'd let himself forget who her father was. While he might respect honesty, a man like August Mortlake would only ever regard it as weakness, and Ophelia had rightly called him out on it. Honesty was dangerous.

Now he'd pissed Ophelia off and he didn't know how long it would be until, or even if it would be possible to get her to open up again.

Fuck.

———

Deacon had been a member of the Bladed for years. Surely, he must know she couldn't afford to open up to anyone. She didn't doubt he had principles, but to make her feel like she was stupid or less than for playing the same games that'd kept her alive all these years was infuriating. And it hurt.

How could he have no notion of the game's vampires played? How could he be blind to the fact that no one said no to a Councilor and lived long to talk about it? Not even if that person was his daughter.

She'd thought he'd understood her position since he'd seen what no one else had seen—how her father controlled her, and how her life was not her own. And he'd made her laugh, and the only person capable of making her laugh was Selene.

She sighed.

He'd tried to apologize. She'd seen it in his eyes, the regret, but she'd cut him off and flung his humanity in his face just as she'd seen Lenore do. Had in fact spoken to him like the thing she'd always swore she'd never be, a bratty, snobby vampire princess.

She needed to say sorry.

She was pulling the front door open when Stanley's voice stopped her.

"Mistress?"

As she turned, she smoothed her face into a calm mask. "Yes?"

"I believe your father made it clear you were not to leave the house alone."

Right. Because she was a prisoner. How could she ever forget that?

For a second, she considered lying. But then shook her head. Maybe honesty, in this case, would serve her better than lies would.

"I said something to the Bladed. Something that he didn't deserve. I need to apologize."

Stanley blinked at her, for a moment surprise flickered across his face. And that was when she realized how much she was changing, how much she had changed already.

When she'd still been human, she'd always been the one trying to get her friends to apologize for their cruel treatment. Stanley, who'd helped raise her, knew that.

The silence lengthened and then he turned away,

retreating the way he'd come. "Don't be long. Your father will want to know where you went—"

"And you'll have to tell him, I know. Thanks, Stanley."

There was no response, and she slipped out, heading for her white Porsche 911 in the garages. Tonight, she wouldn't need a driver, nor did she want one. Tonight, she craved the freedom that came with driving.

She was drawing stares as she made her way down the hallway of Bladed Headquarters set among the flashing lights and music and noise of the Vegas Strip, and within sight of the Vampire Council building.

The decision to have the two buildings so close together was not accidental from what she'd heard over the years.

The Council wanted to keep a close eye on the Bladed, and it was to their benefit to have the Bladed close enough to defend the Council building should it ever be necessary.

After she'd left home, it hadn't taken long for her to realize she couldn't remember how to get to Deacon's apartment.

She'd been so out of it that although she knew what his apartment looked like, and that it was somewhere downtown, getting there was a mystery. She could have turned back and had her driver take her, but it'd taken less than a second before she changed her mind.

It was one thing going or being taken to Deacon's house when she had the excuse of being out of it, and his protecting her. It was another thing entirely making the decision to go to his apartment when she should be at a pre-wedding event.

The sound of metal clashing against metal grew louder as she approached the doors to the gym.

Anticipation spurred her on, and the sharp tap of her heels echoed loudly as she traversed the hallways with its harsh fluorescent lights.

Pushing the double doors open, she stepped inside and found herself enveloped by the smell of sweat, man, and of Deacon.

Her mouth went dry when she saw him.

His movements were sure and fluid as he fought another Bladed, and shoulder-length blonde hair, usually tied at the nape of his neck hung loose around his face.

Clothed in nothing more than a pair of black sweats that hung low on his hips, sweat clung to golden muscles rippling with his movements.

Desire hit hard. Her stomach clenched. She'd never wanted a man as badly as she wanted this one.

Drifting closer, ignoring the glances from the other Bladed using weight machines and treadmills dotted around the room, she moved toward the canvas mat.

Then she glimpsed something she hadn't expected to see. A tattoo, a large one on his shoulder. It looked, she frowned, like a snarling dog wearing a helmet.

Huh. Strange.

"Impressive, isn't he?"

Turning, she came face to face with an older man in the black-on-black uniform of the Bladed, his salt-and-pepper hair marking him out as older than anyone else in the room. And human.

, Nodding, she shifted her focus back to Deacon's muscled form as he met and parried each of his opponent's attacks with a speed she had never expected a human to possess. "I didn't think anyone could come close to vampire speed," she admitted.

"If anyone can, it would be Deacon."

The voice was familiar and it didn't take her long to figure out where she'd heard it before.

"You're Pierce. Deacon's boss."

"I am. I know who you are, and I'm more than a little surprised to find you here."

There was a question in his voice, but she pretended not to hear it.

"That man he's fighting? Why am I getting the impression this is more than just a practice bout?" she asked.

As if Deacon and his vampire opponent had heard her, their pace increased and the aristocratic-looking vampire Deacon fought ramped up his attack, lunging at him, and the sharp point of his blade arcing dangerously close to Deacon's neck.

Breath catching in her throat, she could only stare as Deacon whipped his head back at the same time his blade came up to clash against the vampire's sword.

It looked so effortless, she struggled to believe Deacon, a human, could not only go toe-to-toe with a vampire wielding a sword but that he could make it look so easy.

Pierce shrugged but avoided answering her question. "He's one of the best. One of the most naturally gifted swordsmen we've ever seen."

"He's amazing," she murmured.

She felt the sharpness of Pierce's gaze on her and mentally shook herself. She couldn't let slip to anyone, least of all Deacon's boss, a hint of her attraction. Especially in the middle of the Bladed gym. That would have been the height of stupidity.

"He is that," Pierce agreed.

Nodding, she watched as Deacon went on the attack. Slowly, he made his move forward, his blade slashing out, opening up a cut on his opponent's chest before he could block the attack.

The vampire retreated with his face twisted in a snarl, and Deacon followed. His face was calm, and his movements were confident as he seemed to anticipate each of his opponent's responses almost as soon as he'd made them.

But she wasn't the only one absorbed by the fight. Around the canvas mat, Ophelia caught sight of other Bladed abandoning their training, and falling silent in favor of watching Deacon fight. He fought with such perfect grace, she found it impossible to look away.

"Is it usual for them to train with metal swords?" she asked Pierce, imagining there must be severe injuries if they did, especially for the human Bladed. She'd have thought they would use wooden swords, or at least blunted metal ones to prevent severe injuries, or even death.

"Not usually. But not today," Pierce said.

But before she could ask him to explain, Deacon swept his foot out at the same moment he slashed out with his sword. His opponent, distracted by the sword slashing at his face, attempted to parry, and missed Deacon's footwork.

He thudded to the mat, his back slapping against the mat so loudly it echoed in the room. But Deacon wasn't still, no, he followed him down.

An angled slice from Deacon's sword sent his opponent's sword skittering across the mat, and then his sword tip was pressed against the fallen man's neck.

"Do you yield?" Deacon's voice was cool, unaffected. Though sweat covered his chest and dampened the hair around his face, he didn't sound out of breath or tired in the least.

The vampire on the ground glared up at him, his muscles tensing as if preparing to launch another attack.

Deacon pressed the blade harder against his neck. "Yield."

The room was silent as they watched. The seconds ticked by, and the vampire let out a breath. "I yield," he said, his voice low.

And just like that, most of the watching Bladed turned back to their training, or turned their attention to her.

She felt their eyes on her as if they'd only just noticed her presence and Pierce, while she'd been distracted watching Deacon, had slipped away.

In the sudden silence, she started toward Deacon, the men around her stepping out of her path. She said nothing, didn't call out to him, but she didn't need to, not when Deacon seemed to suddenly be aware of her presence.

He looked up from the vampire lying at the point of

his blade, and frowning, he pulled the sword from the vampire's neck and started toward her.

"Ophelia? What's wrong?"

As he padded across the mat like a golden jungle cat, his movements sinuous and smooth, she fought to keep her eyes on his face, and away from the sharply defined muscles on his chest, or his six-pack abs.

"I need to speak to you," she said, more than a little aware they'd become the sole focus of the men around them.

"Ah, Ophelia, is it?" It was one of the Bladed leaning against a treadmill, a towel slung around his shoulders and his eyes running up and down her body. Not even trying to hide the way he appeared to be undressing her with his eyes.

Automatically, she reached automatically for her ice princess persona but found it took more effort to slip it into than it had before.

What would happen when she eventually grew tired of being that person or outgrew it completely? What mask would she wear? How would she be able to protect her heart then?

"You sure I can't offer you a little something more than this human can?"

Deacon turned toward the leering vampire, but Ophelia beat him to it. She could have let him intervene, but this was something she could handle since she'd been dealing with situations like this since she was sixteen.

This was one battle at least she didn't need anyone else to fight for her.

"I don't think so," she said, her voice frigid as she ran

her eyes over him, making it clear she didn't see a whole lot she had to be impressed by.

Bristling, he moved toward her. But she didn't retreat. Instead, meeting his eyes, she smiled her coldest smile. The one she'd inherited from her father.

The vampire paused, doubt drifting across his face.

He was trying to place the smile, trying to remember where he'd seen a smile like it before.

She held a hand up, her engagement ring sparkling under the harsh lights of the gym.

"I'm engaged."

"Engaged?" His eyes narrowed in thought.

"Yes. I'm sure you must have heard about it?" She raised her eyebrow. "Or about my father. Councilor Mortlake."

Naked fear filled his eyes as he backed up a step, and Ophelia tilted her head a little as she examined him as if he were a bug under a microscope.

He must be a new arrival to Vegas for him not to recognize her. There weren't many vampires or humans in Vegas who didn't know who she was. Or rather who her father was.

But she was silent as she watched him. Should she continue to make him feel even more uncomfortable? She could draw things out a lot more than she was already after he'd tried to embarrass Deacon. He deserved to suffer a little.

"Ophelia?" Deacon asked, placing a hand on her arm.

She looked up at him. Saw the humor lighting his eyes as he shook his head a little, as if trying to tell her the vampire had suffered enough.

"I need to talk to you. It's important."

"This way," he said, starting for the far end of the gym, to another set of doors, handing his sword to one of the Bladed on his way.

Stepping into the room, through doors he held open for her, the door slammed shut behind them, and then Deacon was right there in front of her as she stood with her back to the door.

"You wanted something?"

"I did." Resting her head on the door, she tilted her head up as she studied him in silence. "You look different."

He waited for her to speak.

With his hair falling about his face, she wondered what it would feel like to have him laying over her, his sweaty skin flush against hers as his weight pressed hers into a soft bed. At the thought, her nipples beaded and she fought to keep her breathing steady.

It didn't feel like her expression had changed, but he must have noticed something because his eyes turned liquid gold. "What," he said, his voice a husky growl as he leaned one hand on the door over her head, "were you just thinking?"

"Something that's none of your business?"

Though it didn't look like he'd physically moved, suddenly he seemed closer and she inched back against the door. Or at least she tried to. Given her back was against the door already, she didn't get far.

"Princess, it feels like it has everything to do with me."

"I told you not to call me that."

His lips quirked in a smile. "Yes, you did."

When he fell silent again, she remembered she was

here for a reason, and he was waiting to hear it. But she hesitated as her gaze shifted to the side, to the door beside them.

Deacon had taken her to the locker room, and although they were lucky enough to be alone, it wouldn't be hard for anyone outside in the gym to hear them, or for someone to enter at any moment.

He must have read the thought in her eyes because he leaned closer. "Soundproofing," he said. She fought to focus on his words and not how much closer he was. And how he good he smelled.

"Soundproofing?" she repeated, her eyes latching on his full upper lip. She wanted to bite it.

"There are too many secrets, and too many vampires in this building for them not to be. No one will overhear, and no one will come in while you're here. What did you want to tell me?"

She forced her gaze back up to his eyes and released a breath. He was staring at her mouth in fascination. Gulping, her eyes went to a spot just over his shoulder. "I... I wanted to apologize."

"Princess..."

"No. I shouldn't have said what I did. It was bitchy and you didn't deserve it. I was being bratty. And I'm sorry."

He said nothing for so long, eventually she shifted her gaze back to his face. Found him staring down at her with a blank expression on his face.

Sighing, she slipped out from under him, intending to leave. "You don't have to accept it, I'll see you—"

"Fuck it," he muttered.

Before she could ask him what he meant, a hand

snaked out and caught her arm, yanking her back, and then warm lips were on hers, hard and firm and insistent.

For a second, she stiffened. Shocked. Then slowly, her hands came up and clutched at his shoulders as she parted her mouth, his tongue taking advantage to slip inside.

Held flush against his hard body, she moaned into his mouth as one of his arms wrapped tight around her waist, locking her against him, while the other tangled in her hair.

And then she remembered where she was, and pressing her hands against Deacon's sweat dampened chest, she shoved him back.

For the longest time they stared at each other, her breath panting out of her. But she wasn't alone in fighting to slow down her breathing.

Deacon cleared his throat. "Ophelia—"

"No." She shook her head, raised a trembling hand to her mouth.

She could still feel his lips on hers, and her eyes dropped to his, wanting more. Knowing she shouldn't. It was dangerous. Least of all in Bladed Headquarters.

He moved forward a step.

Spinning around, she grabbed for the door handle.

CHAPTER SEVEN

"You surprised me, which doesn't happen often."

With his arms folded behind his back in a resting pose, Deacon wrenched his mind back from the last place it should be in the presence of August Mortlake —in the locker room kissing Ophelia—and focused on Mortlake sat at his desk.

There is something not quite right with him.

While Ophelia wasn't feeding, August was looking positively rosy in comparison, all red-cheeked and ruddy. Like an alcoholic. And there was something, some strange shadow lurking in the depths of his eyes, that he didn't recall seeing at his first meeting with the Councilor.

"Your speed was... unexpected for a human."

Deacon's mind drifted.

Kissing Ophelia had been sweet, intoxicating. But holding her softly curved body against his had been something else entirely. He'd had a taste of something forbidden, and now it was all he could think about.

He knew nothing good could come from it. Not when the only thing he could look forward to was a few sneaky kisses before she got married, and then they'd never see each other again.

She'd be busy playing the aristocratic wife and mother, and he'd be… doing whatever it was he decided to do with his life.

Exactly how that worked when vampires couldn't have children, he didn't know, but Ophelia was insistent a kid was in her near future, and she would know better than he on what vampires could and couldn't do.

"You appear to be distracted."

Deacon didn't blink. "I'm just thinking about tonight's event. Ophelia will be late if we don't leave soon."

August leaned back in his office chair with a shrug. "It doesn't matter if Ophelia is late, the only thing that concerns me is that she attends. I've looked into your progress in the Bladed, and from what I can see, you haven't moved past door guard."

Deacon forced himself not to react.

Had Pierce said something to August?

"I understand it's a rare thing for a human to climb the ranks in the Bladed," he said, noncommittal.

"It's impossible."

He knew it.

"I see."

"So, if you were hoping for promotion then you'll be waiting in vain."

"And the reason you're telling me this, Councilor Mortlake?"

"Because as my guard your position wouldn't be as

limiting as it is in the Bladed. And of course, I would reward you far better than the pittance you receive. Think of the bonus you'll receive once Ophelia weds as a… small taste of things to come."

Deacon stilled. "You're offering me a job."

"I want you to think about it." August smiled.

Deacon looked at that smile, and he didn't like it. Didn't trust it in the least. "I can do that."

There'd be a cost, some hidden price to pay. And the second he stepped out of line, his head would be rolling across the floor of August's office.

While there was nothing to stop him from losing his head now, the idea of being under the sole employ of August Mortlake didn't seem like a good idea. And that was putting it mildly.

"If that's all?"

A narrow-eyed nod and Deacon was turning, crossing over to August's office door, ready to pull the door open when August stopped him.

"In the future, when I order you to do something, I expect to see it done. Taking my daughter to whatever hovel you call home is unacceptable. Don't let it happen again."

"Yes, Councilor," he said to the office door, and pushing the door open, he stepped out. Glancing up, he froze, swallowing hard.

Ophelia stood leaning on the upstairs railing, wearing a white one-shoulder toga style dress, her hair a flaming red-gold coronet around her head. Looking for all the world like a Grecian goddess.

She was quiet in the seat beside him, her gaze pointed out of the window, but Deacon could feel her tension. It wouldn't surprise him in the least if she were thinking about their kiss.

Embarrassment had seen her breaking their kiss, face flushing as she turned to leave. Slipping his arm around her waist, he'd bent to murmur into her ear.

"If you rush out looking like this, all the Bladed will take one look at you and know exactly what we were doing in here."

She stopped, and although he felt her shiver, she didn't turn around, and she didn't speak a single word.

Seconds passed, a minute, then she was reaching for the handle as she smoothed her hair down with her other hand, and his arm slipped away from her, stepping back as she pulled the door open and strode out, her head held high.

He hadn't seen her face, but when the Bladed parted around her as she stalked toward the exit in her high heels and silk dress, the first thing he did was head straight for the showers. A cold, long one. Yet even that hadn't done a thing about the raging erection the kiss that didn't come even close enough to being long enough, had left him with.

"Tonight. This cocktail party, I'm assuming your fiancé will be there for it?"

His question startled her, and she swung her head to look at him. "Uh, yeah. He will, why?"

Nodding, Deacon turned to stare out of the window.

So that was the reason for the strain around her mouth and the ring spinning.

"No reason," he said, staring out of the window.

He could feel her curiosity even though he couldn't see it. But when he said nothing else, he felt the heat of her gaze leave him.

Tapping his fingers on the hilt of his sword, his thoughts turned to August. He couldn't even begin to guess what was going on with the vampire, but whatever it was, Ophelia and Selene knew about it. Something, he was sure, had to do with the reason Ophelia wasn't feeding.

Was he regretting having kissed her? He usually talked to her in the car, but he was quiet, staring out of his side of the window, his fingers tapping on his sword hilt.

As much as she wanted to admit the kiss had been a terrible idea, and she should have pushed him away the second he'd pulled her against him, she couldn't. At least she couldn't and mean it.

Not when it'd felt good. So good, it'd felt like the most natural thing in the world to slide her arms around him and kiss him back.

But then reality had reared its ugly head.

She was getting married, and she was kissing the guard hired by her father behind a door that wasn't even locked. A room where any Bladed could walk in on them. If that didn't send her father crazy, then at a bare minimum it would cost Deacon his job, if not his life.

Their car slowed, and she worked to shove her emotions down deep enough no one could glimpse them in her eyes.

By the time they'd turned into the Cosmopolitan hotel and she was climbing out of the car, her face was free of emotional turmoil and she was just another bored heiress on a night out.

She couldn't even remember who'd organized the cocktail party. All she knew was that Byron would be there and that it was in honor of their nuptials. It was a toss-up between someone trying to impress her father by throwing money around, or Byron's parents who had no intention of returning from Paris for their only child's wedding.

Paris in winter was apparently too magical to abandon mid-season. Not that she felt any sympathy for Byron having such self-absorbed parents. He was just as bad as they were.

Deacon caught her above her elbow, and she turned with a frown to him as their car pulled away and headed toward the parking area.

That was weird. Deacon didn't usually—

"Uh…?" Her eyes widened when instead of leading her inside, he steered her into the yellow taxi that'd pulled up behind them. Jumping in after her, he slammed the car door shut as the driver was turning around with a frown on his face.

"I know you don't usually do pick-ups here, but we need to get to Desert Pines. It isn't far. You don't mind, do you?" Deacon asked, fishing notes out of his pocket and shoving them at the driver.

The driver took one look at the bunch of notes and grinned.

"Not at all. Not at all," he said, grabbing them.

"Deacon," she murmured, out of the corner of her mouth as the driver pulled away from the Cosmopolitan. "What exactly are we—"

"Shh, we'll speak in a minute. Where we're going isn't far."

And it wasn't. Minutes later, they were pulling up in front of Desert Pines Golf Course.

"Uh…"

"Come on." Then he was climbing out, holding his hand out for hers, and confused she let him lead her past an empty car park, and a dark building down a stone path.

Stopping when a man wearing a navy security jacket came out of nowhere, she glanced at Deacon.

"Hey, Terry," Deacon said, grinning at the man.

"Deacon, hey," the guard said with an answering smile.

The security guard unlocked a side gate and beckoned them in, saying nothing about Deacon turning up with a woman dressed up for a party. If anything, he seemed to be going out of his way to pretend he hadn't seen her at all, as he waved at Deacon before disappearing back where he'd come.

What was Deacon doing? And why had he brought her to a golf club of all places?

"You might want to take off your heels," Deacon said, stopping at the edge of the grass.

"Look…"

"I'll tell you why we're here in a minute, but first, we

need to be over there." He nodded toward the white dune bunkers a few feet away near a small lake.

There were more reasons to leave than to stay. If Father discovered she'd dodged another pre-wedding event, he'd kill her. Then there was this… attraction between her and Deacon. Was it the smartest thing in the world to be alone with him in a deserted golf club?

She'd stay for an hour and then she'd insist they go back.

"Okay, fine." She sighed, slipping out of her shoes before following him across the grass.

Years ago, when she'd still been human, a couple of her friends had invited her to go golfing, and it'd been the most boring two hours of her life.

But at night, with the sound of the wind blowing through the trees, the fresh scent of pine in the air, and the way the moon and stars reflected on the lake, it was beautiful. Even the feel of damp grass under her feet was refreshing, cooling.

"This is where I come to think," Deacon said, his voice low as if he didn't want to disturb the silent tranquility.

"It's peaceful. I can see why you'd want to come here. But Deacon, my father—"

"Come sit here."

Her gaze moved from him to the sand, and then back again.

"Uh, yeah, I'm not sitting on wet sand. Especially not in a silk dress."

His grin was boyish as he unstrapped his sword and tossed it on the sand, and after slipping off his black suit jacket, he laid it down. "It's not wet. Only the grass is damp from the sprinklers. Sit here."

With that, he pulled off his boots and socks and stepped onto the sand, letting out a deep sigh of contentment as he wriggled his bare feet in the sand.

"You don't know what you're missing," he groaned.

"Deacon..."

"Sit down, princess, and I'll tell you why I brought you here, and why I fought that guy in the gym."

Interest piqued, she moved to sit on Deacon's coat, her feet sinking into the cool sand. "What makes you think I want to know about your fight?"

Deacon lay back in the sand, pillowing his head with his arms. "I didn't. Until now that is. But if you want to talk about something else, like what happened in the locker room instead..." He eyed her with a raised eyebrow.

"No. No thank you. I'd rather not," she said, a little desperately, tearing her eyes away from him when he grinned up at her.

"You sure? Or you could feed, if you're hungry that is? I won't say no."

She stared at him. His pose, his words may have been casual but his eyes... they burned with heat. They were anything but casual.

"You want me to feed on you," she said, her gaze not moving from his face. Because if she glanced at his bare throat even once... he'd know she wanted it as much as he did.

Deacon shrugged. "It's just an offer. No need to accept if you don't want."

But looking into his eyes, Ophelia saw the memory of

her last feeding. Of what had happened, or rather what nearly happened in the back of the car.

There was no driver now. They were alone, and if she wanted, they wouldn't need to stop. Her nipples hardened and as if Deacon could read her body's response, his gaze slid down her body and fixed on her breasts.

Just change the subject, Ophelia. Now before you decide to do something stupid like decide the best place to sit is on top of Deacon.

She cleared her throat. "How about you tell me why we're here?"

She hoped. Really hoped the night was enough to disguise her flushed face from Deacon. Because the thought of doing more than talking was making her feel warm all over.

"Lie back," he said. "You'll be more comfortable and staring up at the sky is always relaxing."

"Not going to happen."

He was staring up into the sky, and just as she ran out patience, he spoke.

"Pierce showed me a picture of you. You were laughing with your sister, but even then, I could see it in your eyes."

Wrapping her arms around her knees, she frowned. "See what?"

"That you were trapped. Caged."

She blinked in surprise, opening her mouth to deny it.

He could tell that from a picture? How could he, a stranger, see something only Selene could?

He turned to look at her. "I hope you're not about to lie. Because I thought we'd talked about that."

Closing her mouth, she looked away, struggling to

think of what to say to fill the silence that'd fallen between them.

"I was lonely," Deacon said.

Surprised, she glanced down at him.

"When I first came to Vegas, I missed my family. I didn't know where I fit in and driving past here one night, I saw how peaceful it was. So, I snuck in, lay here just like this, and stared up at the stars for hours. There was something about staring up at a sky blanketed with stars which made me feel a little less alone."

She'd never considered that the Bladed would ever be lonely. More often than not, she thought of them more as machines than as men.

But they weren't, she thought, gazing down at Deacon who stared up at the sky, relaxed, his sword lying beside him, and his feet burrowed under the sand. They were just like everyone else.

"Since I was old enough to understand the world around me, I always knew my purpose was to marry and raise the next Mortlake heir."

Deacon made no comment. His expression was neutral as he shifted his gaze from the sky to her face, waiting for her to continue.

"It'd always been something he said, and it was always there in the back of my head. But I had Selene then, and I knew that as long as I still had her, I'd be strong enough to get through it. Or she'd get Father to change his mind. She always fought my battles for me. Fought Father for me."

She drew shapes in the sand with her finger as she spoke. What she was doing was wrong—telling a stranger things he shouldn't really know about her family, but she didn't want to stop. It felt... *freeing* to talk with someone.

"When I turned twenty-one, Father turned me. Then the next night he threw a big party for me. I thought it was to celebrate my turning. But it was for my engagement to Byron. Everyone else knew of course. Everyone but me and Selene." She lifted her head and found Deacon watching her with a blank expression.

"I just froze. Selene..." She barked out a laugh, and it echoed in the night. "You should have seen her. She went absolutely crazy. Trashed the party, screamed at Father, the things she said..."

Shaking her head at the memory of Selene defending her, humiliating their father in front of all the guests, she laughed again. "Well, he cut her off that night. Then she left, and... that was when something inside me died."

Tugging one arm from under his head, he held it out to her.

"Come lie down," he said.

But she was already shaking her head. "I'm not getting sand in my hair."

"You do realize that's exactly what a princess would say, right?"

She leaned toward him. Stared him right in the eyes. "Asshat."

She didn't swear often, it just wasn't the way she was. But that didn't mean she didn't know how. And obviously, Selene swore like a sailor so it wasn't as if she didn't know a multitude of curses.

He threw his head back and laughed out loud, surprising her. He laughed with his entire body, giving himself up to it completely. And seeing it, she couldn't help but stare.

She hadn't ever seen anything as beautiful before. It fascinated her—he fascinated her. And even though he wasn't a vampire with the ability to enthrall. Somehow, he managed to entrance her nonetheless.

"Suit yourself," he said, once he stopped laughing.

"Tell me about the sword fight at the gym."

"Why? Were you impressed by my physical prowess?" he asked, wiggling his eyebrows at her.

Pausing, she thought about it. "Yes, actually I was."

His flash of surprise was brief. "Is that why you let me feel you up against the door?"

"Deacon, you're being an ass."

"Okay, fine. It wasn't as impressive as it looked. The vampire I was fighting lacked experience. With it, it would've been a closer fight to call."

"But it looked like he knew what he was doing."

"He thought he did. There's a big difference between thinking and actually knowing something. I was teaching him a lesson."

Although Deacon seemed just as relaxed, sounded as calm as he had when he'd first laid down, there was something about the way he said it made her think he was being more serious than he was letting on.

"I spoke with Pierce," she said, watching him closely. "He said it isn't usual to train with steel."

"Did he?" Innocence coated his words, and she frowned in suspicion. He was keeping something from her.

Was this some Bladed secret she shouldn't know anything about?

"Yes, he did. Was there a problem between you and this vampire?"

Deacon sat up. "I guess that's another way of putting it. The thing is, not everyone in the Bladed believe humans are as capable of… well, anything as you vamps are."

She watched him stand, stretching, muscles rippling beneath his shirt. "I never thought you'd have to face discrimination like that in the Bladed. What are you doing?"

Her eyes locked on his hands as he started unbuttoning his shirt.

He flashed a quick grin at her. "Taking a dip in the lake. Join me."

Ophelia didn't have to think about it for even a second. "No."

"It's not that cold if that's what you're afraid of."

More and more of his muscled chest was being revealed as his shirt gaped open.

She forced her eyes away. "Getting cold is not what I'm afraid of."

"Terry's patrolling the other side of the course and other than me, there's no one else around," he said, slipping the shirt off his shoulders before tossing it on the sand beside her. Then his hands dropped to the front of his pants.

Realizing she'd started staring again, she jerked her eyes away. "Deacon, I am not swimming in a lake."

A long moment passed in silence.

Since she wasn't hearing his zipper, she took a calculated risk and peeked at him. Found him studying her with a seriousness she'd rarely seen in him.

"Ophelia," he started. "When do you ever have fun? I'm not talking about organized fun, or a party, or shopping. I'm talking unscripted, fly-by-the-seat-of-your-pants fun? You know, just letting yourself go?"

She thought back over the last few days. Remembered meeting Selene with a bottle of champagne at her bridal shower and opened her mouth.

"Something Selene organized doesn't count," Deacon interrupted.

She glared at him. "But this does? Even though it's your idea?"

He said nothing, just continued to stare at her as he waited for a response.

Not quite ready to admit he was right; she said the first thing that popped into her head. "We don't have any way to dry off."

Though his expression didn't change, she could see what he thought. He didn't think she would. She was too much of a vampire princess—had too much of August Mortlake in her to do it.

She rose. Not letting herself think for too long, or too hard about what she was doing, she slid the strap of her ivory and gold Marchesa gown down her shoulders and wriggled out of it.

Keeping her eyes firmly pointed away from Deacon, she unclipped her hair and shook it. Then, when she was standing in a white strapless bra and a white thong, her hair around her shoulders, she turned to Deacon.

"I'm ready. Let's—Deacon?"

He hadn't moved. His eyes were fixed on her body and they were filled with utter absorption. His hands were still on his pants zipper.

In the time she'd been undressing, he must've just been standing there, watching her undress.

"Uh, Deacon?"

"I was waiting for you to finish so you wouldn't be too distracted to watch me," he quipped, lazily lifting his eyes to wink at her.

Rolling her eyes, she started for the lake. "Come on. And quit staring at my butt."

He muttered something beneath his breath, and then she heard him unzipping his pants. It took every ounce of self-control to not turn around.

At the edge of the lake, she hesitated.

Did she really want to go through with this?

Behind her, she heard Deacon's fast approach, and alarm shot through her. If she didn't walk in on her own, she had a feeling he wouldn't think twice about tossing her in.

Sucking in a breath, she waded in, not stopping until the water came up to her shoulders, then floating, she turned and nearly crashed into Deacon.

"Hey! How did you get in so quietly?"

"Training," he said, swimming closer.

She paddled backward, but he reached out and after wrapping an arm around her waist, pulled her closer.

"Wrap your legs around my waist," he said, his voice husky.

"Uh, that sounds like a bad idea."

"But you want to." He drew her closer, and her hands

went up, clutched at his shoulders, thinking she'd push him away.

Instead, her fingers curved around the hard muscles there and she wrapped her legs around his waist, just as he'd said, bringing her core flush against his erection.

At the intimate press of him, she swallowed as heat pooled in her belly and she pushed at his chest, intending to move away. His hand on her hip tightened, and he brushed a hand along her jaw.

"You're so beautiful," he murmured, his eyes drifting from her eyes down to her lips.

He was going to kiss her. It was in his eyes, and instead of backing away as she knew she should, she was waiting, anticipation coursing through her, for him to do it.

Her lips were suddenly dry, and she licked them, sucking in a breath when his eyes darkened and he pressed himself against her even harder.

"You didn't think that—"

His lips brushed against hers, one hand sliding around the nape of her neck and holding her against him as he angled his head for a deeper, more intimate kiss.

He was coaxing a response from her. It was the only way to describe what he was doing to her, and it was working she thought as she wrapped her arms around his shoulders and leaned into the kiss.

There was no real urgency in him. As with the kiss at the locker room, there was something about it, something about the way he kissed her that made all resistance fall away. The man knew how to draw a response from her like no one else ever had.

Her lips parted and his tongue slid against hers.

Moaning into his mouth as his hand tunneled into her hair, their tongues stroked against each other, their kiss deepening.

His erection pressed against her, thin wet material the only barrier to his slipping inside. She ground herself against him and sighing into his mouth at how good it felt, she did it again. And again, as a pressure started to build inside her. She could come like this.

Groaning into her mouth, he broke their kiss, and after resting his forehead against hers, pulled away from her.

"Deacon?"

His eyes were burning as they stared back at her, and her stomach clenched at the intensity with which he studied her.

"How about we swim for a little bit, then we should see about getting you back."

It made little sense to her, his stopping. Not when she could see in his eyes he didn't want to. Not really. But forcing a smile she didn't feel on her face, she swam back. Created more distance between them.

"Sure," she said, a tension rising between them as they swam.

They didn't stay in the lake long. And relaxing was out of the question, not when all she could think about was kissing him again.

Forcing her mind away from kisses she shouldn't want, they stepped from the lake, Deacon disappearing to retrieve a couple of towels from somewhere.

A short, silent cab ride saw them back to the Cosmopolitan.

There she booked a room so they could use the hotel's dry-cleaning service, and she could re-do her hair. But she couldn't face going to the cocktail party and seeing Byron, not after what she and Deacon had shared.

She told him to take her home. She'd rather face her father than spend the night playing excited bride-to-be.

CHAPTER EIGHT

*D*eacon's back slapped against the mat. The sound, echoing loudly in the Bladed gym. A bokken, the hardwood training sword poked him in the gut and he grunted, knocking it aside.

"What's wrong with you?" Pierce snapped. "I shouldn't be able to beat you."

"Maybe you've just improved," he mused, grinning up at him. "Or I'm getting old?"

"Get up. What I have to say to you, I'd rather say in private."

To his surprise, Pierce turned to walk away, thrusting his wooden practice sword at one of the Bladed who took it since Pierce wasn't giving him much a chance to refuse, before he stalked out of the room.

That he did so in bare feet, and without heading to the locker room to change out of his sweats, clued Deacon in on the state of mind his boss was in.

At the low whistle beside him, he turned to find Julian, the new vampire recruit he'd fought, smirking at him.

"And here I thought Pierce was impossible to piss off. You been doing something you shouldn't have?"

Never were any truer words spoken, Deacon thought as he backflipped to his feet. Not that he was about to admit it to Julian.

"I'd tell you," he said with a wry grin. "But your sister swore me to secrecy, and you'll have no choice but to challenge me to another fight. And I think we all know how that would turn out."

Ignoring the snorts of laughter as he headed after Pierce, he grabbed his duffel bag and shoes on the way.

"Screw you, Chase," Julian snarled.

"I'm assuming you must have heard the rumors circu-lating about the... disunity among the Councilors'," was Pierce's opening gambit, the moment Deacon stepped inside his office.

Shrugging, he dumped his bag on the only space large enough beside the door and leaned against the wall, crossing his arms over his chest. "Nope. Just know someone was eager enough to separate Mortlake's head from his shoulders that he didn't even try to hide his intent."

Lacing his fingers together on his desk, Pierce nodded.

"Yes, well. The consensus seems to be that he believes another Councilor was responsible."

"That sounds exciting. And this news concerns me, how?"

Pierce leaned toward him, making his desk wobble.

"The last thing the world needs is anything else setting him off," he said with a pointed look. "You *do* understand what I'm saying, don't you Chase?"

Ah, it looked like rumors of Mortlake's assassination attempt wasn't the only thing making the rounds.

"That I should be more vigilant in case of more assassination attempts?" he offered helpfully.

Pierce narrowed his eyes. "Something like that," he muttered.

Those cool gray eyes that seemed never to miss a thing focused with unnerving intensity on him.

At the probing stare, Deacon fought the need to straighten or look away. He'd seen that same look, or many versions of it many times over the years. They hadn't fazed him at eighteen, and they didn't faze him at twenty-eight.

Raising his hand, he yawned as if bored.

"Fine then. But I'm warning you, Deacon, the second I catch even a hint of anything untoward going on that shouldn't be. I think it's clear enough to both of us what I'm talking about, then that's it. End of assignment."

It was harder now to keep his expression neutral when Pierce was threatening to replace him with another Bladed, potentially Julian. He'd seen the way the vampire had been watching Ophelia, and he hadn't been the only one. There was no way anyone was guarding her but him.

"There's no need. I can do the job."

Pierce's eyebrow shot up. "Can you?"

"You know I can. Not trying to change the subject or anything, but you're in more of a pissy mood than usual. What else is going on?"

For a second Pierce studied him. "Cracks are starting to appear among us. There are at least a couple of fights each night."

Usually, Deacon stayed away from the training center for that very reason. The human contingent in the Bladed wasn't large, and with his reputation, more often than not, there seemed to be vampire eager to test himself against him. When all he wanted to do was work out before his shift, he wasn't always in the mood to be dealing with a vamp with something to prove.

He took a moment to think over what he'd seen when he'd arrived at the gym. It was strange to find Pierce working out, but now that he thought about it, there were more of the Bladed supervisors observing than usual.

But that wasn't all he'd noticed. After his usual stretch, he'd jumped on the treadmill to warm up and taken the opportunity to scan the room.

The wealthier and well-connected vampires only associated with other wealthy and well-connected vamps, and the same with those who'd gone through training together. There were other splits and divisions among the Bladed he couldn't even begin to understand, but from what he'd seen, there was even more space between the groups than usual.

Some of the groupings had stuck out in his mind as being odd.

"Yes," he said. "The usual groupings are different. Some of the more self-obsessed guys in there were hanging with a couple of the newer guys. Some of them would never make time for the new ones. Not ever."

Pierce nodded. "The Bladed leadership meets with the

Council regularly to receive our orders, and it is with all the Council or none. But that meeting didn't happen this week. Now I'm hearing whispers individual Councilors are attempting to break apart the Bladed and keep little parts for themselves."

Deacon thought back to August's offer. How many of his fellow Bladed had said yes? Was this the beginning of the end for the Bladed?

"So, you know who the other Councilors are? You've met them?"

Pierce's expression went blank. "I know enough. And now there's a woman—a human woman—sniffing around. Asking questions about a dead Bladed. Questions it's best she doesn't know the answer to."

"Mm, curious."

"You don't want to go there, Deacon," Pierce warned.

"And the reason the vamps haven't enthralled her and sent her on her way already?"

"She's resistant to it. That and she hasn't done anything to draw the attention of the command yet. But I have a feeling it's only a matter of time, and I'd rather she not wind-up lying dead in an alley because of it."

"Why not pass it onto one of the Bladed?"

"You think I haven't considered that already?" Pierce's voice was dry. "There's more work than there is Bladed to do it. I can't spare any men—human or otherwise."

"Get a recruit to do it."

Pierce stared at him. "The recruits are here to learn, to train, and to prepare for their role out there," he said, jabbing his finger in the general direction of outside.

Deacon shrugged. "Sure, I get that. But weren't you

just saying there were more fights than usual? So, make it a punishment detail. Pick someone, it doesn't matter who as long as it's a vamp, to babysit this woman. If that doesn't go some way to dealing with some of the problems at least in the gym, I don't know what will."

Pierce blinked at him. Then he opened his mouth, and Deacon waited for the arguments—the reasons it was such a bad idea. He was sure there were plenty.

If he were being honest, he hadn't been thinking about the woman, or about anything other than having someone, namely Julian, tied up doing something else. Because if Pierce was going to replace him, it damn well wouldn't be with the vamp.

"You know what Deacon. I think that just might work. But who will I…" His eyes narrowed. "This isn't just some way for you to—"

"Pierce. I'm just offering you a solution to one of your problems. You do with it what you want, but I have to go. I'll catch you later."

Suiting action to words, he retrieved his duffel from the floor.

"I'll think about it. And you—don't you forget what I told you."

"I won't."

He glanced at his watch as he left Pierce's office. As he headed for the locker room to shower and change, his thoughts turned as they always did to Ophelia. He was becoming obsessed, there was no other way to describe what was happening to him.

Mid-fight with Pierce and he'd had a flashback of her

slow wiggle as she slipped her dress down over her hips. And then *bang*. His back was hitting the mat.

A part of him couldn't believe he'd found the super-human strength to pull away from her in the lake. But the last thing he'd wanted was for her to feel like he was rushing her into having sex when she wasn't ready. And she wasn't. Not yet.

He'd felt the tension in her body as he'd gathered her in his arms. A tension that'd faded away once he'd started kissing her until she was grinding her pussy against his cock. And her ass… the perfection of her ass in his hands?

He deserved a fucking medal for not nudging her panties aside and burying himself inside her. But she was worth more than that. Ophelia deserved more than that. When he took her to bed, it would be on a bed with silk sheets, not in the middle of a lake on a golf course.

"Ophelia. In my office. Now."

Ophelia paused with her hairbrush, mid-stroke. Her father only called her to his office for one reason, and one reason only.

She was in trouble.

"Yes, Father," she said, lowering the hairbrush to her dressing table.

Deacon would be here to pick her up in another half an hour, but at least she'd changed already, she thought as she smoothed her hands down the front of her pale-green silk dress.

She'd planned on braiding her hair and coiling it

around her head, so the heavy weight wasn't falling into her face, but since her father wasn't known for taking his time when he was shouting at her, it didn't look like she'd have time.

So, quickly twisting her hair on top of her head, she secured it with a silver clip before she started downstairs and to whatever fate awaited her.

After stepping inside his office, he didn't even wait for the door to close behind her before he started speaking.

"You weren't at the Cosmopolitan last night. Byron noticed your absence."

Right, she thought. *The party.*

"I was at the Cosmopolitan," she hedged. She had been, she just hadn't stepped foot into the party. Now for the actual lie. "But I saw Byron with—"

Her father blinked. It was slow, predatory as he stared at her from across his desk. "Ophelia," he said, his voice soft. "You remember I can tell when you lie to me, don't you?"

"Yes, Father."

This was it. He was about to tell her someone had seen her and Deacon at the lake.

He leaned toward her over his desk, his eyes narrowed in suspicion. "Did you think I wouldn't find out?"

"Uh, I didn't mean. I mean it wasn't—"

"Do you think I'm stupid?" He half rose.

Backing up a step, her hand searched blindly for the door handle she'd closed moments before. "I, er—"

"Have I not made myself clear how important this wedding is? Not just for me, but for the Mortlake line? Have I failed to make you understand?"

Her hand paused.

What was he talking about? Why wasn't he already ripping her head off for what Deacon and her were doing in the lake?

"Father—"

"I will not have you dodging events thrown in your and Byron's honor. Not anymore, Ophelia. Do you hear me?"

"Yes, Father."

"Because whatever else happens, Daughter, this wedding is going ahead. In fact, I've moved the date up for your appointment with the doctor. You and Byron will attend the day after the wedding." He reached for his diary and resettled in his chair.

"The next day? Isn't that a bit... soon, Father?"

"There's no reason to wait. It's not like you and Byron are heading off on some honeymoon. Might as well get things started with the surrogate as soon as possible."

Fear blossomed in her belly and quickly spread. Regret was a foul taste in her mouth. Byron had suggested a honeymoon, maybe a few weeks in Europe, but the thought of having to spend that much time alone with him had turned her stomach. She'd vetoed the idea straight away. Boy, was she regretting her hastiness.

Now if things went smoothly at the hospital, which, considering the amount of money Father was throwing at the private hospital and the doctors, how could it not? In about seven months she'd be holding a baby. Her and Byron's baby.

"You look pale," her father said, snapping her out of herself.

She swallowed. "I haven't fed yet."

It was clear he didn't believe her. But since she'd been putting off feeding, she hoped there was enough truth in her words to cover up the taint of her lies.

"Hmm. Well, you know now what I expect from you in the coming days?"

"Yes, Father." She took a step back.

"Because if you fail me… if you let me down, you'll force me to do something you will not like." There was something in his eyes, something that seemed excited by the prospect. As if he wanted her to step out of line so he'd have a reason to punish her.

"I will do as you ask, Father.

He bent his head to the diary he'd flipped open in front of him. "You may go."

Swallowing a deep sigh of relief, she turned to leave.

"Ophelia?"

She closed her eyes. "Yes, Father?"

Oh god, why couldn't he just let her go?

"Why aren't you wearing your ring?"

Opening her eyes, she frowned. Her ring? Her engagement ring? She always wore her…

Terror, blind panic raced through her at the sight of her naked finger.

Where was *her ring?*

She'd been wearing it when she left for the

Cosmopolitan. As always, it'd become a habit of hers to twist the ring around her finger.

But coming home she'd been staring out of the window, so conscious of Deacon sitting close beside her, terrified her father would see something—some hair out of place, and guess what'd happened between them.

It was only yesterday. How could she forget something that only happened last night? How could—

The lake.

What if her engagement ring was at the bottom of the lake?

She swallowed again, nearly choking on her panic. "It's, uh, feeling a little loose and I thought I might lose it."

Clearing her throat, she continued, "So, I thought I wouldn't wear it tonight. You know, just in case."

His eyes were boring a hole into the middle of her back, and it took everything for her not to tense up or run screaming from the room.

But one thing was certain. She couldn't turn around, because if she did... he'd take one look at her face, and the jig would be up.

"Put it on, Ophelia. I see you without it again..."

"Yes, Father," she told the door, forcing her hand not to shake as she pulled it open.

Stepping out into the foyer, she started for the staircase. The office door was still open behind her, so until she got up the stairs and was in her room, she'd be casual. Nothing was wrong. Everything was fine.

Casual steps, Ophelia. Just take it easy. Save the panic for upstairs for when you quietly tear your room apart looking for that stupid ring.

CHAPTER NINE

Ophelia sat staring straight ahead, a ball of palpable energy despite her stillness. Since he'd picked her up several minutes ago, Deacon had tried to ask if she was okay, but instead of answering she'd pointedly ignored him.

Then there was the shawl she'd been clutching like a lifeline when he'd arrived to collect her. Since vampires didn't get cold, he didn't understand why she'd need a cover-up now.

Was this because of what had happened between them at the lake? Was this Ophelia freezing him out?

When their car pulled up to the entrance of the Bellagio for the courtyard private party, Ophelia was out of the car almost before it had stopped moving, slamming the door shut behind her.

It wasn't like her to be this eager, he thought as he climbed out.

Frowning as he followed at a more leisurely pace, he skirted around the back of the departing car.

He'd barely reached her side, when without turning to look at him, Ophelia grabbed his arm and started at a brisk walk toward the taxi stand outside the lobby, dodging tourists and guests gathered outside.

"Uh… Ophelia?"

She didn't even look at him.

But instead of stopping at the stand, she yanked open the door of the first taxi and scrambled in, leaving him no other alternative but to follow.

"The Cosmopolitan." Her voice was odd.

"Ophelia," he said, "how about you tell me what's going on?"

Although his voice was low, mild even, the eyes Ophelia turned on him were stark with panic.

"I've lost my engagement ring."

Glancing down at her hand, the lace shawl suddenly made perfect sense. With the grip she had on it, it was impossible to see her ring finger.

"I don't remember you taking it off," he said, as the car crawled down the Strip.

"I didn't. Which means it's at the bottom of the lake, or it fell off while I was getting dressed, and if I don't find it Father will kill me."

"Why didn't you just tell him it must have fallen off in the lobby, or something?"

Ophelia stared at him. Her mouth opened but no sound came out.

"Hey, it'll be okay," he murmured.

"And how do you know that? Oh god, what if I don't find it in time for the wedding and I have to walk down the aisle without it? He'll kill me. Do you understand? Because I don't think you do."

She had him by the front of his shirt, was shaking him with naked fear in her eyes.

"Hey, lady?" It was the driver.

Ophelia whipped her head around to face him.

"We're here."

"Right." Dropping her hands, she pulled away. "Thanks."

Watching, bemused as she plunged her hand down the front of her dress to retrieve a handful of notes she thrust at the driver before scrambling out. He was a step behind her as they stepped into the Cosmopolitan Hotel.

She was conscious of his eyes following her as she all but tore the luxurious Moroccan style suite apart searching for her engagement ring.

Dropping to her knees on the handwoven Berber rug, she lifted the bedsheets and peered under the bed, trying to see if it'd rolled underneath.

"I think they would have cleaned under there," Deacon said, from above her. "Well, I would hope they had, given how much this room costs."

Rising, she glared at him stretched out on top of the sheets, one ankle crossed over the other. "That doesn't mean it isn't worth me looking. Just in case."

"Ophelia…" Deacon's voice was a sigh.

"No. It's here somewhere. It has to be."

"If it'd been here, someone would've handed it into the

concierge, or the cleaners would have found it when they cleaned the room."

"But what if—"

He patted the bed beside him. "Come lie down. Since you booked the room, we may as well relax while we're here."

She raised an eyebrow. "Relax, huh?"

Amusement lit his eyes. "Why not? About that. Aren't you worried August is going to wonder why you've been booking hotel rooms all of a sudden?"

She picked up a cut-glass vase on the desk in front of the floor to ceiling glass windows overlooking the Strip, and after yanking out the peach roses, peered inside. "I have an account he hasn't paid attention to since... well... since ever."

"Ophelia?"

After shoving the flowers back in the vase, she glanced at him. "Yeah?"

His eyes were on the vase in her hand, and there was a strange look on his face. "The vase? Really?"

"I'm desperate, okay?" she snapped.

"Come here."

"No. We need to go to that golf course because if it isn't here, then it's at the bottom of the lake."

Deacon was already shaking his head. "You were wearing it when we came back here."

Narrowing her eyes at him, she ignored the hand he held out toward her. "How can you be so sure?"

"Bladed. Was in the military. I'm sure."

He was in the... No, Ophelia. Now is not the time to be thinking of Deacon in uniform.

But despite herself, her eyes slid down his chest, remembering all the tanned rippling muscles she'd be clutching when they'd been at the lake, as she felt her body warm, barely containing her sigh at the image.

Good lord, with all those muscles he must not have been able to go anywhere. Women must have just been throwing them- selves at him wherever he went, and who could blame them.

"How can you say no to silk sheets?" he tempted her, drawing her gaze back up to his face.

He was watching her with a look in his eyes that told her he knew where her thoughts had gone, and he didn't disapprove. "What could be more relaxing?"

It was the way he said it that made her aware of how much danger she was in.

They'd kissed twice. Sheer terror someone would disturb them had made her run after the first time. And the second... if Deacon hadn't been the one to break things off, they would have had sex in the lake. No doubt about it.

Now they were in a hotel room with silk sheets and arousal spiked through her at the thought of all the things he could do to her in a bed with silk sheets. There was only one thing for it.

"Princess? Where are you—"

She slammed the bathroom door shut behind her and leaned against it, staring at her reflection in the mirror above the glass double sinks.

"Is there a reason you're hiding out in the bathroom?" There was more confusion than humor in his voice as she heard him climb off the bed and approach the door.

"I'm not sleeping with you," she blurted out.

There was silence on the other side of the door.

"Princess..." He sounded like he was choking. That or he was about to burst out laughing.

She glared at her reflection. "Look, you may be in the habit of sleeping around, and used to women throwing themselves at you." She paused.

Had that sounded like I was jealous? Maybe a touch.

"But I refuse to be one of them." *No matter how badly I want to be.*

"I am not," Deacon bit out, "in the habit of sleeping around."

"So, what is this then?"

"This is... something else. You're something else." He was leaning against the door.

"I don't know what that means."

"It means, princess, that you are one of a kind."

"You mean, I'm Ophelia Mortlake and you get to brag to all the Bladed—"

"Princess." His voice was dangerously quiet. "Open the door and look me in the eye before you accuse me of something like that."

She closed her eyes. "I shouldn't want you as much as I do." It was a whisper, a guilty admittance.

"Open the door, princess." His voice was low, husky and there was such heat in it, she was powerless to ignore it.

She opened the door.

Deacon stood just outside with one hand resting on the door frame.

He gazed down at her. His eyes burned with an intensity that made her warm all over.

"I'm getting married to another man, Deacon. This is —we can't do this. We shouldn't be doing this. It's wrong."

"It doesn't feel wrong to me." He stepped closer, close enough to touch. "It feels like something I've been waiting for my entire life."

She felt the impact of his words in her gut like a punch.

Searching the hard planes of his face, her eyes fixed on amber eyes that gazed back at her with naked need. It was a look she recognized. She'd seen it in her face moments before she'd opened the bathroom door.

Her hands tightened into balls at her side, nails digging into the palms of her hands and she swallowed.

Soon her life would be over. She'd have nothing to look forward to except rare nights at Eros and hours shopping at the night mall to pass the time. When she wasn't raising the next Mortlake heir that is.

But before August and Byron snatched away what little freedom she had, she wanted—no, craved—this. One night of freedom. One night of having what she'd wanted since she'd turned to see him leaning negligently against the wall, his amber eyes on her.

Surely it couldn't be wrong to give herself to a man who desired her, and who didn't view her as just another notch on his bedpost. Didn't she deserve that?

Raising one hand, she placed her hand over his heart. Felt his heart leap in response to her touch.

His eyes never left hers as he caught her hand. Raising it to his mouth, he pressed a heated kiss in the center of her palm. Her breath caught in her throat.

Tugging her hand free, she took a step back and

reached for the tie on her right shoulder. One tug later and the silky material was sliding down her body to pool on the ground.

The heat in his eyes turned into a raging inferno as his gaze dropped to her bare breasts before they lowered to her thong.

He murmured something beneath his breath, something vaguely Italian. But before she could ask what it meant, he was stepping forward, his arms wrapped around her, lifting her off her feet as his mouth came down on hers.

His kiss was *everything*.

All fire, tenderness, and sweet heat.

She melted under the onslaught. Lost all sense of anything and everything beyond the taste and touch and feel of Deacon's lips against hers. As his tongue stroked against hers, and her arms coiled around his shoulders, all she could do was hold on for dear life.

She was vaguely conscious of his moving, then her back was pressing against silk sheets, and his weight was coming down on top of her.

Moaning into his mouth, suddenly, she was greedy for him. She needed to touch, to taste his bare skin. Ached for him to fill the hole deep inside of her.

Her hands worked at the buttons of his shirt, peeling the material from him. And then she rolled, stopping when she was sat astride him.

Kissing her way down his jaw, she nuzzled at his throat. Felt him harden which triggered her hunger, and ravenous, desperately she sucked at the skin on his throat and smiled at Deacon's harsh growl. Fangs extending, she bit down. His hand tightening in her hair was almost painful as she drew the decadent taste of him into her mouth.

He groaned, and with one hand gripping her hip, he thrust hard against her, his erection butting at the entrance of her sex. Grinding her body down on him, she fed, luxuriating in the rich taste of him. He was addictive. But tonight wasn't about her feeding. No, what she wanted was so much more than that.

She lapped at her bite, sealing the broken skin, before easing back as reluctantly his hand slipped from her hair, his eyes, a liquid gold, fluttered open. Then shifting until she sat on the top of his thighs, she reached for his pants, unbuttoning him, her fingers brushing against his hardness.

She didn't look up as she released him from his pants, pausing for a moment to eye the thick length of him jutting up between his muscled thighs.

He was... bigger than she was expecting. A lot bigger.

A faint stirring of wariness crept through her. Just like Deacon, she wasn't in the habit of sleeping around either. She had never been interested in having sex with Byron, and her last relationship had been a couple of years ago.

"Princess?"

Her gaze shifted to his face.

"I haven't…" She felt herself flush. "It's been a while since…"

A smile tugged at the corners of his mouth. "Are you trying to tell me I have a big c—"

She clapped her hand over his mouth. But below her, his body shook with silent laughter. It was crazy, she thought, fighting back her own laugh. There was something about talking about sex which she'd always found embarrassing.

She'd had former lovers who'd tried to talk dirty to her, and instead of turning her on, it'd done the opposite. And right now, the last thing she wanted was for anything to ruin their time together.

Deacon's laughter made no sense. And for that matter, neither did hers, but the utter ridiculousness of it all chased away her apprehension.

Taking her hand off his mouth, she slipped off him, dancing back when he moved to stop her with a frown on his face. "Princess, where—"

A frown that evaporated when she, holding his gaze, slid her panties down her legs, stepped out of her heels, and turned her attention to his pants.

He lay back as she returned to sit astride his thighs. She swallowed hard when she caught sight of the searing heat in his eyes as he stared with naked lust at the exposed heart of her femininity.

Reaching for his erection, she wrapped her hand around him and stroked her hand up and down in a smooth glide. He was hot to the touch. A contrast of hard and silky soft heat in her hand.

"*Fuck,* Ophelia!" The need in his harsh growl had her shivering in anticipation. The muscles in his neck were taut with strain as he forced himself to lay still beneath her.

Heat pooled inside her.

She released her hold on him.

Rising onto her knees, she shifted forward and pressed

the tip of him to her sex. But before she could lower her body on him, his hand squeezed her hip. Stopping her.

Lifting her eyes, she saw the visible strain in his face, the tension in his neck as he held her still. A question in his eyes.

"Wait, are you ready for me? Let me—"

Her body was crying out for him. She needed him now. "I don't want to wait," she breathed, already sinking down on him. "I can't…"

He slipped inside her one slow inch at a time and, moaning, she tossed her head at the heavy fullness of him invading her body. His body shuddered beneath her as he held himself still, giving her time to adjust to his size.

Then, with her hands on his shoulders, she started to move.

His hands, those strong slightly calloused fingers skimmed her curves, kneaded her breasts, applying the perfect amount of pressure as he tugged at her nipples. Her eyes locked on his, as she rode him, rising and sinking down a little more each time.

But it wasn't enough. The ache deep inside her grew more intense, not less. She wanted… no, she *needed* more. Frustration beat at her.

"Deacon…" she moaned, as she ground down on him.

"Let me," he murmured, keeping their bodies joined as he rolled them, so he lay above her. "I know what you need."

Lifting her legs to rest on the top of his shoulders, his hands spanned her waist as he tilted her lower body the tiniest degree. Then he was on his knees, bending over her as his hands caressed her breasts.

He sank into her, so deeply into her she sucked in a breath at the feel of all that hardness filling her. Then easing back, he thrust into her with a deep groan, and she grabbed desperately at his arms, her back arching. He did it again, and again, and when the tip of him touched her womb, she writhed beneath him.

More. Just a little more, and she was there.

"Oh, god, *please*… Deacon…"

He stopped moving, his eyes locked on her, his body trembling with his own need as he curved a hand around her nape. *"Tesoro mio…"*

That Italian phrase again. "What? No, don't stop. I need more."

Each withdrawal had her panting, and each hard thrust was enough to have sounds, desperate hungry sounds spilling from her mouth. And all she could do pinned beneath him was squeeze her muscles around him as he thrust.

Soon, she felt her stomach tightening as a heavy warmth spread over her. His jaw locked, and his face was a harsh grimace of concentration as he thrust with increasing speed.

And then it was all too much. Her body, coiled so tight, exploded.

Throwing her head back, she screamed as every muscle tightened and released, back bowing as Deacon tensed above her, and then he was shoving himself so deep inside her, he threw her into another release. He jerked helplessly inside her, and then eyes closing, he sagged over her, spent.

She didn't remember falling asleep. But she must have because when she opened her eyes, she was lying sprawled on her belly with Deacon behind her, his fingers drawing lazy circles on her lower back.

"That was…" She stopped. Wasn't sure how to describe what had just happened between them.

"Yeah, I know."

"You made me scream," she said, her voice still not quite steady. "I never scream."

His body shook with his laughter. "Mm, and you were *loud*. If I'd had any idea, I'd have, you know covered your face with a pillow or something."

She yawned, feeling too good to be anything other than content. "Next time."

"Over here, *tesoro mio*. I think you're too far away." His murmur was all sated man, as he curled his arm around her waist and hauled her flush against him.

"You called me that before," she said, wiggling a little to get more comfortable, feeling a certain something hardening in response to her movements.

"I have," Deacon admitted.

When he said nothing else, she wriggled until he groaned, hardening even more. "Woman, you must be trying to kill me."

"So, tell me what it means." She tried to hide her smile.

He nuzzled his face in the hollow of her neck and shoulder. "Don't think I can't see that smile on your face."

"Deacon," she said, letting him hear the warning in her voice.

"Okay, fine. It means *my treasure* in Italian," he grumbled against her neck.

Without warning, she rolled over to face him, nearly head-butting him in the process. Just in time, he jerked his head out of the way. "Hey! Careful."

"So that's your new nickname for me?"

As she waited for his response, a slow, decidedly smug smile crept across his face. But before she could even think of moving, he clasped her around her hip and tugged her closer. "You like it."

How did he always seem to know what she was thinking?

Making a sound of frustration, she flipped over to lie on her back. "No, I don't, I'm just surprised you speak Italian."

It was his turn to roll over. The smile on his face widened as he bent closer, his mane of blond hair framing his face as he braced himself on one hand over her.

She wanted him again. How could she be craving him already?

"You do like it."

"I didn't say that."

"Didn't have to." One hand stroked the line of her jaw. "You're blushing. It's adorable."

"Shut up," she said, poking at his chest.

The smile on his face grew until he was radiant, and looking like some kind of sun god. Her heart ached at the sight of it.

"Tell me how an all-American jock like you knows even a single word of Italian."

"My great-grandmother was Italian," he said. "So, I

happen to know a little more than that. If you're nice to me, I might tell you more."

Finally giving in to her need to touch, she ran her hands over his sweat-dampened skin on his back and over his wide shoulders. "Italian, mm? Who knew?"

Groaning, he closed his eyes as she combed her fingers through the soft strands of hair, settling his weight more firmly on her. "Mm."

"Deacon?"

His eyes opened, a satisfied smile in their depth. "Hmm?"

"Say it again," she murmured, her eyes fixed on his stubborn chin. Not quite daring to meet his eyes.

A hand, his, tilted her head until they were eye to eye. "Look at me."

His face was serious as he forced her to meet his eye. "Never be afraid to tell me what you want. Not when I would give you everything."

Oh god, he meant it.

Then his lips were on hers and his tongue was invading her mouth. His kiss was demanding, probing hers as if determined to taste every corner of her mouth.

As he settled more of his weight on her, sighing, she massaged the heavy muscles of his shoulders and wound her legs around his waist.

His erection hovered at the entrance of her sex, but he didn't move. Breaking their kiss, he stared down at her for a beat.

"*Tesoro mio,*" he murmured, and then he thrust into her.

Eyes fluttering closed as Deacon kissed her, she rode the waves of pleasure each new movement brought her.

When his lips traced a path away from her lips and down to her neck, she sighed, even as her gut clenched in anticipation.

He wasn't a vampire. His bite couldn't give her the same pleasure a dark kiss could. At least that was what she'd thought the second before his teeth bit down on the sensitive hollow of her throat. Jerking, she came so violently she barely felt his own release following hers seconds later.

CHAPTER TEN

*H*e wanted nothing more than to grab Ophelia, find some dark corner, muffle her screams with his kiss, and fuck her until she was coming all over his cock.

But Eros didn't have any dark corners. And he'd seen no opportunity to drag Ophelia anywhere, especially with her dealing with an endless line of acquaintances since they'd arrived.

To his eyes, they appeared to be nothing more than hangers-on desperate for the opportunity to secure an invitation to the most talked about wedding in the city.

None of them, from what he could see were friends. And none of Ophelia's smiles were real. He'd seen the real thing, had heard her laugh, and what he was seeing was nothing more than a mask she used to hide her true self.

They'd been at the private vampire only club Eros for a couple of hours already, and from the way Ophelia was slowly but unmistakably inching toward the front entrance, evidently she'd had enough. He followed close behind, ignoring the glances from the elegantly dressed men and women.

It was unusual his being there since the only humans to be found in the expansive rooms glittering with chandeliers and diamonds, and full of the sweet lyrical strings of a harp from a musician tucked unobtrusively in one corner, were the servers. And him.

Some of the glances were hungrier than he would have liked, but one glance at the sword strapped around his waist soon disabused them of the notion he was on the menu.

Ophelia had just replaced her empty champagne glass on a passing server's tray when Deacon spotted him. Byron. Cutting a path through the crowd, his eyes fixed on Ophelia.

Clearing his throat, when Ophelia glanced his way, he subtly tipped his head toward Byron bearing down on them.

There was no visible change on her face. The neutral, but bland expression she'd been wearing since they'd stepped out of the car remained fixed in place, and Deacon couldn't help but feel disturbed seeing it.

Had this been her life all along? Dealing with people who cared more for what she could do for their societal standing, than whether she was happy?

"Byron!" Delight filled Ophelia's voice as she raised her hand for him to kiss the inside of her wrist. "What are you doing here? I thought Eros was much too stale for you."

"I heard you were here. And that, future-wife, changes

everything. You're looking ravishing tonight." Byron's eyes didn't move from her cleavage.

Ophelia was looking beautiful in an ice blue, long sleeve sequin dress with a deep V-neck. But clearly, Byron's interests lay only in the skin the dress revealed rather than the woman wearing it.

"How sweet. I wish I could stay, but I was just about to walk out the door. You're lucky to have caught me."

"Leave? Where?" Byron's eyes narrowed as they fixed on him, but Ophelia's hand on Byron's arm drew his attention back to her—or rather to her breasts.

"Oh, to Hakkasan," she said airily, taking her hand off his arm.

Although Deacon had never visited Vegas before, friends of his as well as some of the guys who'd served alongside him in the Marines, had. From what little he could recall, Hakkasan had been a famous restaurant, and there was a club as well.

The nightclub still functioned much as it had before. But the restaurant now catered to a different clientele entirely, and what was often served on the menu wasn't entirely fit for human consumption.

Byron's eyes glinted. "A blood-feast? I'll come with you."

Ah, so it was the restaurant then that Ophelia and Byron meant.

Her giggle was a happy bubble of sound.

"In a Naeem Khan dress? Don't be silly, Byron. No, Madelaine and Violet have booked a private room."

Deacon had no idea who Madelaine and Violet were, but he couldn't help but marvel at her quick thinking.

"Private room, great idea. Let's go," Byron said.

Ophelia grinned up at him. "Perfect. Since you'll be the only guy there, you can give us a man's opinion on whether you think all the bridesmaid dresses look ridiculous matching. Or, should I have listened to Marta, and had them all in contrasting colors?"

She hooked her arm around Byron's and started for the exit.

Byron paused mid-step. "Bridesmaid dresses?"

Ophelia nodded. "I think I prefer them matching so no one stands out. I mean, I wouldn't want anyone to say one of the dresses is prettier than the rest, or for anyone to accuse me of playing favorites, but—"

Byron gently removed Ophelia's hand from his arm. "My sweet, I've just remembered there's somewhere I need to be tonight. You know how it is? But I'm devastated I can't join you and your friends."

As far as Deacon could see, Byron was doing a terrible job of hiding his relief. But Ophelia blinked up at him, pretending not to see it.

"Oh, how sad. Are you sure you can't—"

"I'm sure."

Nodding, Ophelia drifted toward the exit. "I'll see you later, then."

"Ophelia? Why aren't you wearing your ring?" Byron's eyes narrowed in suspicion.

They would have to do something about Byron, Deacon thought.

He'd gone back to the Cosmopolitan earlier just in case the ring had turned up, but no one at the front desk had seen it. Which meant that it could be anywhere.

She shrugged. "I'm having it cleaned. I want everything to be perfect for the wedding."

For the first time since Ophelia had opened her mouth and the lies had poured out, Byron didn't look convinced.

"But I have to go now." She raised her hand for another kiss, and started for the exit, pausing to say a few words to the vampires she passed on her way out.

But Deacon felt the weight of Byron's eyes at his back, following them as they threaded their way through the crowd.

"You made him suspicious," Deacon murmured.

"It was the only way to get rid of him, and the absolute last thing I wanted was to spend hours playing happy fiancée all night. Not when I could be here with you." With her head resting on his bare shoulder and his arm wrapped around her waist, she resumed tracing the tattoo on his shoulder with her finger.

She felt his smile when he pressed a kiss against her forehead. "Mm, the feeling is mutual, *tesoro mio.*"

As ever, when he called her his treasure, a part of her melted.

The bed in his apartment wasn't as big as her bed. It was small, could even be less than a twin, she didn't know. All she knew was, she'd never loved a bed more. Or maybe it was the man she was sharing it with that made it so special.

After her driver had left them outside Hakkasan at the

MGM, it had taken little to convince her they should head to Deacon's downtown apartment.

He was right when he said staying in a hotel was eventually going to get them into trouble.

"So, about that tattoo on your shoulder…"

"You mean the one you've been dying to ask me about?" There was a smile in Deacon's voice.

"No, I haven't," she lied.

"Your eyes have been burning a hole through my shirt since the moment you saw it."

She stopped stroking, and he groaned in frustration.

"Okay, you haven't. If you keep doing that, I'll tell you all about it."

She was so relaxed, so content that for a moment she let herself enjoy the feel of his bare skin flush against hers as she smoothed her fingers over his skin.

Now with the need she'd felt for him building all night satisfied, she wanted to know more about him. She wanted to learn all his secrets. The things he told no one.

"Deacon," she murmured, poking him in the chest. "You better not be asleep."

"I was in the military," he said, sighing in contentment. "The Marines. The tattoo was one a bunch of us guys got after basic training."

"I don't understand what a snarling dog has to do with the Marines. The helmet, I get. The dog, I don't."

"It's a Devil dog." His words came out at a near purr as she brushed her lips against his jaw. "And the British bulldog is a kind of mascot."

"Devil dog?"

It felt so good to cuddle with him. She'd never thought

of herself as someone who would enjoy intimacy like this. Sex in the past had been more akin to scratching an itch, and it'd always proved to be a disappointment.

"Hmm. From the first world war."

"Is that where you learned how to use a sword as well? In the Marines?"

"No. That was before. I was always into martial arts when I was a kid, and my parents encouraged it since I was a skinny, little runt who kept being beaten up."

Lifting her head, she blinked down at him in astonishment. "You're lying! Even your muscles have muscles."

Grinning, he shifted her before rising. "Wait here."

Her mouth went dry as she watched him pad naked out of the bedroom, completely unabashed. When he returned seconds later, her eyes dipped to his semi-hard arousal. And as she stared, he hardened under her gaze.

"Here," he said.

"Hmm?"

Would they have time to make love again before they had to leave?

"Here." There was a smile in his voice as he blocked her view with a worn photograph. Sighing as she took it, she shifted to allow Deacon back into bed.

When he'd gathered her into his arms again, she examined the picture of the skinny little boy with a thick blond fringe, and a sweet smile.

"This is you?"

"Hmm mmm."

"You were so cute."

One of his fingers poked her in the side and she giggled.

"What do you mean, were?"

"You know what I mean. So, you started martial arts to defend yourself?"

"Yep. I ended up loving it. Started with the usual Karate and Judo, and long story short, I ended up being introduced to Kenjutso, and the moment someone handed me a katana, that was it. I never looked back. I trained every single day throughout high school for hours. It's a wonder I graduated at all."

Listening to him, it was hard to miss the respect, and the love in his voice. She couldn't imagine what that was like, to find a passion like that.

Growing up, she hadn't had anything that came even close to resembling his experience. She had a role to play and that was that. It'd seemed pointless to want anything else, not when her life had already been mapped out for her.

"I'm surprised the Bladed didn't offer to turn you," she mused.

Vampires, the Council in particular loved to hoard talents. And even though she didn't know a whole lot about martial arts, what little she'd seen of Deacon, she knew he was crazy talented.

The hand gliding up and down her lower back paused. "They offered. But I have no desire to sacrifice my humanity for the sake of being promoted. I didn't come to Vegas for that."

"Even if you'd be faster with a sword?"

"Even still. Now, I have a question for you. Something I've been curious about for a while now."

Her heart stuttered. If he asked her about her father,

what would she say? She didn't want to lie, but she wasn't sure she was ready to spill all the Mortlake secrets just yet, and this one was dangerous.

"This baby your father is so eager for you to have," he said, ignoring her sudden tension, though he had to have felt it. "How is that supposed to work given—"

"Vampires can't get pregnant?" she interrupted, hiding her sigh of relief.

Of all the questions he could've asked, this one at least was the one she could be most open about.

"Hmm."

"It's done with a surrogate. It's a little more complicated because of what we are and how different our cells are, but our genetic information is transplanted into a surrogate—a human woman and the result is always an earlier delivery date than usual. The entire process is so expensive, so few of us are born that way. That and the fact the process is ninety-nine per-cent of the time guaranteed to kill the surrogate."

Deacon's arm tightened around her and he pressed his lips against her hair. "Your mother?"

She sighed. "Dead. Selene said she didn't get a chance to hold me before... before. So, yeah, I killed her."

"Princess, you didn't kill her."

"So, who's to blame, then?"

"How about no one."

"Deacon, you can't ignore the fact that she would have been alive if she hadn't given birth to me."

Deacon was silent.

"Is that why August didn't push you into marrying

Byron when you were human? I'm assuming you could have gotten pregnant then?"

She snorted. "He didn't push because if anything would've happened to me, Selene would have made it her life's mission to kill him. That and there was no guarantee the baby would have survived. If I'd died, Selene would never have agreed to the procedure."

"Why couldn't he—"

She shook her head. "He's old enough it wouldn't work. It shouldn't have with me, and that was over thirty years ago. I'm his last chance for a Mortlake heir."

He was silent as he considered her words. "But you were born human?"

Conscious she was telling him more than she should. More than he should know, it wasn't enough to make her stop. All her life, the only person she could talk to—really talk to was Selene. She couldn't—refused to not enjoy every last second she could with Deacon.

"Kind of. Maybe not completely. We're—those of us who were born this way—are weaker. Even though I could be out during the day, I was still really sensitive to light, and I could never stomach a lot of food."

"And if August hadn't turned you?"

"I don't know. I could have stayed like that, or I might have died. Selene said I was a sickly baby. I guess that explains why she's so protective of me—"

"No. She's protective over you because she's your sister and she loves you."

"She stopped him from killing me, you know," she heard herself say.

He went still at her words.

"He's only ever wanted a son. An heir. A blood heir to be precise. But when it turned out I was a girl, he was going to kill me. It didn't matter that I was a baby."

His hands tightened around her reflexively, and she swallowed. "It was Selene who convinced him that I was such a pretty baby, wouldn't it better to keep me alive so I could marry and give him what he'd always wanted."

"To keep you alive," he murmured against her forehead.

She nodded. "She's smart. It's the only thing that would have convinced him to let me live."

"As I said, she loves you. Even then, she loved you."

A smile tugged at the corners of her mouth at his words, but it didn't last. Because soon it would be over. A doctor would hand her a baby created from her and Byron's genetic makeup, and she'd be trapped, imprisoned in a new life.

One she'd never escape from. And one she'd never hope to see Deacon ever again. There'd be no more freedom to come and go as she'd had before. Her father and Byron would see to that.

It was unexpectedly painful to think about it, so swallowing, she moved to stand, not looking at him. "We should start getting dressed."

But Deacon used his larger body to press her back into the bed. He stared down at her for a moment without saying a word.

"Ophelia…" he said, voice soft.

His hand curved around the side of her face and she leaned into his touch, her eyes closing. Relaxing into the touch, her body softened, and when Deacon lightly brushed his lips across hers, she sighed.

When he lifted his head, she opened her eyes.

"More?" His voice was husky as he searched her face. Looking for what, she couldn't say.

Nodding, she wound her legs around his hips and slung her arms over his shoulders. "More."

Bending his head, his lips found hers, capturing her moan when he slipped back inside her. Giving her more, much more, than she'd ever thought she'd have.

CHAPTER ELEVEN

*W*hy had he asked her about the baby? All the rest of the night and the following day, the question had plagued him.

Why had he mentioned something that would only remind her of her future life? A life that left her eyes clouded with shadows and despair if she let him see it at all that is. Which is why he'd known she'd needed the quiet peacefulness of Desert Pines.

They'd made another brief appearance at Eros, and fortunately this time there was no sign of Byron. And while he'd craved nothing more than spending the next few hours in Ophelia's arms as he breathed in the scent of her skin, there was more between them than just sex.

"Run away with me." The words burst out of him. Surprising even him.

Lying beside him on his jacket in the dune, Ophelia twisted to face him, wide-eyed. Stunned. "What!"

Shifting to lie on his side, he waited for her to do the

same so they faced each other. "Run away with me. Leave Vegas, forget the wedding—forget Byron."

"Deacon... I can't. We can't, it just wouldn't work." She was shaking her head, a deep line creasing her forehead.

"Why not?"

"Well... how about where would we go? What would we do for work? Or live? And you're a Bladed, they won't just let you—"

"I don't care about any of that. It's just details. You can't want to go through with the wedding?"

"You know I don't. It isn't anything I ever wanted."

He moved until he lay on top of her, framing her face with his hands, his eyes searching hers for even the slightest hint she might want this as much as he did.

"So, say yes. Run away with me, and we can make a new life—a life we both want—together. Just you and me."

"This is crazy. It's too soon... What if it doesn't work out?" she whispered. "What happens then?"

Keeping his eyes locked with hers, he lowered his head and kissed her, pouring out all his need and all his want in a searing kiss until they were both breathless.

When he lifted his head, he found her eyes closed and her lips were red, plump from his kisses. And as he watched, her eyelids fluttered open, revealing eyes hazy with pleasure as she licked her lips.

"Does that feel like something that won't last? Something that won't work out?"

Because to him, it didn't. When he kissed her, it felt like a homecoming, like Ophelia was everything he'd ever wanted, achingly beautiful and sparkling with life, but somehow soft and strangely shy.

He wanted her, needed her more and more with each passing day.

"Ophelia? *Tesoro mio?*"

Her silence was agony.

Terror, sheer terror filled him she would tell him no, would tell him he was wrong and that she wanted this marriage—craved stability and security with Byron more than she wanted him.

She swallowed hard. And when she spoke, she stopped his heart.

"Yes."

Her single word was soft. So soft, he wasn't sure he heard it over the harsh drumbeat of his heart.

"What did you say?" It was an order. He needed to hear her say it like he needed air.

"Yes. I want this. I want you. Yes."

And then a sweet smile was curving her lips. The most beautiful sight he'd ever seen his entire life. His own smile was wider, full of amazement as an unfamiliar ache clenched his heart.

"God, I need to be inside you right now," he growled, and then he was kissing her again. His hands were frantic, yanking her dress up over her hips as her hands, just as desperate, just as eager as his tore at the front of his pants, freeing him as he shoved aside her lace panties.

Then he was sliding into her warm heat. Feeling the muscles of her sex squeezing around him. As always, that first moment of being inside her choked the air from his lungs. He didn't think he would ever get enough of it. Of her. It was like heaven. All honeyed heat and desperate longing.

For a moment, he lay panting, his forehead resting against hers. But when she made a soft sound of complaint as she shifted restlessly beneath him, he lifted his head, drew his hips back, and tunneled back into her.

Her breathy moan had his hands tightening on her hips as he gritted his teeth, his eyes searching her face to make sure pleasure was the only expression on her face.

With her head tipped back to stare up at the sky, she curved her legs around him, her fingers digging into his ass as she lifted her hips to meet each of his hungry thrusts with a gasping moan. His answering groan was loud in the quiet darkness of the night.

Staring down at her, despite his body trembling with need for her, his hips slowed, and her eyes shifted from the stars in the sky to his face.

He didn't know what she saw in his face, but her eyes, the warm hazel-green of them softened and she reached a hand up to his face.

"Deacon..." His name was a soft gasp on her lips.

There was something in her eyes, something in the desperate way she clung to him that called to his need to claim her. To possess her.

His playful side slid away, his expression now a harsh grimace of concentration. This hidden side of him, fierce and possessive, usually tucked out of view spilled out.

He prepared himself for her withdrawal. Conscious he was gripping her hips too tight and that he had to ease back, needed to be gentler. But even as he thought it, his hips continued to drive into her, hard, unrelenting.

His control was shot. She'd stolen it away from him the second he'd slid into her, and getting it back was an exercise in futility. He'd never been as out of control as he felt when he was in Ophelia's arms.

He told himself Ophelia was delicate. She'd grown up with silk sheets, classical music, and pretty vampire princes.

But despite his fear he was being too rough, beneath him her body softened even as her eyes darkened with heat.

Her eyes begged him for more, and in response, his body swelled at seeing the desperate need in her. His body had known it before his mind had: A gentle loving wasn't enough for her. She wanted something more from him. Something only he could give her.

Rocking against her, his hands gripped her hips tighter, angling her body to give her even more pleasure, so he could penetrate deeper until she was shuddering beneath him.

She stared up at him, her eyes turned glassy as her breath spilled out of her parted lips. She was close. So close, he could feel the way her inner muscles of her pussy clutched at him greedily.

"Now," he murmured against her lips, capturing her scream in his mouth as she came apart in his arms.

Her back bowed beneath him, and he swore as the muscles of her sex clamped so tight around him, the pressure of her grip made every muscle tense.

He forced himself to hold on just a little longer, draw the pleasure out a little longer, but it was impossible. Groaning deep in his throat, holding her still beneath him he thrust once more, his body straining as his cock jerked inside her.

Not once did he look away from her.

Lowering his head, his full weight pressing her down into the soft sand, his tongue swept into her mouth in a lazy lingering kiss that had her hands stealing under his shirt to stroke at his back. Wanting nothing more to live inside of her forever.

Back at home and in her bed with the sheets pulled up over her breasts, and the sand from the dune long since washed away, it didn't take long for doubt set in.

She wasn't spontaneous or impulsive like Selene was to suddenly decide to run away with a guy she was…

Just what was she and Deacon, exactly? Was he her boyfriend, or was this turning into something more?

It was feeling like something more. Had started to the moment he'd kissed her in the locker room at the Bladed gym.

The feeling was new, soft, like the wings of a butterfly fluttering against her chest, she thought as she pressed a hand to her heart.

Was this love? Had she fallen in love with Deacon?

She couldn't deny sex between them was beyond anything she'd ever experienced before. He seemed to know exactly what she needed, and she couldn't deny how arousing it was to be with someone who never tried to hide his own response from her. If anything, he went out of his way to show her how good it was for him too.

Whatever it was, nothing else seemed to matter anymore. Not her father, not the wedding, and certainly not Byron. Glancing down at her naked ring finger, she snorted. Well, at least finding her missing ring didn't matter anymore. She wouldn't be needing it where she was going.

Leaving Desert Pines had been agony, especially when she'd wanted nothing more than to lie in the dune with Deacon and talk. He'd told her a little bit about his family, and about his life growing up in Chicago.

They'd love to meet her, he'd said, and there was no reason they couldn't stay with them for at least a few days once they left Vegas.

They'd left early because of Deacon's plans, and packing was only one small part of the preparations that needed to be done, things only he could do. Helplessness had been an ache in her belly. There was little she could do, not while she still lived under the same roof as her father.

She smiled at his tender kiss when he'd noticed her mood change in the aftermath of their loving, as they'd still lain wrapped around each other. He'd picked up on it instantly, known what had caused it without her having to say a word, and his kiss warmed her even more than his assurances he could handle everything fine on his own.

Try as she might, her imagination struggled to bring into sharp focus what their new life would look like. As she'd showered and dressed for bed the vision remained blurry, indistinct.

What that life might look like, and where they might end up was still a mystery to her. She'd never left Vegas except to attend boarding school on the east coast, so she hadn't even been able to tell him where she'd want to live when he'd asked.

But she liked the sand, even if it got into places that she'd rather it didn't. And she liked the water, so it'd be nice to be somewhere near a beach. Grinning at her, Deacon had kissed her knowing it was because of him, because of the happiness he'd given her in a golf course in the middle of the Vegas Strip, of all places.

Wherever they'd end up didn't have to be forever. They could go anywhere, and she'd have to remember to ask Selene where she and her boyfriend Max had visited.

But Selene had had the foresight to take her jewelry with her before she left. And since Father had always valued expensive gifts over love and affection, both she and Selene had hundreds of thousands of dollars' worth.

Selene had pawned a lot of the jewelry gifted to her, and she'd been smart enough to invest a lot of the proceeds. All of which left her in a position where she could live comfortably, renting a new place in Vegas and often traveling around the states with Max.

Investing sounded far more complicated than she could ever get her head around, and since math had never been her strong suit, that didn't surprise her.

She'd never had to think about money ever. All she'd have to do was request to have whatever she wanted to buy put onto the account of Ophelia Mortlake, and the manager of whatever shop or boutique she was in dealt it with, just like that.

She kept a few notes for paying tips to staff, something Father could never understand. He'd always told her people were there to serve her, and tipping would only encourage people to expect payment even when they didn't deserve it. But that was Father.

It would be a different way of living and she'd have to rely on Deacon a lot to learn about how to budget, and how to live without the vast Mortlake fortune. But this looming change to her life didn't fill her with as much fear the way change always had.

After all, it wasn't like she wouldn't have Selene to rely on for help. And she'd be with Deacon, and a change that filled her with such warmth could never be a bad thing.

Smiling, she turned onto her side. As long as she had Deacon, she would be happy whatever happened, she thought, closing her eyes, and no matter where they ended up.

CHAPTER TWELVE

*T*hrowing himself onto his couch, Deacon let out a deep sigh as he thumped his feet on the coffee table.

It wasn't often he was awake before midday, not anymore. Especially not when more often than not he was working until five in the morning and getting home at six. But today he had more to do than he had time to do it.

Exhaustion beat down on him, but he'd been up at ten in the morning making calls—making plans with a large steaming mug of coffee to keep him going and doing it all with a massive grin on his face.

He'd asked Ophelia to run away with him, and she'd said yes.

If anyone had told him a year ago, or even a couple of weeks ago that he'd be planning on running away with the daughter of a Councilor, he'd have laughed in their face. But this was Ophelia, and Ophelia was… special.

There was something between them, some rare and unexpected gift he couldn't walk away from. And somehow, without his noticing when it'd happened, she'd crawled under his skin and made a home for herself there.

He wanted—no he *needed* to know more, learn more, and see where it took them because he could guess what it was that she was feeling. Because when he stared deep into her eyes, what he saw reflected right back at him was an echo of what must be shining out of his own eyes.

The fallout of their running away would be messy, and that was putting things mildly. But if he let Ophelia marry that idiot Byron, he would regret it every single day for the rest of his life.

Then there was the not so small matter of August Mortlake. August would have people working for him in Vegas that Deacon couldn't afford to let on what he and Ophelia planned. And that included Pierce who already suspected something was going on between them.

Pierce wouldn't be happy when he heard what he'd done, but his boss would try and stop him, regardless of how he felt about Deacon. He'd been a Bladed for over ten years, and there was no question his loyalty lay with the Council.

And Byron. He couldn't ignore Byron's increasing suspicion.

There wasn't much else he could think of that he had left to do. He'd spent hours researching hotels before he'd realized it would be the first place August would look for them. Better they stay in an apartment. At least then he'd be able to spot any pursuers, something he'd struggle to do in a busy hotel.

Gazing around his apartment, he saw he was leaving more behind than he'd be taking with him. It'd come fully furnished, and over the years he'd filled it with household essentials, but with limited space in his trunk, he had little choice.

He'd picked up some ultra-blackout blinds and drapes in case the apartment he'd found for them didn't have any, and he'd filled any remaining space in his car with a few changes of clothes for himself, and Ophelia as well.

Tonight when he picked her up, there'd be no way for her to leave the house in anything other than a party dress. He'd tried not to think about her giving up everything to be with him. Her home, her closet full of designer clothes, her wealth and life of ease, everything.

And she was trusting him. Most especially with her life. There was so much trust in what she was doing. He wasn't about to do anything to shatter the trust she'd given him.

They'd agreed to do what they'd been doing the last couple of nights. The only difference was, instead of driving to the Mortlake mansion, he'd take a cab. After Ophelia's driver dropped them off for her event, they'd jump into a cab and head straight for his car.

From there, they'd leave the city and by the time August—or anyone else realized Ophelia wasn't where she should be, they'd be hours away and it would be dawn. Too late for pursuit, at least that first night. Unless August sent Pierce or another human Bladed.

He glanced at his watch. Five o'clock.

Rising, he bent to pick up his short sword. He'd already packed his katana in his car. He would need it because August would send someone after him. After them. It was only a matter of time, and he would need all the weapons at his disposal. The katana was his, but the wakizashi—the short sword, the black steel weapon of the Bladed was not. If they wanted that back, well, they'd just have to come and take it from him.

———

After shrugging into his jacket, Deacon grabbed his sunglasses and keys and was heading out the front door when his cell phone started vibrating in his pocket.

Narrowing his eyes at a number he didn't recognize, he decided to answer it anyway. "Yeah?"

"Deacon. It's August Mortlake."

Deacon paused at the front door. "Councilor Mortlake? Is there a problem?"

August laughed. "Oh no. No problem. I'm sorry to be calling you at the last minute, but Ophelia's event this evening has been canceled. We won't be needing your presence tonight."

Deacon frowned. "I hope it's nothing serious."

"Not at all. But since Ophelia and I have spent so little time together recently, and you haven't had even a single night away from your duties, tonight gives me the opportunity to spend some quality time with her before she marries."

It sounded so reasonable, so believable. But Deacon found his suspicion stirring.

"Of course. I will see you and Ophelia tomorrow night then."

"Yes," August said, and just like that he hung up.

For a second Deacon stared at the phone in his hand.

He knew things like this happened. People canceled events at the last minute all the time, but a part of him couldn't help but wonder why it had to be tonight of all nights. And since when had August cared about spending quality time with Ophelia?

Had August realized what he and Ophelia were about to do?

No.

If August had even the slightest idea of what they planned, there was no way he'd have called him to give him the night off. He'd be dead.

There wasn't even a way for him to reach Ophelia to speak to her, not when she didn't have a phone, and turning up out of the blue after August's call would only make the man suspicious.

He should have bought her a phone and helped her to hide it. At least he'd have been able to make sure she was okay, and he could convince himself his unease was paranoia and nothing more.

But there was nothing either of them could do. So, toeing off his boots, he headed for the kitchen and grabbed a beer. Tonight would be a long night. But at least everything was ready to go for tomorrow night. He'd have a few beers, get takeout and watch TV.

It was one more night after all, and in the grand scheme of things one night wouldn't change anything.

Halfway down the stairs, Ophelia paused with a frown on her face as she listened in to the phone call.

That didn't sound like Father. At all.

He'd never shown the slightest inclination in spending quality time with her or Selene. For him to start now was more than a little suspicious.

Over the years she'd laughed, but quickly changed the subject whenever any human reporters had asked if August Mortlake was as charming in real life as he was during interviews on TV.

No one needed to know what he was like and how little she knew about him. It was bad enough already they looked at her with hungry eyes, eager for her to spill the secrets about the Council, because living with a Councilor, she must be the holder of so many secrets, right?

There was no way she was about to admit she was as much in the dark about the Council and her father's role in it as everyone else.

When she'd been younger, it had frustrated her no end, but now she couldn't be more relieved to know so little.

Had she known anything of any substance about the Council, there was no doubt in her mind her Father would see her dead before he let her go even a single night with Deacon.

"Ophelia?"

"Yes, Father?"

"Come here, please."

Right, she thought. *Quality time.*

Maybe he'd finally realized after the wedding he'd be all alone since she couldn't think why else he'd be interested in spending time with her.

Whatever the reason, she wasn't about to ignore this

rare opportunity. A chance to breach the divide between them. Breach, but not heal. Too much had happened between them for that. He'd hurt her too much for her to easily forgive and forget.

She wasn't naïve enough to think everything would be different, but at least for one night, she might have something that resembled a father-daughter relationship before she and Deacon left.

In her heart, she knew Father would never accept Deacon, and she saw that a life without Deacon in it was colorless and devoid of warmth.

She'd had a taste of a new way of living. Of laughing and skinny dipping, and making love. There was no way she could go back to the way her life had been. Not now.

"Father, since I'm already dressed, maybe we could—"

She stopped. Stared.

On his desk sat her engagement ring.

"Where did you find that?" she asked, her mouth dry, her face flashing from hot to cold, and then back again.

"Perhaps you might tell me?"

Finally, she lifted her gaze from her diamond ring and met her father's eyes.

Leaning back in his chair with his dark eyes fixed on her, he looked relaxed, at ease even. But that wasn't what had her heart racing. It was the excitement she saw stirring in their depths.

She'd seen that look before. Knew what it meant. It was a look that promised her something bad was coming. Something that would hurt.

"You did something." Her words were low, and when her father's lips curved in a smile. The same smile he'd given her at the vampire Lucian's blood feast, just before the doors had opened, her heart started pounding harder.

"I warned you, Ophelia. Did I not warn you to do as I asked?"

"What did you do?" Her voice was sharp and just a little shrill, and loud. Far, far too loud.

He continued to study her in silence before slowly lacing his fingers together.

"You should have heeded my warning." His voice was gentle, could've been mistaken for being kind by someone who didn't know him as well as she did.

The last time he'd looked at her like that was something she'd never forget. It'd been years since she'd defied him by continuing to secretly meet with the friends he'd ordered her to cut out of her life. Friends he'd considered too human, and too poor for the daughter of a Councilor to have.

If she could dream, if she could have nightmares, then without a doubt she'd still be having nightmares over what Father had done.

"Who did you send after him, Father?"

The phone call made perfect sense now. Her father would have wanted to make sure Deacon was home. The lack of outdoor noises, gym sounds, and even the time would have told him where Deacon would be.

Deacon wouldn't have seen the attack coming until it was too late. How many Bladed had he sent? Deacon was good with a sword, but her father would know that. He'd have seen how good he was at the sunset terrace party the night he'd saved her life. Would he have sent two, or three? More?

165

"Did you send the Bladed after him?" Her voice was shrill in the quiet office.

What would she do? *Oh god,* what would she do without Deacon?

Her father laughed. "Him? Do you think I would do something to that human guard of yours? How would you learn your lesson then?"

She blinked in surprise as relief surged through her that Deacon was okay.

But was he telling the truth? Was he just playing with her?

It doesn't matter Ophelia. Deacon's alive.

As long as he's alive she'd be okay. She could breathe.

"I don't…" She shook her head. "I don't understand."

"My instructions to you were most explicit about who you are to see and who you are not. Your focus was to be on the wedding, and on spending time with your fiancé."

She frowned, confused. "But I have been, I haven't—"

Then it hit her. Who he must have hurt to punish her if it hadn't been Deacon. There was only one person who she had seen he'd warned her away from. Her sister.

Selene.

Strength left her, and she was falling even before she realized what was happening. Desperately she grabbed for the door.

"What did you do?" Her words came out in a harsh whisper as she clung to the door. "What did you do to my sister?"

Leaning toward her, slowly. Taking his time doing it, her father folded one hand over the other on his desk, examining her coolly. Clinically.

"As I said before, Ophelia, you do not have a sister. Perhaps you will understand better now."

Her grip wasn't enough to hold her up, and she stopped trying. What was the point? She fell heavily to the floor.

"No… *No!*" Shaking her head, she raised her hand to her face as tears streamed down her face.

He was suddenly there, her father. The man who'd killed her sister. Killed Selene. Right there, crouching in front of her pressing the engagement ring toward her.

"No!" she shrieked.

She lunged at him as she'd never done before, not knowing if it was agony or rage which fueled her attack. The ring went flying. Where it went didn't matter. Nothing mattered but her need to lash out at the man— the monster who'd taken her sister from her.

"I won't marry Byron. I won't ever do anything you ask. I hate you. *I hate you.*"

He moved faster than her eyes could follow. His counterattack came with no warning. It was only after he had her pinned her to the ground, his hands gripping her arms, forcing her to stillness, that she was conscious he'd even moved.

"You will do whatever I tell you to do, Ophelia, even if it kills you to do it. I will give you tonight to return to your senses. Tomorrow, you have an event at Eros, an event you will attend in a pretty dress, with your engagement ring on your finger and a big smile on your face. Unless you wish to spend it mourning the guard, that is?"

She stopped struggling. But the tears sliding down her cheeks… they weren't as easy to stop.

Just as sudden as the attack had come, it was over and her father was rising, turning his attention to the figure who'd materialized in the doorway.

"Stanley, if you could see Ophelia to her room. Run her a bath, and she'll need a glass, perhaps two, of blood. She's been looking a touch pale of late. I shouldn't need to tell you how important she looks her best."

Gentle but firm hands eased her to her feet. Sagging for a second against the solid weight of their servant, slowly Stanley guided her out of her father's office.

No. She would never think of him as her father again. From now he would only ever be August Mortlake. He was not her father. No father would ever kill his own flesh and blood in order to punish the other.

August was saying something as Stanley led her out, but she wasn't listening. His words only had the power to hurt her, and she never wanted to hear his voice ever again.

Then there was a pressure on her hand, and instinctively she glanced down. Saw the ring on her finger.

Lifting her head, her eyes met his. August Mortlake's. He was smiling happily at her. As if he hadn't just killed one of his daughters and ripped out the heart of the other. He was enjoying this. Enjoying her pain.

"Tomorrow will be a fresh start for all of us. Good night, Ophelia."

She stared at him.

"Say goodnight to your father, Mistress, and I'll take you up to your room." There was a warning in Stanley's voice.

Had he seen the mad glint in August's eyes, or was he

concerned only about saving his job? Perhaps he didn't want to have to deal with cleaning her blood from the foyer.

"Goodnight... Father."

She hated him. With every fiber of her being she hated him, and even if it killed her, she would destroy him for what he'd done.

CHAPTER THIRTEEN

*S*tepping into the foyer of the Mortlake mansion, Deacon paused, surprised at the sight of Ophelia standing outside August's office. In front of her, with his back to Deacon, was her father speaking in hushed tones.

Even though she must have known he was there, that Stanley had let him into the house, neither Ophelia nor her father paid him the least bit of attention. Instead, head bowed, nodding periodically, Ophelia remained hyper-focused on what August was saying.

She was okay. The important thing she was okay, and all his unease the previous night had been for nothing. Nothing but paranoia. Quietly, he let out a slow breath of relief.

Last night had felt like the longest night in the world as he'd tried to distract himself with TV, beer and some Chinese food. Neither had worked out to be too much of a success. Not when all he could think about, all he could concentrate on was freedom—forever with Ophelia waiting for him just around the corner.

Finally, at about three in the morning, he'd brushed his teeth and climbed into bed. Had she been in bed thinking about their future together as well?

Once they'd gotten away from Vegas and shaken off any pursuers, he'd take her to the beach—a real beach. And after, they could settle in a city big enough for them to get lost in the crowds, somewhere like New York, and he'd have an easier time picking up a security job.

He'd find something that would mean Ophelia wouldn't need to work. Even so, the new life they'd have together wouldn't be anything like she had now.

There would be no designer dresses, expensive jewelry, and no entrance to the hottest and most exclusive clubs.

But they'd have each other, and he'd spend every night making sure Ophelia never regretted for a single second everything she was turning her back on.

"Yes, Father."

Ophelia's soft murmur reminded him now, in the presence of August Mortlake, wasn't the time to let himself be distracted.

Watching as August bent to brush a kiss against Ophelia's cheek, he frowned when her face went colder than he'd ever seen it before. She didn't like him kissing her. Just as she hadn't the first time he'd seen August do it. There was something about the act, something that made it seem more of a threat than a sign of affection.

But then August stepped aside, and Deacon had his first sight of the rest of her. She wore a white semi-sheer corset-style dress, with a puffy full skirt that had his mouth hanging open.

With her gold-red hair curled and sweeping over one shoulder, white-silver eyeshadow dusting her eyes, she looked like an ice-queen.

All thoughts tumbled out of his head.

She was beautiful, her skin radiant. Angelic. And she was his.

"I see Ophelia's made quite an impression on you this evening." Dark humor coated August's words, snapping Deacon back to attention.

Shit.

Had August caught him gaping at Ophelia? Had he seriously forgotten the danger August represented?

"I hadn't been expecting something so elaborate for a night at Eros," he said, turning to face him.

August smiled. "Of course, you weren't. Now, perhaps you'd better get going. I believe Byron was most excited to dance with Ophelia this evening."

"Of course, Father." Ophelia started for the front door, her gaze sweeping past him as if he were invisible.

He tried not to read too much into it. Not when her father was right there, his eyes on both of them. They'd talk later, not in the car with the driver listening in but either in Eros or, even better, in his car as he was driving them out of Vegas.

"Goodnight, Councilor," Deacon said, opening the door for Ophelia.

"Goodnight. I'll see you later."

No. No, you will never see either of us again.

"We'll see you later," he lied.

The car ride to Eros was as silent as he'd expected it to be.

They couldn't talk. Not about anything that would end up being reported to August.

But at Eros, climbing out first, he reached inside to help Ophelia out. And that was when he saw it. The ring. Her engagement ring on her finger.

"Ophelia?" he murmured, his eyes searching her face.

She didn't look at him. Instead, her gaze remained fixed on something over his shoulder, and gently pulling her hand from his, she stepped around him and started for Eros's front entrance. He slid his sunglasses and turned to watch her walk away.

"Byron!" she called out, sounding delighted.

A frown creased his forehead as Ophelia lifted her hand to Byron who stood waiting just outside, a smile on his face. Taking her hand, he pressed a lingering kiss onto her inner wrist before turning to lead her inside.

His frown deepened at the sight of the couple disappearing inside.

Since when was Ophelia excited to see Byron, and where had she found her lost engagement ring?

Byron's hand on her waist was making her feel sick.

August had said Byron would expect a dance from her. Ophelia had stupidly thought he meant one, as in a single dance and she could spend the rest of the night gazing into the distance, pretending she was on a beach with Deacon.

She should've known better.

Byron's hands were possessive, and they were never still for even a second. He'd grabbed her ass at least twice already, and he hadn't been gentle about it. And she couldn't do a thing about it.

If she made a scene, or snapped at him or showed even the slightest sign she felt anything other than disgust, he'd be on the phone to August in a heartbeat, and she knew how that would end up. With Deacon dead.

He had his mirrored sunglasses on now, but she knew the frown that'd been on his face when he'd helped her out of the car thirty minutes ago was still there. He'd be trying to work out what was wrong. Likely trying to figure out a way he could get her on her own so they could talk. So, they could run away together.

How would she tell him? How could she make him believe that would never happen? Not now. She'd spent hours crying, mourning her sister, mourning her future with Deacon already.

The sharp pain of what she was about to do pierced through her mask, and for a second, a single second, her fixed smile wobbled, and losing concentration, she forgot the steps of the dance and froze.

Deacon stepped toward her.

August could never learn how she felt about Deacon. He could never discover something she'd only began to see herself—she'd fallen in love with him. If he did, he would kill Deacon in front of her if only to make sure she never defied him again.

She would never survive it.

Forcing a cool smile on her face, she raised her head.

Deacon stopped.

Byron's hand drifted down, and he squeezed. *Again.*

"Byron," she said tightly, speaking out of the side of her mouth. "I don't think that's appropriate behavior on the dancefloor."

She watched as Deacon's hand twitched toward the hilt of his sword and turned so there was no way Deacon could see any more than he had already. Because going by his reaction, he'd seen exactly where Byron was groping her.

"As my future wife, I doubt anyone minds," Byron murmured into her ear, holding her even closer.

She chose not to respond. She didn't trust what would come out of her mouth if she opened it.

———

"Babe, sorry but I have someplace I need to be," Byron said, glancing up from his phone.

Her face was awash with disappointment. "Are you sure? I was just getting to my plans for the gardens."

"We can talk about it later," he said, bending to press a kiss on her lips.

Seeing it coming, quickly she raised her hand, using it to block his kiss. No matter what August said, there was no way on this earth she was letting Byron kiss her on the lips.

"I guess if you have to?" she offered in her sweetest

voice, hiding her shudder as he kissed the back of her hand instead.

He probably had a girl waiting for him at home, or he'd made plans to meet her in a hotel somewhere. Or she'd done a good enough job of boring him he'd decided he didn't care where he was going, as long as it was away from her.

Since Byron couldn't seem to dance without groping her, she'd complained about her feet hurting. Once they'd settled at one of the tables on the periphery of the room, she'd begun her campaign in earnest.

There she'd gone into minute detail about her decorating plans for their new home, closely monitoring him, waiting for his eyes to glaze over. She made sure she had an opinion about everything: the color scheme for the reception rooms, the master bath, the flowers she wanted planting, leaving nothing out.

It took close to an hour before Byron had had enough. Longer, much longer than she'd thought it would take. August must have spoken to him as well; maybe he'd promised August they'd spend all night together.

"You won't... mention this to your father, will you? I wouldn't want him thinking I'm neglecting you, or anything."

Yep. August had definitely said something to Byron.

Painting a smile on her face, she shook her head. "Of course not. It's not fair for me to expect you to always be on hand to entertain me. I'll be fine here, you know, resting my feet."

Relief swept across his face, and rising from his seat, he glanced at his phone. "Great. I'll, uh, I'll see you later."

He disappeared into the crowd, and she stared after him. And then it hit her what she'd done. She'd successfully gotten rid of Byron, but that meant she and Deacon were alone. At Eros, yes, but there'd be no buffer between them now. He would want to speak to her, figure out what was wrong with her.

It was too early to go home. August would demand to know why she was back, and he wouldn't be happy if he thought she was trying to avoid Byron. And she couldn't go anywhere with Deacon, not after…

No. She couldn't let herself think about what August had done. She couldn't think about Selene. Not here. Especially not now.

Too late. Her eyes burned with unshed tears, and she rose. She needed to find a bathroom and deal with the tears threatening to fall before Deacon realized something was wrong with her. Stumbling into the crowd, she tripped and nearly fell.

A large warm hand wrapped around her arm. "This way."

Deacon. She'd recognized his touch anywhere. And then he was pulling her through the crowd, leading her… somewhere.

Blinking furiously, she followed him blindly. Her head lowered in case anyone saw the naked anguish on her face. She couldn't afford to let anyone see any of it, least of all Deacon.

Then they were outside, surrounded by fresh air and lush greenery and flowers. The Eros gardens. The door to the main room slammed shut behind him, cutting off the classical pianist mid-note.

Deacon had brought her outside.

She hesitated. Was this the best idea? What if someone had seen them come out here together? What if they said something to August?

"This way. We need to talk." He led her deeper into the enclosed garden.

At once her heels sank into the soft earth, but Deacon was already stepping onto a stone path.

Behind a towering tree near the center of the garden, he stopped and turned her so her back pressed against the tree. It wasn't hard to figure out why. This way at least if anyone were to step outside, they wouldn't immediately see her or Deacon.

"What's going on, princess? Tell me," he asked, sliding his glasses off his face.

She stared at his chest.

"Ophelia. Did your father say something? Did he threaten you?"

"I changed my mind."

He was silent for a beat. "You changed your mind? About what?"

His voice was quiet and serious. So serious it was strange to hear him speak without the smile she was used to hearing in his voice as if a laugh were always lurking just below the surface. He knew what she meant; he was waiting to hear her say it.

"About us. It was just a bit of fun, certainly nothing serious. I admit I might have gotten a little carried away, and let things go on longer than they should have." Her voice was empty-headed heiress, shallow and false.

"Look at me, Ophelia. Where did you find the ring?"

Shoving her fear, her pain, her agony somewhere deep down inside her, she forced a smile on her face. A careless one. The one she reserved for persistent guys who tried it on with her she had no time for.

"I'd like to go back inside now."

The hand on her arm tightened, and she glanced down at it.

His eyes searched hers, trying to read her. "What happened, princess? You agreed to—"

Panic spiked. Oh god. He was going to mention their plans. Here. Where anyone could overhear.

"I appreciate it must be disappointing for you," she interrupted in her coolest voice. "But this was nothing more than a quick tumble in the sheets. Also, can you let go of my arm now?"

He bent close, close enough for her to feel his breath against the side of her neck. "I don't believe you," he whispered.

Closing her eyes at the feel of him, at the scent of him, wanting nothing more than to wrap her arms around him and hold him to her, instead she leaned back against the tree and stared over his shoulder. Why, why was this pose reminding her of their kiss in the locker room?

Their first kiss.

"You've gotten attached, is that it? I could see if Lenore has some time on her hands if you want some attention. Maybe you'll be able to keep her more entertained than you did me?"

It took everything she had to pitch her voice with just the right level of casual cruelty, and when she saw him flinch, she nearly crumbled.

His eyes were stark, his pain right there for her to see. "This isn't you."

She forced a harsh laugh. "Of course, it is honey. Think about it, I'm Councilor Mortlake's daughter and you're nothing more than a Bladed, a human one at that. Did you imagine we had some kind of a future together? *Us?* How sweet."

"The ring." Slowly, the pain in his eyes faded, was replaced by the emotionless stare she'd only ever seen the Bladed wear. "Where did you find the ring?"

She forced a casual shrug as if her heart weren't breaking. As if she knew she wasn't breaking his. "Father said someone found it in the lobby. Surprising, isn't it? And here I thought all you humans were nothing more than thieving, lying—"

He turned and stalked away from her.

She clamped her hand over her mouth as she sagged against the tree at her back, using it to hold her up, struggling to choke back her cry. Her body trembled with the need to call him back, to take back what she'd said. To tell him she loved him.

He hated her. Oh god, she'd made him hate her.

But she didn't have time to mourn or to cry. Her guard had gone back inside, and she had to follow. She couldn't stay out here and let someone find her falling to pieces.

Forcing her hand from her mouth, she straightened from the tree. Several deep breaths later and she was a little closer to regaining her composure.

She'd be okay because Deacon would be alive. That was what mattered the most. Even though Deacon hated her, and they couldn't be together, she could live with it because he'd be alive. As long as she remembered that, she could get through this.

Somehow.

Raising her head, she fixed an expression of cool indifference on her face, pausing to take one more breath at the doors before she followed Deacon inside.

CHAPTER FOURTEEN

"*D*on't you think you were a little hard on him?"

Deacon didn't look up from lacing his boots. "This is the Bladed. If he can't keep up, he needs to ship out."

"That's pretty cold."

Standing, he shoved his workout clothes in his duffel, still not meeting the eyes of the vampire who stood at the entrance of the locker room. "Is there a reason you're here, Julian? Perhaps looking for another fight?"

"I came to see what was wrong with you. You don't have a reputation as someone who likes to beat down on the recruits."

Julian was right. He didn't.

Deacon had been ruthless on the mat, not letting up on the recruit for even a second before dumping him on his ass again and again. But right now, he didn't particularly care. Not with how he was feeling. Not after Ophelia Mortlake had reminded him that they belonged in two different worlds. Worlds distinct and separate.

He should've known better than to think there was something between them, and that they had a future together. She was right, what future could someone like him have with someone like her?

It was time he left Bladed headquarters. The longer he stayed, the more chance there was for someone or something to set him off since nothing had been enough to take the edge off his anger.

Time spent on the treadmill had just given him more time to obsess over Ophelia's rejection. He'd lifted weights until his muscles burned, but no matter how hard he pushed himself, nothing could silence Ophelia's voice in his head.

All this time he'd been thinking of, planning for, their future. He'd been picturing waking up beside her. Making love to her. But all he was to her was cheap entertainment. Just something to pass the time.

Pushing past Julian, he shoved the locker room door open and started for the exit. If he didn't get out of here. Didn't get somewhere where he could be alone, he'd be challenging Julian to another fight. And if he did that, he knew he wouldn't be able to stop.

"Look, man." It was Julian again.

"Whatever it is you want. Just say it and fuck off already," he snarled.

Eyes turned toward him, more than a few wide with surprise.

"I don't know what's happened, what's eating you up… but you ever need to talk, I'm around."

He raised an eyebrow at the offer. "Is that right? You?"

Julian scratched at his shaved head. "Yeah," he said. "Me."

Deacon stared at him.

Julian couldn't have made it more obvious he thought vampires—he thought himself—a league above anyone and everything.

Then he shook his head. What did it matter whether Julian was suddenly being less of a dick than he had been before? Thoughts of Ophelia were once again invading, and that meant getting the hell out of the gym before he lost it.

Swinging around, he stopped short of crashing into Pierce who'd approached so silently, he hadn't been aware he was even there.

"Deacon—" Pierce started.

"I have to go." He stepped around Pierce sparing him little more than a brief nod of greeting.

"Deacon!"

"I can't talk."

He kept on going. One day, probably soon, Pierce would pin him down, but it wouldn't be today. Today he didn't have the energy or the patience to deal with anyone or anything.

Expecting Pierce to chase him down, he glanced behind him before the double doors slammed closed and saw his boss had turned his attention to Julian.

Back at his apartment, he dumped his duffel on the tiny dining table he used only for that purpose and headed straight for the refrigerator. He needed a beer.

For him to drink before his shift was beyond reckless. Deacon had been in more than enough fights in the past to know first-hand just how much alcohol dulled his senses and slowed his reactions.

In any other job it wouldn't matter so much but going up against vampires he didn't need anyone to tell him how dangerous it was.

There'd already been an attack on Ophelia—or rather August, and there was every reason there could be another attack since experience had taught him assassins rarely quit until they got the job done, or someone stopped them.

But, even knowing that, knowing he was risking his job and even his life, he couldn't bring himself to care.

Sinking into his couch, he propped his feet up on the coffee table in front of him and took a long draw of his beer. He should at least get up and put something on TV, something that might distract him. But he didn't move. Dropping his head onto the back of his couch, he stared up at the ceiling.

He still wanted her.

There'd been such agony in her eyes when he'd met her. So much hidden pain. He was rarely ever wrong about people. How could he have been so wrong about her?

And how the fuck was he going to get through the next few days guarding her? Could he watch her being groped and do nothing?

Then there was Byron. His lips tightened at the thought of him groping at Ophelia like she was nothing more than a drunk hookup in a club. He didn't give a flying fuck about her. She was, and would only ever be, a possession to a guy like Byron.

And Deacon was supposed to just stand there and watch it happen?

Raising his head from the back of the couch, he downed his beer and went back for another.

———

Deacon spoke not a single word to her.

From the moment he collected her, there was a heavy silence between them. An oppressive weight that left her on edge all night. It was impossible to ignore the feel of his eyes tracking her movements as she danced and chatted about meaningless things with people who weren't her friends and never would be.

And then, she'd fought a losing battle trying to pry Byron's hand off her ass all night. In the end, she'd given up. What was the point when this was the way the rest of her life would go? Better to conserve her energy for the battle's worth fighting, because being Byron's wife? She didn't doubt for a second there wouldn't be battles.

Exhausted with the effort to maintain her false smile all night, it was almost a relief to close the car door behind her and step through the front door. At least until she realized she'd stepped into someone's nightmare.

Blood coated the marble floor in the foyer, and the air was rich with the unmistakable stink of terror.

Quickly, she closed the door behind her.

Her eyes didn't move from the sight before her. The woman lying sprawled on her belly on the floor in a mustard-yellow waistcoat stared at her with vacant eyes.

When the young woman suddenly blinked, and her heart lurched, Ophelia couldn't stop herself from jerking in surprise even as she raised a hand to cover her mouth, horrified.

Her skin was white. So white her large brown eyes were like bruises on her face.

With the amount of blood covering the woman's shirt, Ophelia couldn't believe she was still alive.

As she approached, the woman's lips moved soundlessly, her lips a blueish tinge. Finally, reaching her at the base of the staircase, she ignored the blood and sank to the floor beside her, gently gathering her head into her lap.

"It's okay," she murmured, bending her head over the woman as she gently smoothed her hair back from her face. "Everything will be okay."

"Help...."

Even with her preternatural hearing, the whisper on the dying woman's lips was barely audible. It couldn't be long now, not with the way she was fighting to draw breath into her lungs.

The silence when it came was sudden. Sharp. And then the woman went still in her arms.

"Oh, was she still alive?" Disappointment coated her father's words.

Raising her head, she glared at him. "You're a monster."

187

He laughed, emerging from his office where, evidently, he'd been waiting for her arrival. "You're being dramatic. Did you not have fun at your party? I'd have thought you'd be in a much better mood."

Gently, Ophelia lowered the dead woman's head back to the floor and rose, never taking her eyes from him. "What did you do to her? All I can smell is her fear."

His inhalation was loud. "Mmm. Delicious, isn't it? I've learned I prefer the taste of terror best of all."

"You know it's only a matter of time before the rest of the Council come after you, don't you? This is just another sign you've gone too far."

The smile slid off his face and he stalked toward her. "Where's your loyalty, Ophelia? And your respect. I don't believe I've been seeing a great deal of that of late."

"Loyalty? Respect? What would you know about that?" she sneered.

"Are you feeling brave because you're on your way out of this house? Do you think you'll be free to do as you like under Byron's roof?"

His hand curled around her neck before he shoved her against the banister, hard enough to make her gasp. But not enough to keep her silent. Her universe was becoming one of silence and she felt the cage as she'd never felt it before. Because of Deacon. She'd been silent too long. It was time to make her voice heard.

Blood dotted the collar of his shirt and her eyes latched onto it. The woman's blood most likely, but seeing it, all she could think about was Selene.

"What did you do to my sister?" Her voice was low,

controlled, even as she struggled in his grip. "Did you hurt Max as well? Tell me."

"You are not indispensable, Ophelia. You would do to remember that. I will have an heir, but you do not need to be the one to raise it. Remember that."

His hand squeezed and for a second her feet left the ground. Gasping for breath, her fingers scrabbled at his hand, trying and failing to tear him from her.

But his grip was too tight, and just as the edge of her vision started turning black, she was suddenly free and falling to the ground.

Coughing and spluttering as she rubbed at her throat, she watched as he walked away from her. Lazy steps across the bloodstained foyer, as if he was enjoying a casual afternoon stroll. As if he hadn't nearly choked the life from his daughter.

He disappeared into his office, and the door closed firmly behind him.

The second it did, Ophelia leaned back against the stairs, her legs stretched out in front of her, and her gaze fixed on the large white door.

A part of her. A tiny part of her had always hoped that one day she'd find some way to escape him. The man who called himself her father but acted as if he were anything but.

Laughter spilled out of her mouth, but there was no pleasure in the sound. She massaged her abused throat, conscious that it was already healing.

Hollow.

It was the only way to describe how she felt. Nothing felt real anymore. She almost wished Selene hadn't stopped August from choking the life out of her when she'd been born a girl instead of the male heir he'd longed for. Maybe then she would have been spared the hell her life had become. Because this wasn't living.

Selene had said once, "You're a fighter, Fee. I can see it in your eyes. It's there. You just haven't found the thing worth fighting for yet. But make no mistake, little sister. When you do, even the great August Mortlake won't be able to stand in your way."

Her sister had lied.

And now she was dead, and Ophelia was alone. How could she take on August on her own?

The man she loved hated her, and it was only a matter of time before August killed her. Where was this strength Selene had told her she had inside her? All she felt was hopelessness. Weak.

Covering her face with her hands, not caring that August would see her or could hear her, she bent her head and wept.

CHAPTER FIFTEEN

*L*eaning against the side of his fridge, Deacon downed two beers, one after the other in such quick succession he barely tasted them.

The thought of going through another night of watching Byron and Ophelia together had him reaching into the fridge for another bottle. But his hand encountered nothing.

Scowling into his empty fridge, he slammed the door shut as he growled in frustration. Then he remembered the night before. Hadn't he had a couple when he'd gotten in last night?

Shit. How could he forget that? Downing beers at four in the morning with his jacket and shoes still on wasn't exactly something he made a habit of doing.

But last night had called for a beer.

He shook his head. Who was he kidding? It called for a bottle of whiskey, but since he wasn't a big drinker, he didn't keep liquor in his apartment. So, two beers had gone some way to dulling his nightmare night. Some, but not all the way.

He'd lost count of the number of times he'd had to watch Byron slide his hand over the sweet curve of Ophelia's silk-covered ass.

She didn't like it. Not one bit.

A blind man could've seen it. But had she said anything? No.

Had she pushed Byron away? No.

She'd pasted a ridiculous smile on her face that made a mockery of the word smile. And he'd done nothing. Oh, he'd wanted to…

More than once he'd found his hand on the hilt of his sword before he realized what he was doing.

But he could see where this was going. Any more of this guard duty and he'd either take Byron's hand off or something a little more permanent. Like his head.

Tonight though, there would be no Byron to deal with. No. Tonight would be much worse than that.

It took less than two minutes to decide to hit up The Rising Sun Pub. Damn the consequences.

"I didn't think the Bladed got drunk," an amused female voice said.

Raising his hand to get the bartender's attention, he waited until another glass was in his hand before he spoke.

"Everyone gets drunk."

"Aren't you Ophelia's guard? Shouldn't you be working tonight?"

He paused with the glass against his lips. The woman was right. He should be. But the thought of watching Ophelia try on her wedding dress demanded more of him than he could handle.

The last thing he needed an image of was Ophelia in a wedding dress. Even though she'd rejected him, told him nothing between them was real, he couldn't stop thinking of her as his.

So, for the first time in his life he'd called in sick, and the second he'd hung up he was on his way to the pub. And if anyone saw him and reported him?

Well, he couldn't bring himself to care about the fallout.

"I don't see that it's got anything to do with you," he slurred.

He blinked at the counter. Just how many drinks had he had? He'd wouldn't exactly call himself a lightweight but seeing the four empty glasses in front of him confused him. Four drinks were nothing, or rather, they shouldn't be.

"If you think you've had just four, you must be drunk." The woman laughed.

Shit. He hadn't been talking out loud, had he?

"Yes. And you still are."

He swore again.

"Yeah. This isn't going to work. Come on. We need to talk, and to do that you need to sober up."

He raised his head, blinking at the woman blearily.

Long dark hair and a pale face swam in his vision. He

squinted. Leaned toward her... and promptly tipped off his stool.

Effortlessly, she caught him and put him back on his feet before she started leading him out.

"Selene?"

"Bingo. Wondered when you'd realize who it was."

Before he could say anything else, Selene was shoving him inside a cab outside and slamming the car door in his face. A slow blink later and Selene was jumping in the passenger seat.

He didn't think he'd closed his eyes for longer than a second, but he must have, because how else had he missed the car ride? And how were they suddenly outside a three-story brick townhouse?

It wasn't until they were inside said townhouse and Selene had forced a steaming mug of coffee in his hand, that he realized how drunk he must be. The entire journey from the pub to... wherever they were was a blur.

Taking the mug from her, he sank back into the couch Selene had pushed him into. It wouldn't hurt to listen to whatever she was so desperate to say since he was here, and the couch wasn't exactly uncomfortable.

Selene paced back and forth in front of him in their open-plan elegant surroundings. It wasn't anything like the antique-filled Mortlake estate, no, this was a little less monied. Even still, it was several steps up from his apartment. The Mortlakes did seem to like the finer things in life which helped put things in perspective. He'd been crazy to think he could keep someone like Ophelia.

"Something's wrong with Fee."

Taking a reluctant sip of the steaming coffee, he grimaced at the bitterness of it. It was tar, pure and simple. Foul tasting tar. Tar he had to find a way of getting rid of.

He eyed the coffee table and tried to work out how he could reach it without having to move.

"Nothing is wrong with her. She's the same cold vampire princess she's always been."

Selene stopped pacing to stare at him. "Ophelia never has and never will be a cold vampire princess. I don't know who you're talking about, but that isn't my sister."

"And how would you know? It's not like you've been around much." he growled.

She narrowed her eyes. "I'll forgive you this once because clearly you're still drunk. But be careful, Bladed," she said, her voice dangerously quiet.

Seeing the darkness in her eyes, hearing the threat in her voice, he took another gulp of coffee. If a fight was brewing, he needed to be a damn sight more sober than he was right now.

Selene's lips curved in a smile as if she knew what he was thinking, and after shaking her head, she resumed pacing.

"I have been around if you must know. Trying to keep an eye on Ophelia since it's not like we can openly meet up. Which hasn't exactly been easy since you started eating up all her time, and I had a distinct impression Fee wouldn't thank me for interrupting," Selene said with a knowing smirk.

He felt his face heat. Lifting the mug, he took another

swig of the revolting coffee, feeling it burn away a layer of his stomach lining.

"But something's different. She's different. I look in her eyes, and it's like… like somethings died. Something is wrong. I need to see her, speak to her, and you have to figure out a way for it to happen."

Deacon was already shaking his head. "No way."

"You will, or I'll tell Father you called in sick to go get drunk."

He stared at her. "What the fuck is it with you Mortlakes?"

"What do you mean, us Mortlakes? I'll give you August. I'll even admit that I can be a bit of a bitch when the occasion calls for it, but Fee… she's—"

"The worst of all of you." His anger drove him to his feet.

"The best, actually. And you don't get to criticize my sister like that and leave. You don't get to criticize her at all. Now sit down and tell me what you're talking about."

That was when he realized he'd had enough. The coffee Selene had given him was making him want to throw up, he was still drunk, and the last thing he wanted was to be dealing with another Mortlake. Shoving the coffee cup toward her, he started for the front door.

"No can do. I'm busy."

In a move he completely missed, he found himself back on the couch with Selene stood over him, glaring at him with the coffee cup in hand.

For a second, surprise held him immobile.

"Speak, Bladed, because you're not going anywhere until you do."

He didn't have his sword, and he wasn't in any kind of condition to be taking on a vampire. And not just any vampire. Ophelia's sister. Could he—would he fight her sister?

Trying to figure out how he was going to extricate himself from this situation gave him time to think. Which is was when he saw it. The thing he'd been missing all along.

Selene's eyes were the same shape and color as August's, but that was about all they had in common. There was something in her eyes he doubted he'd ever see on August Mortlake's face. Fear. It was fear swirling in the dark depths of Selene's eyes.

Shifting his focus from attack to examination, he studied her in silence for another long moment. "You're that worried about her?"

"You don't know Fee like I do. She was more than upset, she's more closed off than I've ever seen her before. And without a doubt, Father is responsible for it."

Distracted, she took a sip of his coffee and grimacing, wrinkled her small straight nose, the copy of Ophelia's as she stared into the cup.

"Ugh, that's *terrible,*" she said, gagging. "God, I can't believe I made that. And that you *drank* it?"

"You're telling me."

With another expression of disgust, Selene deposited the cup on the coffee table and crossed her arms over her chest. "So, speak. What do you know?"

"That she dumped me."

Selene frowned. "Really? But she likes you. Like *really* likes you."

197

He raised his eyebrow.

"Look, I'm her big sister. You think I can't tell when my little sis likes a guy?" She paused and eyed him. "And you think I don't know when a guy likes her right back?"

"Yeah, well. After being told she was slumming it until her wedding with her equal and there was no hope of any future between us, you'll forgive me if I don't believe you."

Selene's eyebrows disappeared into her hairline. "Ophelia said that? I don't believe you."

"I'm sure you'll understand why I'd rather forget all about it and get on with the rest of my life." He moved to rise but narrowed his eyes with Selene blocked him.

"Wait a second. What about her ring? I know she was freaking out over losing it. I searched for it myself but couldn't find it."

He shrugged. "Said it turned up."

"But *where* did it turn up. Where did she say she found it?"

What did it matter where she found it? It wasn't like it made a small bit of difference either way. "I don't know. The lobby of the Cosmopolitan maybe?"

Selene was already shaking her head. "No. I checked. Max checked. We spoke with the staff. We even went to the golf course you took her."

"Max?"

"Not important right now. Think carefully, Bladed. Did she say Father found it? Because if he did. If he was the one, then I guarantee he said something or more than likely did something to teach her a lesson. It's the only thing that would explain her breaking things off with you and that look in her eyes."

He told himself he didn't care. He and Ophelia were over. But the knowledge did nothing to stop his mouth opening and words from pouring out. "What do you mean, he did something to her? She didn't look hurt."

"Father doesn't always need to use physical violence to cause you pain. Like years ago, he didn't want Ophelia hanging around with some human friends she'd made, but she was at that rebellious age. I think she was back home from a break from boarding school, and I don't know, maybe she'd forgotten what he could be like."

He wasn't going to like what he was about to hear. Something in Selene's eyes warned him before she spoke a single word. Dread formed in the pit of his stomach and he began to feel a whole lot more sober than he had before. "What did he do?"

"Had one of her friends enthralled. Made her the central attraction of one of Lucian's games at those disgusting blood feasts. I'm sure you must've heard about what happens there?"

Deacon blanched. He couldn't help it. There weren't many Bladed who hadn't heard what the vampire Lucian was capable of, and the games he liked to play with the both willing and the unwilling.

"I've heard rumors."

"Well, whatever you've heard, I'd multiply it by a hundred because what goes on in his house of horrors is a million times worse. Only the sickest, the most depraved of our kin venture up there."

"But how did Ophelia—"

"Father took her. Forced her to sit through her friend's torment and wouldn't let her leave."

"And after?"

"What do you think happened? She cut those friends right out of her life and went back to Ravenborne early."

"You think—"

Selene cut him off again, "I do."

He rested his head on the back of his seat and examined the woman in front of him. She didn't seem like the sort of woman who you ordered about. But she was staying away—had been staying away, and not once had August asked him to report on her.

"But that's not the only reason you think something is wrong. He hasn't done anything to you, has he?

She flashed a brief hard smile at him. "You're perceptive for a human."

Deacon raised his eyebrow.

"No offense meant," she said, with a heavy sigh, her smile falling away. "A couple of days ago, Father sent some Bladed to ambush me and Max, my boyfriend."

Shock didn't come close to explaining how he was feeling. "The *fuck*?"

She resumed pacing. "Fortunately, we can defend ourselves. And we had some unexpected help."

"Against how many of the Bladed?" he asked, stunned that August was using the Bladed as his personal guards. Surely this went against rules or regulations. Weren't the Bladed supposed to serve the Council as a whole instead of individual Councilors?

"Five."

For someone to survive an ambush against one Bladed was rare. Against five was unheard of. It shouldn't have been possible. "That's… impressive."

"It was close. Very close. But since there's been no pushback or anything from Father, or from the Bladed headquarters I'm guessing it's something he's hushed up."

"You're right. I've heard nothing about any Bladed being injured."

Her eyes were dark. "Oh, there were no injuries. But I need to speak to Ophelia before August messes with her head any more than he has already, and trust me Bladed, I know the signs."

"I'll think about it."

Before Selene could argue, he raised his hand to silence her. "This isn't going to be straightforward. She broke things off with me, and despite everything you've said, I'm not a hundred percent convinced things are the way you say they are. Since it's my life on the line if August finds out, I'd like to at least sober up first before I agree to anything."

That silenced her for a second, but only a second.

"You're working tomorrow. Guarding her?"

He nodded.

"Fine. Then do your job. Watch her. Ask yourself if you're looking into the eyes of the Ophelia you know, the Ophelia we both know. And if you can't, then you know what you need to do."

Deacon called in sick, and Ophelia wasn't the least bit surprised that he had.

It was a lie, of course. He wasn't sick, he just couldn't

bear the sight of her—not that she could blame him. Not when she couldn't bear the sight of her.

After what she'd said… all she could see when she gazed at her reflection was someone unworthy. Someone who didn't deserve even a crumb of Deacon's affection.

He probably wished he'd never met her. She knew it and going by the smirk on August's face, he knew it as well.

Not that she could blame Deacon. He'd cared about her, and she'd used it to hurt him. Used it to push him away to save his life.

And last night, she'd done nothing—said nothing—about Byron's wandering hands. He thought she was weak. Pathetic. Of course, he couldn't bear the sight of her. She couldn't even meet her own gaze in the mirror.

Any feelings Deacon had for her, any respect was long gone, and she knew if he could find some way to get out of his responsibilities as her guard, he'd run and never look back.

It wouldn't take him long to meet someone. Some other girl who was everything she wasn't. She'd be beautiful, and fearless, and wouldn't hesitate to go after what she wanted. Deacon would fall in love with her, and they'd have beautiful babies and live a life of perfect happiness.

No. She couldn't think about any of that. Not anymore.

But that didn't stop her from lying in bed all night tormented by thoughts of Deacon with a beautiful human woman by his side, having picnics in the park, and at the beach with their equally beautiful kids.

It was late. Too late before she'd driven herself nearly mad with visions of a future she could never have when, finally, she closed her eyes and stopped her heart. Grateful beyond measure no dreams, and no nightmares could follow.

The next night he was there, waiting for her punctually at six in the evening beside the front door.

She couldn't bear to turn her gaze in his direction and see what was in his eyes. And August, evidently not bored yet of playing his cruel games stood outside his office, his eyes twinkling with malicious glee. Her stomach twisted in warning. She knew August's expressions. And this one was setting off all kinds of warnings.

"You'll be taking Ophelia to the night mall," August said to Deacon, in place of greeting.

"Yes, Councilor Mortlake."

There was a pause as if August was waiting for Deacon to ask why.

Deacon would've been expecting to take her to Eros for yet another event celebrating the looming wedding, but behind her, he didn't respond.

Impatience flickered across August's face. Deacon, it seemed, wasn't playing the game the way August wanted it played. And since no one could argue patience was August's strong suit, it was only a matter of time before he lashed out at either Deacon or most likely, her.

"With the wedding only around the corner, I thought

it prudent to keep Ophelia at home last night. For her safety. I'm sure you'll agree her safety matters most."

He was good. *Convincing,* Ophelia thought. A stranger would be hard-pressed to hear the underlying malice beneath his words, picking up the note of fatherly concern in his voice and nothing else.

If she were brave enough to meet Deacon's eyes, she knew he would've seen right through August just as she had.

This was all a game to August, and he wanted Deacon to suffer. He wanted her to suffer. Ophelia tried to brace herself for what was coming.

"But, as this is such an important occasion, and her mother couldn't be with her, I've decided I will join you."

Briefly, she closed her eyes.

Oh my god.

This was even worse than she could've imagined. Not only was she going to have to find a way of struggling through her final wedding dress fitting with Deacon watching her, she had to do it with August there as well?

He was watching her, a hint of a smile twisting his lips.

"How kind of you, Father. Shall we leave now?"

Behind her, she heard Deacon opening the front door, not reacting in any way she could hear. The sound of his heartbeat in the same steady rhythm it always did. How could he be so calm?

August was breaking her heart. *Had* broken her heart into tiny little shards and she was being forced to smile through it.

"Councilor? Mistress Mortlake?" Deacon's voice was cool as he stood beside the open door, waiting for them to leave. There was nothing to suggest this was—she was anything more than just a job to him.

She could have had forever with him. He'd offered her that and more, but all of that was gone now.

Keeping her eyes on the ground in front of her feet, she headed past him, down the steps, and into the waiting car.

They were on their way to Vera Wang for her final wedding dress fitting, and she was being taken by a man she hated, and her former lover who hated her.

Great. Just fucking great.

CHAPTER SIXTEEN

*D*eacon would never be able to get the image out of Ophelia in her wedding dress out of his head.

The sight of her in the almost-sheer corset dress she'd worn days before had been like a sucker punch. But her slender form encased in a strapless dress with a beaded bodice, full puffy skirt, and a fine lace veil that did nothing to hide the touch of green in her eyes was like being gut shot. He had no defense against her haunting beauty.

None.

He didn't know how he'd held himself together back at the Mortlake estate in the face of August's little surprise, somehow, he had. But this? There was no way he could pretend to be unaffected by the sight of Ophelia in a wedding dress.

His heart twisted at the thought of her saying her vows to Byron. Byron dancing with her. Taking her—his wife to bed to consummate their wedding. This was torture.

And he'd been a Marine.

Even if he lived to be a hundred years old, he would never forget the way she'd looked when she first stepped out of the changing room.

They had the store to themselves, which meant there was nothing and no one to distract him. He guessed that was the benefit of being a Mortlake, or being rich enough you could afford to buy out the contents of a shop without blinking. Not that he would have been able to pay the least bit of attention to anyone, even if the brightly lit wedding dress-lined boutique was bursting with people.

But this was the night mall, the outdoor mall frequented by the wealthiest vampires in the city. Still, the introduction August and Mortlake had received couldn't be described in any other way than fawning adulation.

The store manager had whisked Ophelia into the changing rooms at the back of the store leaving Deacon to plant himself a couple of feet from the front door, and August to make himself comfortable in a cream quilted couch in front of the mirrored wall and the entrance to the changing room.

Now, the sleekly dressed manageress buzzed around Ophelia, straightening this, smoothing down that. All of it was completely unnecessary. Ophelia was perfection.

He was staring. He knew he was staring, but it was impossible to tear his eyes away. Even knowing August was right there, sipping on a glass of blood-spiked champagne wasn't enough to make him stop.

Ophelia was careful to avoid as much as a single glance in his direction as she stood in front of the mirrored wall. And if Deacon hadn't spoken with Selene, if he didn't still have Selene's words rolling around his head, he would have shrugged it off as nothing.

"What do you think, Bladed? Does Ophelia not look beautiful?"

The smugness. The touch of cruelty in August's voice suggested he was playing games. Whether it was with him, Ophelia, or both of them, he couldn't be sure. But for the moment he let it pass. His gaze was still full of Ophelia's beauty.

"Like a princess," he murmured.

Her head lifted, and through the mirrored wall in front of her, their eyes clashed.

He didn't take his dark mirrored glasses off. He didn't need to. Ophelia's gaze pierced through the glass and connected with his as if his face was bare.

For a second the mask fell away, and the cool vampire princess was a young woman being forced to do something she didn't want to do. Despair. Stark hopelessness swirled in the depths of hazel-green eyes.

She wanted this even less than he did.

What had August said? What had he done to make her turn her back on him and go through with a wedding that filled her eyes with such agony?

Throughout the rest of the night and the beginning of the next night, Deacon pondered the question of what Ophelia's father had done to spark such fear in her eyes. Because it was fear driving her to go through with the wedding.

No, it was more than that. It was terror.

Even now, as he watched her dance with Byron at Eros, he caught glimpses of it in her eyes. It was in the tightness of her jaw and on the empty smile on her lips. All her excitement for her looming wedding was all a game of pretend. Her laughter as she praised her engagement ring as the most beautiful thing in the world was a hollow sound. False. None of it was real.

How had he missed it? He'd told Ophelia he was observant. Him?

She was bleeding pain and terror out of every pore, and he'd been blind to it.

His eyes never left her face for a second. He watched as Byron danced with Ophelia until he grew bored and abandoned her for something better. As if such a thing, such a person, existed.

But that was Byron, ever in search of something to satisfy his urges. Less than two minutes after he'd typed Byron's name in his computer search engine, all the photographs which filled the screen made it clear what mattered most to Byron. Sex and blood. And it seemed there was an endless parade of beautiful women hungry for Byron as he was for them.

Byron could have them. But Ophelia… he couldn't have her.

The moment Byron disappeared through the exit, Deacon stepped forward.

"Mistress Mortlake, your father has requested I take you home."

Ophelia turned away from her conversation with a woman who'd seemed more interested in convincing

Ophelia to get her an invite to the wedding than saying anything of any worth. Deacon had no idea how Ophelia had lived like this year after year.

"I see," she said, careful not to meet his eyes.

It was as if she'd recognized that she'd exposed herself —exposed her feelings to him at the wedding boutique. But it was too late. If she thought he could unsee what he'd seen, she was about to learn how wrong she was.

"If you're ready?" He raised his arm to the exit.

Her farewells were brief. And it wasn't long before Deacon was guiding Ophelia out of Eros, and past the vampire in the lobby responsible for recalling their driver from the underground parking nearby. Instead, Deacon continued out of the front doors before slipping through the tourists who stood gathered outside, eager for a glimpse of the vampires arriving and leaving.

A couple reached for their phones, to take their picture most likely, but Deacon put a hand on the hilt of his sword, and they backed away again. They continued down the bustling Strip, leaving the black gates of Eros behind them.

"Deacon…" Ophelia glanced behind them. "The car."

"We don't need it."

He was being reckless. No, he was being downright stupid, but that didn't stop him from gripping Ophelia's arm and hurrying her away from Eros. Right now, his only priority was getting Ophelia back to Selene's town-house so he could get to the bottom of whatever August was doing and had already done.

An empty cab was coming toward them and raising his hand, it slowed, and they climbed inside.

"Deacon—"

"Just trust me, okay. There's something I need to show you."

———

August would not stop with killing Ophelia. He was going to kill them both when he found out Deacon had taken her, and not exactly unsubtly, away from Eros.

She hoped to god no one who knew her had seen her and Deacon climb inside the cab. Or if someone had, they wouldn't recognize her. But then her eyes caught sight of Deacon's sword.

Right. Of course, they won't. Because everyone is going around with a Bladed guard.

Ophelia didn't recognize the address Deacon had told the driver to take them. But that wasn't unusual, not since she spent her nights at the clubs and bars on and off the Strip.

Occasionally she did some shopping at the night mall where the most exclusive boutiques in the city stayed open all night serving the wealthiest vampires in the city, or she met Selene at her high-rise apartment. But that had been before. Before August had warned her away from Selene. Before August had killed her.

Deacon's gaze was burning a hole on the side of her face. But she didn't turn to ask him what had changed, because something must have. He hadn't spoken a word to her before, and now he had. Now he couldn't stop staring at her. He must have seen something on her face— in her eyes at Vera Wang's.

She should be arguing with Deacon, demanding he take her home. But she sat placidly by his side, too afraid to turn and betray something else she wasn't ready to have him see. Like how she felt about him. Truly felt about him.

The driver pulled to a stop outside a line of smart townhouses, and after thrusting a handful of notes at the driver, Deacon was out and leading her from the cab.

She tried to ignore the touch of his hand on her bare skin as he tugged her toward the front steps of the brick house.

Who was she kidding, she was leaning into his touch as if she'd been starved of him. As if she craved it, and him. And she did. Had it been days since they'd touched— kissed, made love? Whatever it was, it felt like forever.

Then she remembered what August would do to Deacon if she didn't pull herself together and demand he take her home.

"Deacon—"

"Just follow me," he interrupted, leading her up a short flight of steps.

She expected him to knock or for someone to open the door, but he just twisted the handle and stepped right in. As if it were his house.

Frowning, she glanced up at the house. Deacon had his own apartment, and from what Selene had told her about renting in the city, a place this close to the Strip couldn't be cheap.

"But my father—"

"Ophelia. Come here." His tone was serious, his eyes telling her he wasn't about to back down anytime soon.

Glancing behind her at the sound of a car heading down the street, she sighed. Better she get inside before someone recognized her and spread the word she was somewhere she shouldn't be. She'd give it five minutes, and after Deacon had shown her whatever it was he wanted her to see, she'd demand they leave.

Stepping inside the front door, she jerked to a stop.

It was as if someone had reached inside her chest and grabbed a tight hold on her heart. So tight she couldn't breathe. Couldn't think.

All the breath left her lungs in a whoosh, leaving just enough air to gasp out a single word. A name.

"Selene!"

Her legs crumpled beneath her and her knees hit the floor, hard, before Deacon could even think of catching her. And then everything went black.

CHAPTER SEVENTEEN

*D*eacon leaned his back against the wall, his eyes on the bedroom door Ophelia and Selene had disappeared into a couple of hours ago. Scratch that, the room he'd carried Ophelia into.

The second he'd seen the look in Ophelia's eyes, he'd known Selene had been right. Right about everything.

Fortunately for his state of mind, her unconsciousness hadn't lasted long. Just long enough to stop his heart, that was all. But almost as soon as he'd slung her into his arms and started up the flight of steps, her eyes were flickering open, and her hand reaching out to grab Selene as if she didn't believe her sister was truly there.

At that moment, he didn't exist anymore. Ophelia's entire focus was fighting to get to her sister, words spilling out of her mouth that made his jaw clench tight and his face harden. All the while tears—blood-red tears continued to slide unabated down her face, and her body continued to tremble with the force of her cries.

August had convinced Ophelia that Selene was dead.

That was when he knew with absolute certainty, not only had he fallen in love with Ophelia, but August Mortlake had to die.

It took everything in him to lean against the wall instead of going after August then and there. But he couldn't do that. He couldn't leave Ophelia like this.

Selene had wanted time with Ophelia alone. So, he'd stood outside the room knowing Ophelia was on the other side of the door in front of him, sobbing, falling to pieces. But she needed her sister. It was clear enough even to him she needed Selene more than him right now. But his patience was at an end.

Straightening from the wall, he reached for the door handle. He needed to see Ophelia. Touch her. Reassure himself she'd stopped shedding tears that made him want to gather her tight enough in his arms they weren't two people anymore, but one.

But Selene was pushing the bedroom door open and stepping out, gently closing the door shut behind her. Just before it closed, Deacon glimpsed briefly Ophelia curled up in bed, the sheets pulled up to her neck, her face relaxed in sleep but still ravaged with grief.

Fury pulsed through him. Raw. Violent rage. His hands formed tight fists and he knew with absolute certainty that if he were alone, he'd have punched a hole through the wall.

Ophelia was in pain, and the thought of leaving the person responsible for her suffering alive a second longer than necessary was killing him.

"How is she?" he forced himself to ask Selene in an attempt to stifle his rage.

Selene brushed past him, her eyes warning him not to push too hard. He hesitated.

Everything in him cried out his need to crawl into bed beside Ophelia. But one glance in Selene's eyes was enough for him to see how close she hovered on the edge, just as he did. Right now, they needed each other.

Turning his back on his fury—and his heart—for the time being, he followed Selene down the stairs, through the lounge, and into the kitchen. He found her clutching a half-empty bottle of vodka in one hand, and an empty glass in the other.

"How is she? A fucking mess is how she is." The laugh that emerged from Selene's mouth was hard. A bitter sound that bore testament to her unquenched rage.

Pouring herself a large glass of vodka, she downed it and gently replaced the glass on the counter. But she didn't turn to face him.

Her gaze remained fixed on the cupboard in front of her, as he leaned his hip on a cabinet and folded his arms across his chest. Alert. Raw energy roiled around her and he waited, coiled, ready to get himself out of the way of her fury.

It was obvious what she wanted to do, Deacon thought as his gaze focused on her pale thin hand wrapped tight around the glass. But he wasn't about to stop her, not with his control being what it was.

If Selene wanted to smash her glass, the bottle of vodka or anything else close at hand, he had no complaints. He could understand it. But it would have to be quiet. Ophelia was sleeping.

"I'm going to kill him." Selene's whisper was all leashed violence. A promise rather than a threat.

He nodded. "Yes."

Selene turned to face him. Slowly, almost reluctantly released her tight grip on the glass in her hand.

"I've never seen her like this before. Not after finding out how her mother died. Not after he kicked me out. He nearly destroyed her. He nearly destroyed my little sister." She spoke in a whisper, but the fury, the sheer fury in her voice made her voice tremble.

"We'll need a plan. Killing him won't be easy."

It was Selene's turn to nod. Sighing, as if his agreement had gone some way to calming her down. "He's been… unpredictable. And there's more going on you should know about before we go any further."

She and Ophelia had been speaking of August at the first event he'd taken her. At the sunset cocktail party. The night she'd almost died in his arms.

"You asked Ophelia if he was doing something again? You were talking about August. Does this something have anything to do with his unpredictability?"

Snatching the bottle of vodka from the counter, she crossed into the lounge and dropped on the couch with a heavy sigh. "Come on, Bladed. You look like you need this more than I do."

He didn't hesitate before joining her.

"Father—no. I really should stop calling him that. August hasn't been behaving normally for a while." She took a swig from the vodka. "No, that makes it sound like I'm excusing him for this when I'm not."

Deacon held his hand out for the bottle. "But?"

"This is going too far, even for him. I mean, he's always had a high capacity for cruelty. But for him to have me killed? I never thought he'd actually go through with it. Threatening me? Been there, done that. Sending the Bladed to knock me around a little so I wouldn't dare threaten Ophelia's—or should I say, his big day? Sure, whatever. He's controlling, yes, but I'm still his daughter." The hurt in her voice was faint, but it was there.

"He told Ophelia you were dead." There was no question in his voice. It was clear what Ophelia had been told—what August had let Ophelia believe.

"He did." Selene snatched the bottle out of his hand and took a healthy gulp.

"You think he knows you're alive?" He took the bottle back. Noted how quickly they were draining the contents of it and shot a quick glance toward the kitchen.

"Don't worry, I have more. And yes, I think he believes I'm dead."

He stared at her, waiting for her to tell him why.

"Sorry, can't tell you more. Made a promise."

"To whoever helped you in the ambush?"

Selene's smile was brief, but it was real. "Mm, observant and excellent memory. Even when drunk. I'll have to be careful what I say around you in the future."

"Back to August. You're implying something is making him more cruel than usual?" he guessed. Taking a draw from the bottle, he passed it back.

"He's been gorging," Selene said, her eyes on the bottle in her hand. "Drinking from the vein is a powerful feeling. The emotions, the adrenaline, the pleasure—it can become addictive."

He frowned. "It can make you mad? Then why aren't more vampires—"

But Selene already shaking her head. "It doesn't send you mad. It just… overwhelms you. Like any other addiction. Soon all you can think about is your next fix. You lose focus, become easily distracted. Everything else starts to matter a little less—or rather, blood or I guess emotion starts to matter more. Than anything."

"But why don't more vampires experience it then? I thought August was a Councilor, and an old one at that?"

"It's his age that's the problem." Selene drank and leaned toward him. "I'm about to tell you something we don't tell anyone. Ever."

"I understand."

"The older we get, the more emotion we lose. You must have seen how perpetually bored the older vampires are at Eros?"

He blinked. Thought back to his experiences at Eros. The feel of the place, the music and the elegant dresses put him in mind of something from a Jane Austen novel. Everyone stood around talking, or dancing, or looking bored. He couldn't understand why the place was so popular when everything he knew and had seen about vampires told him they preferred a little more excitement than Eros offered.

"Now that you mention it, yeah, I noticed."

Selene nodded. "That's how it starts. Boredom. They start sniffing out things that will excite them. Usually, the sicker it is, the more novel, the more likely it is to trigger an emotional response. That and pure human emotion— fear, excitement, you get the picture."

"Let me get this straight. You're saying August has become addicted to feeding because he's losing the ability to feel?"

"Yes."

A memory stirred. "Why am I getting the impression this has been going on for a while?"

"Because it has. Over the years there have been rumors, rumors I'm surprised you haven't heard of since no one can go around leaving that many bodies lying around without someone clocking onto what they're doing. Not even a Councilor has that kind of power. And like I said, it's an addiction, and it explains why he didn't push this wedding until now. No matter how careful he was in the beginning, it wouldn't have been long before he became careless. It wouldn't surprise me if the rest of the Councilors see where this is heading and are trying to get rid of him."

This was what she and Ophelia had been talking about that first night. August's gorging, which if he had to guess explained Ophelia's reluctance to feed.

She'd been afraid she would turn into her father. She'd been afraid she wouldn't be able to stop. Those had been her words in the car after she'd nearly bled to death because of it.

The man was a fucking menace. The amount of damage, direct and indirect he'd caused—*was* causing his daughter's beggared belief. Someone had to stop him. And that someone was him.

"The guy who tried to kill him at Ophelia's bache-lorette party?" he guessed.

Selene shrugged, took another gulp of the vodka, and

passed the bottle back. "Heard about that. And it wouldn't surprise me."

"So, he's trying to do what then? Secure his legacy before they take him out?"

"He wants something to hold over them. A way to control them."

Both he and Selene turned at the quiet voice behind them. Ophelia.

Her burnished copper-gold hair hung around her shoulders, her face was scrubbed of her tear stains and the make-up she'd been wearing earlier. With a white sheet wrapped around her slender form and her feet bare, she looked pale and exhausted. Fragile. But that wasn't what held him transfixed. It was her eyes. In her eyes was naked need. For him. No one else but him.

Before he could rise, she started toward him, her eyes never leaving his. When she all but crawled in his lap, burying her face into the hollow of his throat and wrapping her arms around him, his hands smoothed down her back and around her waist, tucking her more firmly against him as he bent his face to draw the scent of her deep into his lungs.

Since he'd walked away from her in the Eros garden, for the first time he felt he could breathe.

But as with anything, the moment didn't last.

Reluctantly he eased his tight grip on her as Ophelia lifted her head, pulling back enough to meet his eyes.

"There's a rumor, a..." She shook her head. "A prophesy? I don't know what you would call it, that a Mortlake has always sat on the Council. Without one, the Council would descend into civil war, and with it the rest of our kin."

Resting his chin on the top of her head, he stroked his hand up and down her back, luxuriating in the feel of having her in his arms again, and of having her hands on him. It felt like heaven.

"Seriously? That seems a little—"

"Farfetched?" Selene interrupted, the hint of a smile on her lips as she watched them.

She liked it. Seeing him and Ophelia together like this. It made her happy.

He nodded. "A touch."

Selene glanced at Ophelia, a sign Ophelia hadn't finished speaking.

"Not necessarily. It was a Mortlake who formed the Council hundreds of years ago, when before it was a free for all. There was a lot of infighting, a lot of disunity. The goal of the Council was, is, to unite us so we would stop trying to kill each other. But now we've revealed our existence to the rest of the world, we can't risk returning to what we were. If we prove ourselves monsters determined to destroy each other at the cost of everything and everyone around us, there is no doubt in anyone's mind the rest of the world would band together to destroy us," Ophelia said.

He hadn't thought Ophelia took an interest in vampire politics, but listening to her speak, he was realizing there was much more about her he still hadn't learned yet. There was a strength in her, still mostly sleeping, but it was there in the controlled way she spoke. She wasn't just the vampire princess others thought her, she was much more than that.

"You think August plans to use this child—your child to, what, force the Council to keep him around?" he asked.

"I do. But I don't think it will work," Ophelia said, pressing closer to him, her hand burrowing under his shirt. He sucked in a breath at the cool feel of her fingers dancing across his bare skin, his muscles coiling tight under her soft touch.

Having her in his lap already had his cock stirring in interest, but her touching his bare skin turned interest into raging, burning need. His eyes dropped to her lips. He wanted to taste them, but not now. Now they had to talk, but after…

He shifted her enough for Ophelia's thigh to brush against his erection straining against the front of his pants. Her eyes locked with his, darkened, and then she was pulling away, turning to face Selene.

"You don't?" Selene sounded surprised.

What was Selene…? Oh, they were talking about August, about his plans for the child he hoped Ophelia and Byron would give him.

"I don't think the failed assassination attempt was a serious attempt. If the Council truly wanted him dead, none of us would've seen it coming. I think whoever planned that attack wanted August to think it was the Council."

Deacon silently agreed. Why else would there be no further attempts made on August or Ophelia?

"I don't understand," Selene murmured. "Why?"

"Because whoever it is wants August paranoid, and the

sooner he goes crazy, the more of an excuse they have to act. He's been on the Council a long time to have no allies. I doubt all of them will be prepared to stand idly by and watch as the other Councilors force him out. And I'm guessing the Council is also in no hurry to stop this wedding because having a Mortlake child as insurance is in their best interest in case things do go crazy. That way they get rid of August and they have a pawn to take his place. Someone they can stick front and center, so they don't have to reveal who they are."

Deacon wasn't alone in staring at Ophelia. What she was saying sounded plausible. More than plausible.

"Well, I'll be, little sister. I guess one of us was born with those famous Mortlake brains after all. I was beginning to think we were both duds."

Ophelia giggled, and Deacon smiled at the sound of her laugh. It was rare. Too rare, and he didn't hear nearly enough of it.

"As terrifying a thought that is," he said, "it sounds like something the Council would do. But regardless of what they want, he has to die. He deserves nothing less for what he's done."

Ophelia went still in his arms, and he glanced at Selene.

"Max and I checked into a hotel last night. I should go check in with him," she said, standing.

He moved to shift Ophelia to the couch. "I can take—"

"No," Selene said, crossing over to grab Ophelia's hand, "I'll be fine. You and Fifi need to talk."

Ophelia sighed but said nothing about the ridiculous

nickname. She'd likely never expected to ever hear it again.

"You'll be okay?" Fear was unmistakable in Ophelia's voice.

"Max and I will be fine. Don't worry about us."

After Selene left, Ophelia tilted her head up so she could meet his eyes.

"Deacon, I'm sorry I—"

He was already shaking his head. "You have nothing to be sorry about."

"But I—"

"Princess…" he interrupted, cradling the side of her face.

"I thought he would hurt you too," she whispered. "And I couldn't lose you. I couldn't. Better I let you go."

Sliding his arm around her, he bent his head and kissed her. Deep drugging kisses that spoke of his love, his fear, and his need. Then rising, he started for the bedroom, her arms circling his neck, her response as heated, and as desperate as his.

Ophelia didn't know how long she'd been soaking in the bath. It couldn't have been over thirty minutes, max. However long it was, it was too long for Deacon.

It was the weight of his stare she felt first, caressing her naked breasts.

Opening her eyes a crack, she saw him leaning against the door frame, hair hanging loose around his face, arms folded across his chest in black briefs, and nothing else.

Eyeing the luscious, tanned skin on show, all the taut muscles she'd spent the last couple of hours exploring, she sighed and closed her eyes. It was crazy how much she wanted him.

They'd done nothing else for the last couple of hours but make love, and with time ticking along as it always did, soon they'd have to leave their little bubble and return to Eros, and from there, back to the Mortlake mansion. Not home. Because Deacon wouldn't be with her, and a place where Deacon wasn't didn't feel like home. Not anymore.

"I'm trying to have a relaxing soak in the bath after you had your evil way with me. You're distracting me," she murmured.

He snorted. "Evil way? As if you weren't as eager as I was. And don't think I didn't see that look in your eyes a second ago."

He'd moved closer. She kept her eyes closed. Easier to hide her need for him that way.

Her breath caught at the light touch of his finger circling the pointed tip of her breasts, eyes cracking open the narrowest bit. "What are you doing?" she asked, trying to sound bored.

"Touching you. You're not fooling anyone, you know? I can hear it in your voice." His finger slid over her wet skin, circled the point of her other breast. "I can see it in your eyes."

His voice was low, husky. He didn't have to tell her what he was talking about, when arousal was slowly spreading through her, her breaths turning heavy, giving her away. Her eyes snapped shut, pointedly ignoring his chuckle.

Then his hand moved away, and despite herself, disappointment stirred. But he'd only moved behind her, his hand urging her to sit up. At the sound of something hitting on the floor, she opened her eyes.

"Uh, Deacon. What are you doing?"

"What does it look like? I'm joining you, of course."

"We won't both fit." It was nothing more than a token complaint as she made space for him to slip into the large claw bath behind her.

"We will." Wrapping his arms around her waist, he urged her back until he'd sat her in his lap. It was only then she realized what she'd heard falling on the floor. His briefs.

"You're naked," she said, her words ending in a moan as he smoothed his hands up her sides, and over her breasts.

She loved the way he touched her. His fingers tugged at her nipples, his hands strong, yet gentle. It wasn't long before she was shifting restlessly against him, her ass rubbing against his erection as her hands covered his, attempting to ease the ache he'd awakened in her.

"Mmm, that feels good," he drawled, his lips brushing against the shell of her ear, making her shiver.

With his hands covering her breasts, stroking and squeezing, she lost the ability to think.

Brushing her hair off her neck, he lowered his mouth to the sensitive skin at the joint between her neck and shoulders and gently bit down.

She sucked in a breath when one of his hands slid

down her body, down the valley of her breasts, the hollow of her stomach and through the folds of her sex. Her gasp was sharp as the blunt tip of one finger slowly eased in and out of her in a slow glide designed to drive her crazy.

Moaning, she ground herself harder against his erection throbbing against her ass. The sound of Deacon's groan made her wetter, and his finger slipped deeper inside her, brushing against a ball of nerves that made her breath catch.

"Deacon," she moaned.

"I love it when you say my name like that." His voice was a husky growl in her ear.

"Like what?" She tipped her head back to grant him better access to her neck. The feel of his breath on her neck, the brush of his lips, and the stroke of his tongue had her stomach tensing in anticipation. Would he bite her?

Please let him bite her.

"Full of need. Want. Like you're hungry for me."

"I want. I always want."

How could he not know that?

"So, take." He slipped his finger from her sex and she started to turn around, but his teeth biting down on her neck stopped her.

"No. Like this. I want you like this."

For a second, confusion reigned. Between his hands on her breasts, his teeth in her neck, and the incessant pressure of his erection nudging at the entrance of her anal passage, she couldn't think. Then it clicked.

"Uh, I don't know if I'm ready for that," she said, her cheeks heating.

He chuckled, his hands sliding down to her waist, holding her still as he thrust against her, close, but stopping short of slipping inside. "Not today princess, but one day. One day I'll have your ass."

She shivered at the dark promise in his voice.

It wasn't something she'd ever been interested in trying, but with Deacon she wanted to try anything. Everything. And at the thought of his heavy weight draped over her, sliding inside her, her legs parted and her back arched as if in invitation. Deacon growled low in approval.

"Lean forward a little." He was shifting her as he spoke, the hands at her waist positioning her.

Anticipation thrumming through her as she shifted forward, his hands spanning her waist. As he spread his legs as far as the narrow confines of the bath would allow, he lifted her and she gasped as the tip of his erection probed the mouth of her arousal.

Then his hands tightened. "Now, scoot back."

Shifting back, she moaned as he slid deep. He was thick, almost uncomfortably so, and she flung her head back, squeezing her eyes shut as her muscles rippled around him, struggling to adjust to the size of him.

With his body curved snug around hers, his lips brushed against her lower back, she started rocking against him as he met each one of her downward strokes with a firm upward thrust. Soon they settled into an easy rhythm, the sound of their groans loud in the tiled bathroom. As she rocked, the pressure at the junction of her thighs built until she was rocking harder, faster.

"*Fuck!* Princess," Deacon growled against her back, his

grip tight around her waist as he picked her up before forcing her back on his erection.

His roughness only made her wetter and her body softened around him, even as her nails dug into his forearms. More. She needed more.

Water sloshed out of the bath and onto the floor. A part of her was conscious of it on a superficial level, but she couldn't bring herself to care about the mess they were making. Not when Deacon was grunting as he thrust with growing force into her, the fingers biting into her waist nearly painful. Grabbing at the edge of the bath, she shoved back harder as he slammed into her.

Her breathing changed. Became jagged gasps of need. His, heavy pants.

"Please… Deacon…"

She was frantic, her muscles coiled tight with tension. Close. So close.

He was pounding into her now. Bending his face to her neck, his teeth clamped down at the hollow of her throat and she exploded around him.

Screaming, she writhed against him as he continued to thrust, once, twice. And then he was spilling himself inside her, clutching her tight against him as shuddering, he filled her with liquid heat.

"You can't go back there."

They were still in the bath, but the water was cooling now. Soon, they'd have to get out. Although she was fine, she didn't—wouldn't feel the cold, he would, and she didn't want him to be uncomfortable.

But right now, with her lying on top of him in the bath, her head resting on his shoulder with his arms wrapped around her, she didn't want to move. Not ever.

"Deacon, I have to. After what he did, I have to do something."

"You'll be safe."

"But it wouldn't be safe. Not for you. At least while I'm still at the house I can see what he's up to, dig around a little. Since he's spending pretty much all his time at Lucian's, there's hardly any risk."

"Or we could leave Vegas. You and me. Just walk away."

She was silent for a second. "I heard you and Selene talking. Even if we walk away, she never will. Not after what he did. We have to do this together. It's the only way we can beat him. But we need someone on our side, someone just as powerful as he is like another Councilor otherwise there's nothing to stop him from coming after us again and again until we're all dead."

"It's dangerous," he said, his hands tightening around her.

She sighed before moving to rise.

Reluctantly he eased his grip on her and she climbed out of the bath and snagged a towel, wrapping it around her. Then turning, she reached a hand out to him, waiting until he'd stepped out of the bath before she stepped forward and slipped her arms around his shoulders, staring up into his face.

"Deacon. Please let me do this. I... I need to do this. For us, for Selene... For everyone he's ever hurt."

Deacon wrapped his arm around her, and bent to press his lips against her forehead, his eyes closing.

"If anything happens to you," he breathed.

"Nothing will. You know he won't hurt me. He needs this wedding too much. But I'll be careful."

It was clear from the deep lines furrowing his brow when he lifted his head and opened his eyes that she hadn't done enough to convince him, but before he could argue, standing on tiptoes, she bussed her lips against his in a brief kiss.

"You know what?"

His eyes flared with heat as he tightened his hold on her. "You're trying to distract me."

She smiled. "A little. But I was thinking..."

"Thinking what?"

"About after. I..." She trailed off. Realizing what she was about to say, she shook her head. No, it was too soon. He would think she was crazy.

"I... Never mind," she murmured, stepping away from him.

Only he didn't let her. Invading her space, he moved with her and kept on going until her back hit the bathroom wall.

"No. I think you were about to tell me something very interesting, and I'm not letting you go until you do."

"Deacon..." Her eyes dropped to his chest, but not even a second went by before his fingers on her chin were raising her head to meet his eyes.

"What did I say about you telling me what you want?"

"To not be afraid. That you'd—"

"Give you anything. Everything."

She softened at the thought. At the memory. How could she feel so strongly about someone she'd known for such a short time?

Taking a deep breath, she released it and forced herself to meet his warm amber gaze. She trusted him not to hurt her. "When I was trying on my wedding dress, the only thing that got me through it without falling apart was convincing myself it wasn't Byron I was marrying. It was you."

The heat from his gaze warmed her as nothing ever had before. Bending his head, he pressed his forehead against hers. "Is that a proposal, Mistress Mortlake, cause it sure sounds like one to me," he joked.

"You have too many nicknames for me, and I don't have even one for…" Laughing as she spoke, her words trailed off as a sudden image inserted itself in her head. So clear, it was like a memory.

She was in a simple ivory wedding dress, more like an elegant cocktail dress than a mass of ruffles and lace. They were slow dancing, and although she knew people watched them, they didn't exist for her. Only Deacon, in a black tux, with his hair hanging loose around his face, a smile lighting his eyes as he gazed down at her, did.

"Princess?"

She blinked and Deacon was studying her with growing seriousness.

"I…"

"You…?" His eyes focused on her with an intensity she'd never seen on his face before.

233

"Would you think I was crazy if I said yes?" Her voice was soft. Hesitant.

Deacon stared. "I don't think anyone's ever struck me dumb before," he murmured, "but I guess there's a first time for everything."

He hadn't answered her question, her proposal, and she prepared to take it back. What they had was special, she knew in her heart it was something not everyone was lucky to ever find. He made her feel alive in a way no one ever had before, like she could do anything. Be anyone. But maybe she'd read too much into things, maybe things were more one-sided than she'd thought. Maybe—

She gasped as Deacon lifted her.

"Deacon?"

He buried his face against her neck. His body was trembling. "Wrap your legs around my waist."

It was an order, but his voice... he sounded... strange.

"Deacon, what—" She stopped when she felt wetness against her throat. Swallowed as her eyes burned.

Not knowing what else to do, she did what he asked and wrapped her legs around his waist, and her arms around his shoulders. Holding on tight.

"We don't have to. I mean, if you didn't want to we could always just..." she paused when she felt him shaking. "What is it? Do you want me to—"

"Ophelia Mortlake, always so quick to assume the worst. *Princess.*" Lifting his face from the hollow of her throat, he pulled the towel covering her free and dropped it onto the floor. She didn't see where because his lips were on hers, and his kiss was soft, and achingly sweet.

Lifting a hand to cradle the side of his face, she sighed

in bliss when he pressed her more firmly against the wall, his arousal fitting snug against her core.

When they finally came up for air, she eyed him hesitantly. "Is that a yes?"

"Tesoro mio, it's more than a yes. Now, where were we?" He drew her head down for another lingering kiss, one that made her melt against him.

CHAPTER EIGHTEEN

*A*s Deacon watched over Ophelia at Eros, he fought to keep his focus on the here and now.

Moments from last night kept intruding. Invading. Ophelia's face pressed against the hollow of his throat as he held her in his lap. Sliding into her tight wet heat in the bath. Her spontaneous proposal.

He'd been rock hard for most of the night already and the potency of Ophelia's attraction—and his response to her was growing rather than lessening. The more he had her, the more of her he wanted. And he wanted her now. Wanted nothing more than to find a bed, or even a wall, strip the lace panties Ophelia was so fond of from her and bury his cock in her.

"I don't like the way the guard looks at you," Byron said, glaring at him.

If the vampire had any clue where Deacon's mind was, he'd like it even less. But at least with his mirrored shades, there was little Byron could do but guess at the look in his eyes the glasses obscured.

"And how would you know?" Ophelia asked, sounding distracted.

"He wants to fuck you," Byron said.

"I don't think my father would appreciate you using language like that here, and to me."

"You're being ridiculous, Byron." It was Lenore drifting over with her usual hangers-on. "What could the Bladed possibly see in Ophelia?"

Everything.

Her friends giggled, and Ophelia rolled her eyes. "Hello, Lenore."

"And even if he was interested, I doubt she'd be able to keep a guy like that for long."

Ophelia laughed as if Lenore's words didn't bother her in the least. She hid it well, but he knew her now, the barb had hurt.

Deacon's eyes narrowed as he eyed the beautiful blonde vampire with the model good looks. The one who took pleasure in lashing out at Ophelia. He should've used his sword when he had the chance.

"What do you mean a guy like that?" Byron interrupted, eyes narrowed as he stared at Deacon, seemingly unable to tear his eyes away from him.

"Well, *you're* not likely to see it, Byron, but animal magnetism. Sheer animal magnetism." Her eyes were hungry as they slid down his body. But when her gaze hit his sword, a hint of fear shadowed her expression.

He wasn't a guy who enjoyed the idea of putting fear into a woman's eyes, but this woman… He found the idea didn't fill him with the least bit of guilt.

She was thinking about what he'd done. How he'd

used his sword on August Mortlake's would-be assassin. And after what the woman with the cold eyes and brittle smile had said to Ophelia, he couldn't help thinking of it too.

"You're making it up," Byron scoffed, moving his chair closer to Ophelia's and placing his hand on her knee. "Anyway, I don't trust him."

"He's a Bladed," Lenore said as if that explained everything. And in a way it did. The Bladed served the Council and it'd been years since a Bladed had betrayed them. They had earned their trust with years of service, and their lives.

Deacon's eyes focused on Byron's hand on Ophelia's knee. It was clear he'd only placed it there to see what Deacon would do. "I've seen the way he looks at you."

"You're being paranoid." She rose, and Byron's hand slipped off her. "I need to check my make-up."

Without another word she started for the bathroom, Deacon falling in behind her as she crossed the crowded ballroom, a path opening up before her.

———

"Just because she doesn't see it, doesn't mean I don't."

Byron's decision to confront him was unexpected. Especially in the busy entryway near the women's bathroom. He hadn't thought the vampire had it in him.

"I'm talking to you." Byron's voice was a cold lash as he stepped closer, poking a finger into Deacon's chest.

It was a mild irritation Deacon ignored. The instant it and Byron became more, he'd deal with him.

"Do you think you have a chance with her? Is that it?"
Yes. Yes, I do.

Byron's finger jabbed at him again. "Well, you don't. It's called slumming it in case you're interested. And that's even if she would even open her legs for someone like you."

Over his shoulder, Deacon caught a faint murmur from the vampires who were preparing to enter the main room and those who suddenly decided they weren't quite ready to leave Eros yet. The volume of noise in the bustling hallway lowered noticeably.

Since the only reason vampires came to Eros centered on showing off their jewels and designer clothes, their attention sharpened at this new entertainment Byron was determined to provide.

Deacon refused to let Byron suck him in. He was here to guard Ophelia, not be a source of entertainment for the vampires.

"I see how it is. You think you're better than me."

He didn't even bother to dignify that with a response. Not when the vampire seemed to be doing everything he could to peer down his nose at him, which Deacon's six-foot frame made impossible.

But that wasn't enough to stop Byron from attempting it.

"Well, let me tell you something, *human,* you can look but that is all you'll ever be able to do. Ophelia is not for the likes of you. She's for a real man not hired muscle whose only worth lies in the sword he carries."

Deacon's lips quirked. Who did Byron think he was fooling?

The brief flash of amusement on his lips was enough to enrage Byron.

"Are you laughing at me, Bladed?" He stepped closer. "You won't be laughing when Ophelia and I are fucking in our marriage bed. You know what, maybe I'll invite you over, so you can watch me fuck my wife. Maybe then you can learn a thing or two. How about that?"

Behind his sunglasses, he rolled his eyes. Was this guy being serious?

"I can assure you, Hawthorne, I've had no complaints about my ability with my... *sword*." Muffled laughter followed his response.

There was no way Ophelia would ever let this guy anywhere near her. She hadn't been interested in Byron before he was even in the picture. He knew it without a doubt, but he'd let Byron get to him. It was a mistake.

As Byron's face reddened in fury, Deacon braced himself for the onslaught.

"I think that's enough," Ophelia's sweet, cultured tones broke clean through the tension like a knife as she stepped out of the bathroom.

"Ophelia—" Byron started.

The frown on her face was severe, and when she spoke, she was cold power and strength personified, "You are behaving unseemly, Byron. Most unseemly. Listening to your coarse language has me thinking you don't have a civilized bone in your body."

Byron's face flushed with embarrassment, even as the crowd behind him edged closer. With vampires blessed with preternatural hearing, they didn't need to move any closer, but clearly, this dustup was too good to risk missing a single word of it.

"You don't—" Byron's voice was sharp with irritation.

"There will be no fucking. The language of the wedding contract was very clear on that point. It will not be my job as your wife to warm your bed, Byron and if that's the sort of intimacy you're expecting then you will be waiting a long time for it. I'm sure I don't have to tell you there are any number of prostitutes in Vegas for you to get your fill. And failing that, you always have your hand."

Ophelia turned to him. "Bladed. I'm ready to leave."

It took everything Deacon had to hold himself together. Ophelia had ripped Byron apart in front of a crowd who weren't even trying to hide how much they were loving the show, and somehow, he had to keep a straight face? "Of course, Mistress Mortlake."

With that, head held high, and not sparing another glance at Byron who stood trembling with rage, or maybe it was humiliation, she stalked toward the exit with the crowd opening up before her as if she were royalty.

Selene had the front door of the townhouse open before Ophelia could knock.

"What is it?" Selene asked, her smile fading. "Is it August? Did something happen?"

Brushing a kiss on her sister's cheek as she slipped inside, Ophelia headed straight for the lounge. "No, nothing like that. It was Byron. He started a fight with Deacon at Eros."

Settling into a couch, she complained when Deacon immediately lifted her and moved her into his lap.

"It was nothing," Deacon said, ignoring her half-hearted struggles. "No big deal."

"It wasn't nothing. Byron was about to challenge him to a duel."

Selene barked out a laugh. "Byron? Seriously?"

Max sat on the other couch in his usual uniform of white t-shirt and brightly colored board shorts. He had to have an endless supply of them, and Ophelia could never guess which one he'd wear next. Tonight, he had on a black pair with tiny green cacti printed on them.

Giving her a crooked grin, he tugged Selene down into his lap.

"Hi, Max."

"Fee, hey. Deacon," Max said, grinning at her.

"Hey, man," Deacon said.

"Luckily, I got there in time to stop it."

All she'd needed was five minutes to compose herself in the bathroom.

She'd proposed and Deacon had said yes. How was she supposed to pretend something that incredible hadn't happened?

But then she'd heard the things Byron had been saying, the way he'd been talking down to Deacon and it'd enraged her. There was no way she was about to stand by and let anyone speak to Deacon—the man she loved like that. Not anymore.

"It's a challenge, princess, one Byron wouldn't have a chance of winning."

"Do you even know what the rules of a duel are?" she asked with a raised eyebrow.

"There are swords involved?" Deacon guessed.

She glared at him. "Deacon!"

His look was pure innocence. "So, educate me then, princess."

"It's fought with swords. Lucky for you. Usually, it ends with first blood, it depends on what the reasons are for the duel. But it could be to the death," she added warningly.

"And how much experience does Byron have with a sword?"

She thought back over everything she knew about Byron. "Not much. He's someone who puts more effort in styling his hair than working out."

Deacon tugged her closer and kissed her on the forehead. "There you have it then, nothing to concern yourself about. Even if he had challenged me, he wouldn't have stood a chance whether or not it was to the death."

She turned to face him. "Deacon, this isn't just about Byron challenging you to a duel. This is about the consequences that would follow. Everyone would hear about it, and the last thing we need are rumors of you and me getting back to August. So no more antagonizing him."

Deacon's eyes were innocent. "What do you mean?"

"I heard what you said."

"And what about what you said?" There was a hint of a smile on his lips, and she imagined tracing the outline of his smile with the tip of her tongue.

"What Fee said?" Selene asked.

She tore her eyes away from Deacon's lips and turned to Selene. "Byron was talking about me like I was a piece of meat."

"Which is how he's always seen you," Selene muttered, her eyes narrowed.

"Ophelia humiliated him in front of everyone."

"I did not humiliate him. I just reminded him of the sort of marriage we'd have if I was even going through with the wedding."

Deacon propped his chin on top of her head. "Mmm. I think my favorite part was about Byron using his hand if he couldn't find a prost—"

"*Deacon,*" she snapped.

Selene was shaking with laughter. "No, don't stop there. Go on, what were you telling Byron, Fee?"

"It's not important," she muttered, leaning away from him.

"Well, I think it's very important," Deacon murmured against her hair.

Something in his voice had her tipping her head back to meet his eyes.

"No one's ever stepped in to defend me like that before."

Sliding his hand around her nape, he tugged her closer. "I liked it," he murmured, and then he kissed her.

Just as their kiss was getting more heated and she was thinking about heading to a bedroom upstairs, something soft walloped her in the back of her head.

"Hey!" She broke the kiss to glare at Selene.

"You were getting distracted." There was not an ounce of apology in her voice.

"As if you haven't done the same before," she muttered.

Selene's smile was smug as she leaned into Max. "I'm older. I don't get distracted so easily."

Ophelia's eyes narrowed. "Really. How about that time when—"

"Princess?" Deacon interrupted. "As much as I love seeing you and Selene play, we have a lot to talk about and we don't have a lot of time."

Sighing, she pressed her cheek against his. He was right of course. But she also heard what he wasn't saying. A brief kiss wasn't nearly enough. She wanted more. Craved more. But first, they needed to talk about what they planned to do about August. And then they could play. Just her and Deacon.

It felt strange to be sitting with him like this. Surreal. His arm coiled around her the way she'd always seen Selene sit with Max. She'd never been brave enough to admit to anyone how envious she was that Selene had something she would never have. Byron wasn't, and would never be the sort of person she'd ever want to cuddle with, and what he'd said in Eros only proved it.

"August wasn't home tonight so I had a quick look around his office in case there was anything about the other Councilors' in there. But I guess I was expecting too much to find a name in a notebook or something. It was never going to be that easy, was it?"

She thought about that. They were planning on killing him. August Mortlake. Her father. But who would be the one to do it, her? Selene? Deacon? Max?

"He has to die, Fifi." Selene's voice was soft, but it was steely.

Of course, Selene would know what she was thinking. About her doubts. About her. She'd always been able to read her. "Doesn't this make us as bad as he is? He tried to kill you, and now we're planning to do the same to him."

"You don't think we should?" Max's voice was hard. The laid-back surfer had disappeared.

After she'd collapsed and Deacon had carried her to a bedroom upstairs, Selene had told her about the Bladed sent to ambush them. August had tried to kill the woman Max loved. He had every reason in the world to want him dead.

In all the years since she'd first met Max, she'd never seen him lose his temper. But with his jaw hard, and his cornflower-blue eyes liked chipped ice, he looked in a killing rage, ready to go at August at the drop of a hat.

She never would have imagined her short-fused sister would fall in love with a shaggy-haired surfer from Orange County, California who was so laid back, at times he was almost horizontal.

She'd always thought Max softened a little of Selene's hard edges, but studying him, Ophelia couldn't help but wonder if there was more to Max than she'd always thought.

She sighed. "No. I... I know we have to do something. We have to stop him. But he's—"

"Still Dad?" Selene piped up, her lips twisting in a mockery of a smile.

Ophelia shook her head. "No. He was never Dad. I guess I thought it would be... you know, easier, because of everything he's done to us. Everything he is doing. But it's not, and I don't know how I'm—"

"Princess. It won't be you who does it."

There was no room for argument in Deacon's voice as he slid a hand into her hair and tilted her head up to meet his gaze. "Your only role in this is information."

"Which I'm doing a terrible job at. I feel so inadequate —so... stupid for not being able to give you even the tiniest crumb of information. I've lived under the same roof as the man for years, how can I know nothing?"

"He's had decades of keeping secrets, *tesoro mio.* No one's expecting you to uncover them all in the span of a single night."

"*Tesoro mio?*" Selene interrupted.

But Ophelia didn't turn to answer her sister. Her gaze remained locked on Deacon. "It's Italian for treasure," she said in a whisper, remembering the first time he'd told her.

He was studying her in a way that made her feel warm all over, and it had arousal stirring. She realized something then, something important.

"I haven't told you, have I?" She brushed at the stubble on his jaw. Liked the roughness against her fingers, the way it felt rubbing against her cheek when they kissed.

"Oh, boy," Selene muttered.

Ophelia ignored her.

"Told me what?" Deacon asked, his eyes warm, lazy as they searched her face.

"That I love you."

"I thought you might like me since you proposed and everything." Laughter creased the corners of his eyes, but he didn't laugh out loud. "But I could be wrong. Maybe you only want to marry me for my body."

"Ophelia *proposed?*" Selene didn't even try to hide her shock.

"Tempted to do the same, babe?" Max joked. "We could hit up a chapel and do it tonight."

Selene said something, but Ophelia had stopped listening then. Her focus was on Deacon. Deacon who stared down at her as if he was paying about as much attention to Selene and Max as she was. Which was none at all.

Circling Deacon's shoulders with her arms, she raised her eyebrow. "Don't you have something you want to tell me?"

"I don't know, do I?"

Something poked her, and she glanced down. "Your sword is digging into my thigh."

"And on that note," Selene interrupted with a laugh. "We'll leave you to it."

"Selene, that wasn't a euphemism for his—uh, you know." She climbed off Deacon's lap. Was immediately pulled back down. "His sword really is—"

Laughing, Deacon tightened his hold on her.

"Deacon, will you please tell her—"

He only laughed harder as Selene and Max trudged out. "We'll give you some privacy. Come back tomorrow and we'll talk more, love you, sis. And be careful."

"You purposefully let her think something that wasn't true," she said, glaring at Deacon after Selene and Max left.

Deacon nudged his sword belt aside. "The way you

said it, princess, I doubt there's anything I could've said to convince her otherwise."

Then he rose with her in his arms, starting toward the staircase.

Leaning her head against his shoulders, she sighed loudly. "I guess now you want to have your wicked way with me."

"Of course, I do. Byron was right about one thing. I do want to fuck you," he said, waggling his eyebrow.

She poked him in the chest. "Hey! I tell you I love you, and you say you want to fuck me?"

He took the stairs two at a time, heading for the bedroom they'd used the night before, pausing to kick the door shut before he tossed her onto the bed. Unstrapped his sword belt and dropped it on the floor. Followed her down less than a second later.

But he didn't kiss her. Not right away. No, he lay on top of her, his hands braced beside her head. Even though a smile still lingered on his lips, his eyes were serious.

"I love you, princess. A fact you should already know."

Her mouth went dry. "I should?"

He nodded, his eyes sober. "You should. Especially since I've been doing my very best to show you."

She fought to keep a straight face. All she wanted to do was laugh, and cry, and scream to the world that Deacon Chase—the man she loved with all her heart, loved her back. "You have?"

His expression was somber as he slid down her body, his hands stroking over her breasts, along her waist, before he eased her thighs apart, stopping when his face was in line with her core. Her thigh muscles tensed. A low throbbing heat started low down, and she licked suddenly dry lips. It wasn't hard to figure out what Deacon intended.

"Uh, Deacon, what—"

"Just lay back, princess." His tone was coaxing as his hands worked the hem of her dress up over her hips.

He wasn't going to... kiss her there? Was he? No one's ever...

"Deacon?"

"Mm." He nipped at the sensitive skin on her inner thigh. She jerked in response, and once he'd distracted her, he tugged her panties down to her knees.

When he raised his head to look at her, her mouth went dry at the hunger burning in the depths of his eyes.

"You're going to want to grab a pillow, princess. Wouldn't want the neighbors hearing your screams and wondering what I'm doing to you."

Face flushing, she shot up. "That's pretty presumptuous of you, Deacon Chase, not to mention more than a little cocky. What makes you think—"

He bent his head, his eyes never leaving hers as his tongue stroked along the folds of her sex. Her breath caught and she grabbed for a pillow, her hands desperate.

CHAPTER NINETEEN

"You're making Rick uncomfortable," Deacon said, not looking up at the man who'd dropped into the seat beside him at The Rising Sun Pub.

"I have done nothing."

"You're here. That's enough." Deacon finished his drink, hesitating over ordering another.

Time was ticking along and his errand in the city had taken much longer than he'd expected. He still had to get home, get showered and dressed, and be at Ophelia's in a couple of hours, but something told him Julian's unexpected appearance wasn't a casual one.

"Rick, can I grab another one? And one for my friend." He glanced over at the vampire in a leather jacket and ripped jeans perched on the barstool beside him. *Friend was probably being overly generous*, he thought.

"What do you want?"

"Whatever you're having is fine."

"That wasn't what I meant. What are you doing here? Isn't it a bit early for your kind to be about?"

He was only half-joking. Evidently, the vampire was taking advantage of the shorter days in winter to be out, and with the sun setting much earlier.

The vampire had cut it close though, and to Deacon's eye, Julian's nose was a little pink, but otherwise he didn't look to be in danger of being burnt to a crisp.

Julian shrugged before answering, "I heard about what you did."

Uh oh.

"About what I did?" Deacon asked, feigning ignorance.

Rick slid two ice-frosted beers across the counter and Deacon snatched one up, taking a sip. Julian however, merely tugged his over and tapped his fingers on the bottle, showing little interest in drinking.

"Your apology. To Raul."

Oh, was that all?

Hiding his relief, Deacon kept his gaze fixed on the bar lined with a vast array of bottles, and the large gilt mirror reflecting his and Julian's image. A mirror which also caught Rick staring at Julian with undisguised suspicion from the bar hatch at the far side of the counter.

"Don't you have something to do?" Deacon called out.

Never taking his eyes from Julian, Rick leaned over the counter and after snatching up a cloth, did such a piss poor job of wiping at a spot on the bar that to Deacon's eye didn't have a speck of dirt on it, he had to laugh.

Shaking his head, Deacon turned away. He didn't know what Rick thought Julian would do, but whatever it was, it wasn't anything good.

"Most of the guys wouldn't have bothered," Julian said.

Deacon didn't disagree with the vampire's statement. Getting an apology out of anyone in Bladed headquarters was rare. It just wasn't the type of place where anyone was eager to admit they were wrong. About anything.

But he'd grown up in a family where arguments and squabbles were the norm, no less with three older sisters and two younger brothers.

His parents had put their foot down that regardless of who'd done what, or why, apologies were in order. No one went to bed angry in their house. At least that'd been his parents' goal, and though it'd often resulted in more arguments than less, he knew it was a rule born of love.

Much later when he and his siblings had moved out and started families of their own, that was one element of his childhood alongside his memories he'd carried with him into adulthood.

His treatment of the new recruit had haunted him, and he wasn't about to leave the Bladed—leave Vegas without making amends. Something that'd left the recruit gaping at him, too shocked to say much of anything before Deacon had walked away.

Taking a sip from his bottle, Deacon shrugged. "Maybe."

"But that wasn't all I came to talk to you about."

"Of course, you didn't. The Rising Sun is hardly round the corner from headquarters. What, did you follow me?"

"Some of the guys mentioned you sometimes hung out here."

The response was so evasive Deacon raised an

eyebrow as he continued to study the vampire in the mirror opposite.

"Hmm, how about you get to the point you came here to make?"

"There are rumors," Julian said, still not touching his beer.

"Rumors? Oh please, not those. Never those. How will I ever survive?" he intoned, deadpan.

Julian glared at him. "If I were you, I'd be a lot more concerned with what Hawthorne will do if he gets proof of what you've been up to."

"Hawthorne? Isn't that the guy Ophelia Mortlake is marrying?" he asked, playing dumb.

"He has powerful friends, notwithstanding his closeness with Ophelia's father."

Interest spiked.

"Notwithstanding? Who uses words like that?" He grinned.

"You're choosing to focus on my vocabulary? *That's* what's important to you?"

"I'm intrigued is what I am. I mean, everyone knows about the Mortlake lineage, but the Hawthorne's? I reckon I would have to ask five Bladed before I got to one who knew about that line." It was a guess, pure and simple and he waited for Julian to call him out on it. But at the vampire's tense silence, he knew he'd struck true.

"But you, Julian, with no last name and who likes to use words like 'notwithstanding', do. I can't help but find that fascinating."

In a heartbeat Julian's expression was shuttered, and his unusual gray eyes turned cold. Resembling a mask. A mask which put Deacon in mind of Ophelia and her ability to throw walls up to protect herself. He'd watched her do it right in front of him, again and again. Just who was Julian no-name, and what was he trying to hide?

Julian's voice was devoid of all emotion when he spoke. "It's of no concern to you. I was just trying to do you a favor." He stood.

Deacon turned to face him fully now. "Why is that? You haven't exactly tried to hide what you think of the human Bladed. Soft target was the term I believe I heard you use."

"Perhaps I see where this is going, Chase." Julian pierced him with a sharp look. "Perhaps it's something I've seen happen before and have no wish to see it happen again."

There was something about his angled features, the line of his long nose, and the direct way the vampire met his gaze that told him Julian came from aristocracy. But Ophelia had seen him in the gym, and she hadn't seemed to recognize him. He'd have to ask her about Julian.

Still, the vampire had gone out of his way and was warning Deacon of something Ophelia had mentioned already. "I appreciate it. But I know what I'm doing."

"You know pride usually comes before a fall, don't you?"

Deacon shrugged. "I've heard it said before. But, like I said, I know what I'm doing."

Nodding, Julian turned to leave, but after taking a couple of steps he stopped with his back to Deacon. "You're not invincible, Chase. You're talented with the sword, don't get me wrong, but that isn't going to be enough."

The vampire walked away.

Deacon watched him go. There was no doubt in his mind he could take Byron in a duel, and that wasn't pride talking. He'd seen the way the vampire moved, how much he telegraphed his intentions. Yes, Byron had the benefit of preternatural speed, but he didn't make use of it.

And no one had his ability with the sword in the Bladed. Hadn't he been training with and alongside vampires for the last five years? Hadn't he been wielding a sword since he was twelve?

Shaking his head, he took another gulp of his beer and after climbing to his feet, grabbed his bag from the floor.

"I'll see you later, Rick." He tossed a handful of bills on the counter. "Or maybe you won't, who can say?"

He had places to go, and the most beautiful girl in the world to pick up. They'd meet with Selene and Max, talk about their plans, and then he'd have Ophelia all to himself for a few hours. The honeyed taste of her had been exotic, indescribably her and he hadn't been able to get enough of her.

The thought of spending an hour or more lying between her soft thighs, lapping at her essence had his cock straining in his pants, and a wide smile stretching across his face as he walked out.

The slow deliberate glide of Deacon's fingers drawing lazy circles at her lower back was sending Ophelia crazy.

Since she and Deacon had arrived at Selene and Max's rented townhouse from Eros, and Deacon had plopped her on his lap, he'd not stopped.

He knew it too. But every attempt to move away, would see his hand follow her.

Selene was talking, but with Deacon's touch slowly making her want to crawl out of skin with need, there wasn't a hope in hell of her paying attention to what her sister was saying.

Finally, seeing only one way to deal with Deacon, Ophelia decided to fight fire with fire. Lifting the hand she'd splayed on the back of his shoulder, she used her index finger to draw the same shape at the base of his neck.

His jaw tightened and his erection, a hot and hard brand, burning a hole through the thin material of her dress, twitched against her thigh. And although his expression was one of total concentration, she was sure he was paying about as much attention as she was.

"Fee!" Selene snapped.

Spinning around so fast, she twinged a muscle in her neck. "Yes?"

"Are you even listening to me?" The expression on Selene's face; narrowed eyes, tight lips, and the swirling of irritation in the depth of her dark eyes, made it clear she already knew what the answer would be.

"Deacon's distracting me." Her words came out breathy as Deacon's finger edged down toward the crease of her ass.

"Whatever it is he's doing, Fifi, I doubt it can be as important as this discussion."

I don't know about that.

Her eyes glazed over as her thoughts circled back to the previous night. To the feel of Deacon's tongue lapping at her intimately, and the rough brush of his stubble against her inner thigh.

The things he'd done… the way his tongue had probed her… there was no place he'd left untouched. In short, he'd given her the most intense climax she'd ever had.

Even with the pillow to muffle her screams, she knew someone must have heard her.

She had no memory of him removing his clothes, and hers, or of him moving. But the feel of his hard length brushing against her sensitized sex as he'd shifted to enter her, had her coming apart again. And then he'd slid into her. All thoughts scattered. The only thing that mattered was Deacon moving inside her.

"What the hell did you do to my sister, Bladed? Why does she have that ridiculous smile on her face?" Selene's voice pierced her daydream, and she blinked to bring herself back to focus.

Sitting beside Selene on the couch opposite her and Deacon, was Max in a pair of turquoise shorts with tiny black boats. Max's grin was full of mischief. "I might have some idea," he drawled.

Ophelia turned to Selene, ready to apologize. Only the look on Selene's face stopped her short, or rather the dull red staining her sister's cheeks did.

Selene *blushing?* That was new.

"Right," Selene said clearing her throat. "Enough of that. Now, about August. Any luck?"

Ophelia shook her head. "Nothing. I had maybe five

minutes to root around his office and there wasn't anything of any interest there. Just his diary, but it was all meetings with his attorneys and accountant. I don't think he keeps a record of his meetings with the Council."

"And you're sure he's never mentioned any of the Councilors before?" Deacon resumed stroking her lower back until she glared at him until he stopped.

"No. Well, I don't think he has. Selene?"

"Not that I've ever heard. But then again, it wasn't like he was home much anyway." Selene paused, her face creasing in a frown. "The only person I remember him talking about was Mr. Knight."

Ophelia shook her head. "No. Can't be him. August must have needed to speak to him about something else."

"Babe, who is Mr. Knight and why couldn't it be him?" Max asked Selene.

"Mr. Knight's a pencil-pusher. A bureaucrat. He's a Senior Advisor of some department in the Council," Selene said.

She thought back to what little she knew of the man. It wasn't much. She'd never had a reason to be at the Council building, but she had a vague memory of a man with small dark eyes. Maybe she'd met him at Eros.

"I think the only reason I remember him was his age. He was kind of old," she admitted.

Her comment surprised a laugh out of Deacon. "That's harsh, princess."

"I don't mean to be."

At Deacon's look of confusion, she explained. "It's rare for someone older than forty to be turned since the risk of survival decreases the older you are, and Mr. Knight

259

was older than the usual. He looked about middle-aged I think."

Selene, she noticed was deep in thought. "Hmm."

"Selene?" she asked.

"It's nothing, just that…" she shook her head. "No, it's stupid. Ignore me."

"No. Your instincts are usually right, sis, what is it?"

And they were. It hadn't surprised her in the least that Selene had not only survived, she'd thrived after their father had tossed her out. Over the years she'd learned not to discount Selene's instincts.

"Just something I remember August saying. It's probably nothing."

"Maybe not, but I still want to hear it."

Selene smiled. "When did you get to be so bossy?"

"You always said I would one day. So spill."

"Do you remember how sometimes he'd lose his shit and start ranting to Stanley about how much he hated day, and we thought it was his gorging making him say things that didn't make sense? Maybe, it wasn't daylight he was talking about but a person, a person called Mr. Day just like there's a Mr. Knight?"

She blinked in surprise. That hadn't been what she'd been expecting Selene to say. "Huh?"

"I told you it was stupid."

"Wait, just let me think about this a second," she murmured. It was a stretch, there was no denying it, but one of Selene's strengths lay in making connections. And this felt right, it was something she could see the Council doing, hiding their identities behind code words.

"But August is just August Mortlake. If there's a Knight

and a day, why doesn't he have a name?" she asked, thinking aloud. "Because he loves his name and his lineage too much to ever want to hide who he is," she said, answering her own question.

Even though Selene had been the one to suggest it, her face was awash with doubt. "Knight though? Seriously? He can't be—"

A thought struck. "There was a dawn. A woman. You remember hearing him mention her, right?"

Selene's eyes widened. "You're right," she said slowly, "there was. But surely someone would have clocked onto this already? We can't be the first to figure this out."

"No. But who else is going to go shouting about it in case it turns out they were right? They'd be dead by sunrise."

Silence descended as they absorbed what that meant, and what it could mean to them.

"Princess, I think we should walk away from this. It's one thing August coming after us, but if the Council suspect we know who they are, that's another thing entirely," Deacon said.

Ophelia turned to face Deacon and pressed a hand on his jaw. He was trying to protect her. Trying to keep her safe again, but she had to keep him safe too. "Deacon, we need a Councilor in our corner otherwise we'd always be looking over our shoulder no matter where we went."

"So, we kill him."

"And how," she said, her voice soft, "do you propose we do that? He's a Councilor and they're not exactly known for being easy to kill. None of us could do it unless we were lucky. Very lucky."

"Princess…" Closing his eyes, he rested his forehead against hers.

"You know I'm making sense Deacon, it's the only hope we have."

He growled in frustration. "I can't keep taking you back there, *tesoro mio.* Not when I know I'm putting you in danger. If he even suspects…" His eyes opened, and they were dark with fear. Fear for her.

"He doesn't. You saw how he was when you came to pick me up. There wasn't the slightest hint of anything being wrong."

Deacon didn't look convinced. "But he blindsided you with Selene and Max. You didn't see that coming, did you?"

He had a point, but she wasn't backing down. She let him see the resistance in her eyes. The determination. "Deacon, I'm not changing my mind. Not about this. I can't."

You mean too much to me.

"Max and I can go see Knight. Test out our theory. The more that I think about it, the more I'm convinced it's the perfect disguise for him. I mean who would ever suspect Knight of being a Councilor?" Selene asked, her tone thoughtful.

"I get you want to protect her, man," Max said. "But it's one night. Give us one night to see if we're right, and if not you can grab Fee and get the hell out of Vegas."

"We're cutting things close," Deacon warned. "The wedding is in two nights."

"Which I won't be here for," Ophelia said. He was wavering, she could see it, hear it in his voice. "But if we leave now August will know I've run with you, especially after the scene at Eros."

Deacon let out a heavy sigh, looking dejected. "You're very good at this."

She frowned, confused. "Good at what?"

"Convincing me to do things I have no intention of doing," he said, with a dramatic sigh. "But since I agreed to marry you, I guess I'd better start learning to accept this new and terrible fault of yours."

Smiling, she draped her arms around his shoulders. "Sounds like a good idea."

"Okay, so close your eyes," he said.

"Close my—"

"You heard me. And no peeking."

It was her turn to sigh as she slid her hands from his shoulders, and dutifully did what she was told.

With Selene and Max in the room, she knew he wouldn't try anything with her, but when his hands closed around her hips, she sucked in a breath. His lips brushed across hers in a fleeting kiss, but before she could even think about responding, he was pulling away.

"Sorry, couldn't resist, princess."

"Can I open my eyes now?" she asked, once she'd caught her breath again. How could it be, she thought, a brief kiss could leave her breathless like this?

"Not yet," he murmured, his fingers brushing against the back of her neck, making her shiver.

A second later something cool settled in between her breasts.

"You can look now."

She opened her eyes and glanced down. Her heart stopped.

"I know it's nothing like what you have now, but it felt like you. I wanted to give it to you later. After. But you're mine, princess, my heart, my soul—my life. My everything. I can't have you going a second longer without you knowing it, without you carrying a piece of me with you."

As if from a distance she was conscious Deacon was still talking, but her mind was fragmenting. She felt on the cusp of mad tears, or laughter. It was impossible to know which. Later she'd figure it out, but right now her entire focus was on the delicate emerald engagement ring hanging on the end of a matching necklace.

Jade and emerald.

Deacon had said her eyes were like jade and emerald with strands of hazel shot through it when she was aroused. The gemstone on the ring was a perfect description. She'd looked at her reflection every day of her adult life and her eyes didn't come close to being this beautiful.

Tears welled and she blinked them away. It was impossible to tear her eyes away from the ring she held in her trembling hand.

"Princess." Deacon's voice intruded on her thoughts, and although his eyes were full of laughter, as they always were, she picked up the thread of worry he was trying to hide. "You've been pretty quiet for a while. If you don't like it, I can—"

She threw herself at him, her lips latching onto his. Her eyes slammed shut as her tongue stole into his mouth. Hungry. Desperate. Needing him with every fiber of her body, so much her body shook even as tears spilled down her cheeks. Slowly, his hands came up, smoothing up her back and crushing her against him.

The soft snick of the front door announced Selene and Max's silent exit, and then she stopped paying attention because Deacon was shifting to lay her on the couch. Lifting his head, he gazed down at her, his eyes searching hers. Then he smiled.

"There it is," he said. "Beautiful. Mine."

She shook her head. "No." Raised her hand to cover his heart. "Mine. You're my heart. Always."

His eyes flared liquid gold as he shifted so she was cradling his erection in the vee of her thighs. Twining her arms and legs around him, she pulled him even closer. "Make love to me, Deacon."

He grinned. "With pleasure, princess. With pleasure."

CHAPTER TWENTY

*D*eacon had his car packed and his apartment was scrubbed clean. Even though he wouldn't be getting his security deposit back because of everything he was leaving behind, he hadn't wanted to leave a filthy apartment in his wake. His mom had taught him better than that.

If Selene and Max weren't able to speak with Mr. Knight and get him on side, he wanted to be ready to leave Vegas.

Tonight was her rehearsal party at the Waldorf Astoria, the same hotel her wedding was due to take place tomorrow night. Which meant August would be there. But if Selene was right about August's increasing addiction, he'd find some reason to leave early. Then he and Ophelia would play the waiting game as he kept a close eye on his phone to hear what had happened with Selene and Max going to see Mr. Knight at his office.

Deacon still had his doubts about what would happen if Selene and Max confirmed Knight was a Councilor.

Identifying him was only the first step, and in the grand scheme of things, the easiest part of their plan.

Somehow Selene and Max had to convince him to strike at August. And they weren't even sure where Mr. Knight's loyalties lay. There were too many things that could go wrong, and he had a sense there were even more variables he wasn't seeing.

Grabbing his sword and jacket, Deacon swung open his front door and stopped. Julian and an unfamiliar Bladed stood waiting as if they'd been waiting for him to open the door.

"Julian, what is this?"

Had this been what the vampire had tried to warn him about yesterday? Had he been hinting Byron had already made his move?

"Byron Hawthorne is challenging you to a duel." Julian's voice was devoid of emotion, and his face expressionless.

"I see," Deacon said slowly.

"Councilor Mortlake has agreed to hold the duel at his home," Julian continued.

"Now? I'm supposed to fight him now?"

"Councilor Mortlake doesn't believe this matter will delay Byron Hawthorne and his daughter from their event this evening."

"And the rules of this duel?" Deacon asked.

"Will be explained to you on your arrival at the Mortlake Estate."

The unfamiliar Bladed with eyes a deep, deep blue stared at him. His expression never changed, and his hand never lifted from the hilt of his sword.

Killer. Cold-blooded killer.

It was something in the eyes, a dark shadow that proclaimed what he was. Something Deacon had seen again and again in the warzones he'd served in. Death.

He didn't want the vampire anywhere near Ophelia.

"Fine, I'll meet you there."

There was a long pause before Julian spoke, "We're to escort you."

"What, is Byron worried I'll make a run for it?" Deacon joked. Never taking his eyes off the Bladed that he doubted was a Bladed at all. And if he was, he was a commander. The ones who never used the gym. The ones who worked most closely with the Councilors.

No one laughed.

"I'm guessing I'll need my wakizashi. Or do I need—"

"The short sword is fine," Julian interrupted.

"And Byron—"

"Is not your problem."

Right. This was serious. Much more serious than he'd realized.

Stepping out, Deacon pulled the door shut behind him, giving away none of his rising unease. "Well, I guess one of you had better lead the way."

His Bladed guard, because they couldn't be anything else, led him into August's home and through to the same reception room he'd first seen Ophelia. Except the furniture comprised of antique couches, and delicate side tables lined the outer edges of the room leaving more floor space to fight.

And there, leaning against the mantle inspecting a wakizashi short sword was Byron Hawthorne. In a pair of black pants, a black shirt, and shoes. Dressed as if he were a Bladed.

Since Byron was busy examining the sword—clearly a Bladed issued weapon going by the black steel and the distinctive leather hilt—as if the weapon was one he'd never seen before, Deacon couldn't help but wonder who'd given their weapon up to the aristocrat to use.

With their swords forged by master craftsmen in Japan, the weapons weren't cheap. They were highly prized, and by more than just the Bladed. There were collectors out there who made no secret of their desire to get a hold of one of their weapons.

No Bladed would willingly hand their sword over to someone who could inadvertently damage such a valuable commodity. Not unless they'd been ordered to. But by whom?

"Ah, you've arrived. Excellent." August's voice was rich with humor as he materialized at Deacon's side.

It was experience alone that saved him from revealing his surprise in front of Byron who had managed to peel his eyes off his sword long enough to glare at Deacon. Ignoring Byron for the time being, Deacon turned to meet August's eyes.

As he'd thought, the vampire was smiling, looking relaxed in a tailored white shirt, dress pants, and not a strand of his auburn hair out of place.

"Councilor Mortlake."

"All of this must come as a surprise to you," August stated, moving to stand in the center of the room, the bright light from the candelabra overhead lighting his hair a rich coppery-red. As if wanting all eyes on him. Which, considering all the attention the vampire was used to getting from reporters, didn't come as a surprise to Deacon.

"I had some questions." None of which he cared about in the least. He needed to know where Ophelia was. It was after five, past the time he usually came to collect her. Why hadn't she come down to find out what August was doing? Because he sure as shit was up to something. Deacon could feel it in his bones.

"And I have some answers," August said, sounding magnanimous, as if he were bestowing great favor on Deacon. As if he were a king, royalty even. "There has been a... how shall I put it? A threat to Byron's standing."

Deacon shot Byron a glance. Found the vampire staring at him with naked hatred burning in his walnut dark eyes. His hand gripped the hilt of the sword with eagerness, but much too tight.

It was one of the first lessons he'd learned in training. His master had drilled it into him over and over and over again.

"No, your grip is too tight, your sword is not going anywhere. No, too loose, one tap and I'll send it flying. Ease up. Firm but relaxed." Once he'd got the basics of holding a sword down, everything had come easy. A prodigy everyone had called him when within a year he was beating opponents ten years older with the experience to match.

"Threatened?" he asked August, conscious of Julian's eyes on him.

"You see there are… rumors. Of an indiscretion between yourself and Ophelia," August said, offhand.

Deacon opened his mouth, ready to deny everything but August beat him to it.

"Oh, the rumors don't matter one whit to me."

Deacon's suspicions dialed up another notch.

August laughed. "I see you don't believe me. I'll explain, shall I?"

Since the vampire seemed so eager to talk, Deacon let him, nodding for him to continue.

"What concerns me is this wedding. A wedding I can't have dogged with rumors and insinuations. No. Think of this as a performance in a play. A play in which we all have a role to play."

"A performance in a play?" Deacon raised his eyebrow. Did August seriously believe he was buying all this?

"Yes. Since we have an important event this evening, we should get things moving. I believe a round or two will be sufficient. The first to draw blood is the victor. And if you could avoid inflicting damage to Byron's face, I—and likely the photographer at the wedding will be most grateful."

"Yes, Councilor."

Finished with Deacon, August turned to Julian and the mysterious Bladed. "You can leave."

Julian didn't move. "Councilor Mortlake, I believe it's customary for the Bladed to serve as witnesses to duels."

Was it? Why was Deacon only hearing about the rule now?

"Since this isn't a serious duel, there is no need for you to remain any longer." Steel was unmistakable in August's voice; this was no suggestion, but an order. "Get out. Now. You are neither needed nor wanted."

The other Bladed, the one Deacon had never seen before walked out without a word, but Julian remained. "But—"

All evidence of amusement slid off August's face. "I believe I've made myself clear, Bladed."

"Yes, Councilor." Julian's voice was ice-cold as he turned to leave, spearing Deacon with a sharp look loaded with warning before he stepped out.

When the front door slammed shut, August clapped his hands together.

"Now all the formalities have been dealt with, let us begin." August grinned, his black eyes sparkling with excitement.

Yes, Deacon thought, sliding his sword out of its sheathe. He'd been waiting for an opportunity to deal with Byron, and August had handed it to him on a silver plate.

So much for a performance in a play, Deacon thought, dodging another of Byron's two-handed hacks to his neck before shooting August a questioning glance.

August, leaning against the mantle with his arms folded across his chest shrugged, unconcerned.

Fueled by the same rage that'd seen Byron confront him outside the bathroom at Eros, it was a combination of experience and luck which saved Deacon from losing his head under Byron's increasingly furious attacks. They spun across the marble floor, two whirling figures all dressed in black.

What the vampire was doing with his sword didn't come close to resembling even the most basic of martial arts training. And Deacon was finding it was taking more effort to avoid killing Byron outright, when Byron left himself exposed to any number of attacks with each of his wild swings.

White skin peeked through the slashes on Byron's black shirt, and through them, Deacon caught glimpses of bloody and healing cuts. Evidence he'd won the duel several times over.

But there was no call to end the fight from August even though Deacon had drawn blood in his first strike. On and on it went, and August was doing not a thing to stop it. And there was still no sign of Ophelia. Which meant something was wrong. Something he needed to investigate.

Stepping aside from Byron's next attack, Deacon sighed when the vampire lost his balance and stumbled forward. Overbalanced likely, from relying on a two-handed swing which any experienced swordfighter would know not to do with the lightweight short sword.

"Is this really necessary?" Deacon asked, his sword swatting aside Byron's next attack. Reading the vampire's intentions before he could execute. Just like all his other attacks.

Byron's face was a snarl of rage, his aristocratic cold-ness buried under the heat of fire and emotion. "You think you can have your way with Ophelia. With *my* wife and think I'll stand for it?"

Deacon sighed. "Look, I think you're reading too much into things. And really, isn't it a little unfair of you to expect fidelity from Ophelia, when she walked in on you in bed with another woman a mere few days ago? Double standards much?"

Byron's sword was a blur as he slashed at him, but Deacon's sword was already waiting to meet his latest attack.

"Mmm, no response?" Deacon asked.

The snarl that came out of Byron's mouth was barely human.

"You treat people like things, things you can pick up and toss away when you're done with them. Like *toys*."

Deacon thought about the life Ophelia would have lived with Byron. With a man who treated her like a possession. A prison. It would have been a prison devoid of anything coming close to happiness.

Deacon went on the attack. Aimed his next swing directly at Byron's face which sent Byron jerking away, his face white with fear.

"You're like a child. Perhaps it's time I treated you like one." His next swing opened up more of Byron's shirt and his skin.

Byron stumbled back, raising his sword just in time to stop Deacon's powerful slicing cut.

"Now, how about we put an end to this before someone gets hurt?" He shifted his stance, one foot forward, his body turned sideways in a side stance which allowed him to both go on the attack and defend himself at the same time.

Deacon had barely stopped speaking before Byron was stabbing his sword toward his face. Deacon flicked his wrist, blocking the attack instantly.

"Fine, don't say I didn't warn you." He sent his sword up in a diagonal cut, opening a shallow wound along the side of Byron's jaw.

Byron backed up a step. A step was all Deacon gave him before he brought his sword in a vertical downward stroke, which ripped Byron's sword from his grip and sent the blade skittering across the floor.

With no weapon and no idea of how to defend himself against Deacon's next attack, Byron did something Deacon had never seen a vampire do before. He dropped to the floor and raised his arms to cover his face.

Since Byron had just had his ass handed to him, Deacon thought it was the smartest thing the vampire could've done. Relaxing his posture, he kept a close eye on the cowering vampire. He'd been on the receiving end of more than a few sneak attacks at a moment he'd thought a fight was over.

"Excellent," August said, his clapping echoing in the open space. "I heard how skilled you were with a sword, but seeing it is another thing entirely. What a terrible waste."

A frown creased Deacon's face, as he turned to face August. "What do you—"

Searing agony bloomed in his belly, drawing his eyes downwards. The sword slipped out of his hand and the sound of it hitting the ground was loud, sharp. But that wasn't what held him immobile. No, it was the sword August had run through him. It seemed impossible. A nightmare.

Raising his head, his eyes met August's grin, but before he could speak, a harsh gasp was spilling out of his mouth at the same moment August violently ripped the sword out.

Instinctively, his hands clutched at the wound gushing hot red blood. He was dead. No human entered the vampire enclaves high above the city. There'd be no ambulance coming up to save him. Not with August Mortlake staring at him with a dark hunger lighting his eyes.

Ophelia. How would he save Ophelia now?

Slowly, he fell to his knees before just as slowly tipping over onto his side, his hands wet, sticky with blood. And then his vision began to dim.

———

August's voice was the first thing she heard when she woke. Hearing just enough to send fear spiking. He sounded... excited, and right now, August was only excited about the possibility of blood being spilled. And feeding. She couldn't forget about that. And Deacon was there. Alone.

She tried to rise, but nothing worked. Not her arms, nor her legs. Nothing. She couldn't move.

"He drugged me." Her words were soundless. The drug he'd given her had stolen her ability to speak.

She'd been suspicious coming home last night to find

him waiting for her outside his office, two glasses of blood in champagne flutes on his desk. To celebrate her upcoming wedding, he'd said. But what could she do? Say no?

Something in his eyes had warned her she couldn't trust him. But it was too late now.

They were talking about a duel. Deacon, and August and someone else—a Bladed she didn't know. Deacon was going to fight Byron in a duel, and she could do nothing, say nothing to stop it.

All she could do was lie there and listen, fighting with everything she had to break the strange lethargy which held her immobile, leaving her trapped in her own body.

She'd thought it was impossible to drug their kind, but August had found something—some way to do the impossible. Where had he got his hands on a drug which shouldn't exist?

The sharp sound of steel ringing against steel tore her from her meandering thoughts, her face twisting in frustration as she glared up at the ceiling, feeling like a beached whale stretched on its back.

Deacon was good. He was the best swordsman in the Bladed. Byron was... a playboy, she reassured herself.

There was no way Byron could beat Deacon. She was certain of it.

But everything she'd overheard told her August was manipulating Deacon. And he'd made sure there was no way she could warn him.

Maybe if she started small...

She tried to move her fingers. Nothing.

Moved onto her toes. Yet more nothing.

Tears of frustration filled her eyes. Even if she got out of bed, how the hell was she supposed to get down the stairs?

There was a barely detectable snick and as her heart started pounding, Ophelia's gaze shot to her bedroom door, only just visible from the corner of her eye.

Her bedroom door slid open soundlessly. They were still downstairs, Deacon and Byron and August.

So, who was sneaking into her room? Stanley?

No. Not Stanley.

She could only stare as a black-uniformed figure stepped into her room. A Bladed.

Their eyes clashed, and something in his dark eyes, an eye color she'd never seen before—a deeply shadowed indigo, made her heart pound harder. Why was there a Bladed sneaking into her room?

And then he started toward her, his eyes never moving from her face.

The scent of her fear was heavy in the air, bitter, cloying and she was choking on it. But the Bladed didn't react to it, didn't slow his steps.

August had sent the Bladed to kill Selene and Max. Her sister hadn't wanted to tell her, but she'd pushed. Now it made sense what the Bladed was doing here. August had sent him to murder her in her bed.

Tears slid down her face as he came closer. She was begging him to let her go, if he would meet her eyes for even a second, he would read the desperation in them.

He stopped beside her bed, staring down at her. Then his hand dropped to the hilt of his sword.

She fought. Struggling with everything she had. But

she got... nowhere. There was no breaking free, there would be no escape. Tonight was the night she would die.

His sword made no sound as he slid it free from his sheath, and seeing the naked blade, she closed her eyes.

A tear squeezed out between her closed eyelids and slid down the side of her face, as the fight went out of her. It was over. Had been since the Bladed had slipped into her room, only now she accepted it. In her heart, she knew Deacon wasn't walking away from this. And neither, she realized, was she.

Something cool splashed against her lips.

Instinctively, her tongue darted out to touch it. Bitter. Her nose wrinkled, and her eyes cracked open. Was it more of the same drug August had given her coating her tongue? It made little sense unless the Bladed wanted to be sure she couldn't move before he killed her.

The Bladed stared down at her. In his hand was not the sword she'd seen him ease from his sheathe, but a small dark amber medicine bottle. Her eyes went to his sword and saw the top of the hilt was loose—as if he'd unscrewed it. Had he been storing the bottle in the hilt of his sword?

Confusion swirled as her gaze returned to his. As if he'd been waiting for that moment, he leaned over her, and with cool firm fingers, grasped her chin and tugged her mouth open. And then he was pouring more of the clear bitter liquid into her open mouth.

This was... not what she was expecting, and even if she had been, there was nothing she could have done about it.

Seconds passed in terse silence as she studied the

harsh lines of his face, the unusual eyes, and the strange mix of dark and light hair he'd tied back from his face. Who was he?

When no more of the bitter liquid splashed onto her tongue, he drew away from her, sharply and turned to walk away.

Ophelia stared after him.

"Whaa..." her voice was a harsh whisper, but it was there. She could speak.

And was that... was that a tingling she could feel in her feet?

She opened her mouth, and the Bladed paused at her door. Those strange dark indigo eyes narrowed, the first hint of emotion she'd seen on his face since he'd stepped into her room. It was a warning.

Don't speak.

And she realized her mistake, of course, August would hear her. When she closed her mouth, he nodded once, and then he slipped out just as quietly as he'd entered.

Seconds ticked by as movement returned to her body. And through it all, she listened to Deacon and Byron. Heard enough to know Byron was losing, and for now at least August hadn't made his move. For now, at least Deacon was safe and she had time to get to him.

And then she heard Deacon going on the attack. *No, not now. Not yet. Just, wait a little longer.*

She willed herself to stand, but she hadn't recovered yet. Not fully. But when Byron's sword clattered across the floor, she knew she'd run out of time.

For a second, she'd hoped the mystery Bladed would

intervene, but he hadn't. If he was going to do something, he would have done it already. She was on her own.

Rolling herself off the bed, she nearly crashed to the ground. Only her vampire speed saved her, that and a desperate grab of her bed frame, holding on tight until the strength returned to her legs.

If she didn't get down the stairs right now, it would be too late. Everything inside her was screaming in warning, the duel was over, and August would make his move now.

Each step came easier than the last and moving as quietly and quickly as she could, she pulled her door open and started down the stairs, her hands clutching at the banister like a lifeline.

She was halfway down when she heard Deacon's gasp. And then she caught the unmistakable coppery tang of blood in the air. His blood.

Recklessly, she threw herself down the rest of the stairs, tearing across the hall and catching herself on the doorframe before she fell. Getting there just in time to see Deacon, already on his knees, bloody hands clamped over his gut, topple over.

She was screaming. When had she started screaming?

"Really, Ophelia. Is all that noise necessary?" August asked.

Ophelia ignored him. Stumbling into the room, dressed in nothing more than her satin nightdress, she dropped to the floor beside Deacon and gently lifted his head to her lap.

"If you don't stop making that infernal noise," August continued, sounding more bored than anything else.

"You'll force me to make even more of a mess than I already have."

Ophelia looked up at him. Recognized the threat in his words, and saw his hand tighten around the sword in his hand. She forced her screams down her throat until she was near choking, her body trembling with effort.

"Though perhaps," August said, eyeing Deacon coldly, "it might be more of an act of mercy than anything else."

"Father, there's still time for me to get him to a hospital. Please just let me take him, I'm begging you. I've never asked for anything from you. Please, I'll do whatever you want—anything you want."

"I knew there was something—" Byron was speaking, but Ophelia ignored him.

August glanced at him in surprise. "Oh, you're still here? Don't you have a wedding to prepare for?"

"But August, you're not about to—"

"You were embarrassing, Byron. Utterly humiliating in fact. Leave. Now. Before I change my mind about this wedding." August's voice was cold, his lip curled in a sneer. Enough to have Byron striding past Ophelia, his hands clenched into tight fists as he left.

"Father, please. I'll do—"

"You'll do whatever I want regardless. Especially after what you did. Did you think I didn't know what you were up to with the Bladed? Did you think you could run away?"

Deacon's skin was so pale, she could count the thin blue veins spiderwebbing his eyelids. He was always such a bright presence that to see him this weak, terror shot through her. If she didn't get him to the hospital soon, it would be too late. He'd die in her arms just like the woman had.

"He's dying, Father…"

"Sleeping with him?" August continued as if she hadn't interrupted. "I didn't have a problem with that, but telling him about the Council? Betraying me to Knight and the others?" He shook his head, his dark eyes sparkling with rage.

"No. You will get no sympathy from me, Ophelia. You get married in…" He glanced at his wristwatch, "four hours, so get up. We're leaving."

She shook her head, confused. "I don't understand, tonight is the rehearsal. The wedding is tomorrow." August was wrong. He had to be wrong.

Deacon's breath wheezed out of him and her heart leapt in panic, as she clutched him tighter. "Deacon! Deacon!"

His eyes fluttered open. "Go, princess. I love you."

More tears bathed her face. This was goodbye. It couldn't be anything other than a goodbye.

"Ophelia…" In August's voice was a threat.

Her grip on Deacon turned desperate. How was she supposed to let him go? How could she just walk away from him when he was like this?

The answer was that she couldn't and she wouldn't.

"Sire, I will see her to the car." Stanley's sudden presence surprised her, and she glanced up at where he'd appeared in the doorway.

August narrowed his eyes at her. His lips parted, an order already in his eyes.

"There is blood waiting for you in the car, Sire. Fresh blood." Stanley's voice cut through the rising tension.

And just like that, she didn't matter anymore.

After tossing his sword onto the floor, August spun on his heel, making no attempt to hide his eagerness as he stalked toward the front door, snapping out impatiently, "Come, Ophelia."

With August gone, she bent her head to Deacon's forehead. Her heart was being ripped out of her chest, and for a second, she wished she'd never met him.

"Just let me die," she murmured, as tears tracked down her cheeks.

Deacon's hand stroked down her hair and she lifted her head to stare down at him, nearly blinded with tears.

"No," he choked out, blood flecking his lips. "You live. You live for both of us."

"I love you," she burst out. "I love you so much... I can't. Please don't make me live without you." Her voice broke.

The soft smile on Deacon's face was sad, his skin bone white. It wouldn't be long now. She could see the truth of it in his eyes, the acceptance.

"Ophelia." A hand came down on her shoulder and she glanced up.

"Stanley?"

"It's time to go."

Violently, she shook her head. "No... Not yet... No."

"I will see to him." Stanley's brown eyes were sad. It was strange to see it. All her life the old man had been a steady figure, cool—emotionless even. He'd been there when she was born, he'd helped raise her. But it didn't matter now. Deacon was dying. Whether Stanley was sad, or happy, or indifferent was unimportant. Not now.

"I don't want to leave him. I can't," she whispered.

"I was there when you were born, Mistress, and I was there when you were turned. I know what to do. And I have help."

She blinked up at him. What was he talking about? She opened her mouth, the question on her lips.

"*Ophelia!*" It was August outside in the car.

"Now, Ophelia. There isn't much time."

Stanley was right. She desperately didn't want him to be right, but she had to go. If August came back in, she didn't even want to imagine what he would do to Deacon.

Bending, she pressed her lips against Deacon's for the last time. Felt the brush of his fingers in her hair, tasted her tears, and his. Oh god, why was this happening? How could this be happening?

"Ophelia?" Stanley's voice was low with warning. Time was up.

Breaking the kiss, she lifted her head and gently, oh so gently shifted Deacon's head to the floor. His hand fell from her hair, and his heart… oh god, his heart stuttered and slowed.

Standing, Ophelia's legs collapsed beneath her and Stanley caught her, steadied her on her feet.

Then he was leading her out of the room, toward the front door. Away from Deacon. She stopped once, half-turned, but Stanley's grip on her shoulder was firm. He didn't give her a chance to do what she craved with every fiber of her being.

At the front door, Stanley paused, and then he did

something he hadn't done since she was a child. Leaning in close, he gripped the sides of her face and pressed his lips to her forehead in a brief hard kiss.

Stunned, she stared up at him but struggled to shape words in her mind. But before she knew what was happening, he'd pressed her outside and gently closed the door in her face.

It wasn't enough to keep her out. But knowing what August could do, was. She couldn't keep Deacon safe. But she could do something else. She could stop August from hurting anyone else.

Turning, she brushed the tears from her face with the back of her hand as she started for the car waiting for her at the bottom of the front steps. In the back seat, dabbing at his mouth with a white handkerchief was August.

He had to die, and she would be the one to do it.

CHAPTER TWENTY-ONE

*D*eacon would be dead by now.

All the while Ophelia had sat, being assaulted by make-up artists and hairstylists, Deacon had been dying. But hours later they'd left, nodding in satisfaction at their work.

She stared at her reflection in the mirror. Her makeup was perfect. Someone had clipped an antique lace veil to the back of her elaborate styled low bun, and she was wearing a wedding dress worth tens of thousands of dollars. And none of it, absolutely none of it, mattered one bit to her.

Without warning, she tore the delicate lace from her hair and threw it to the floor in the first move she'd made in hours.

Never in her life had she ever worked so hard at forcing emotion in a well deep down inside her. And it had worked. At least until she and August had arrived at the Wynn. By then nothing could contain the explosion she could feel coming.

She hadn't cared about all the attention their arrival had caused. All movement, all life in the lobby of the Wynn had ground to a halt at the sight of her. After all, it couldn't be every day the daughter of a Councilor arrived for her wedding in bare feet and a blood-soaked satin nightdress, with blood-red tears on her cheeks.

Yes, wedding.

As their car had hurtled toward the Strip and crawled through the traffic, August's naked pride had threatened time and time again to wrest away her fierce control over her emotions. He'd laughed out loud at the thought, at the knowledge that she'd had no idea about what he'd been doing. Had not even the faintest inkling he'd moved the date of the wedding forward.

But she wouldn't be marrying Byron today. She wouldn't be marrying anyone.

Once again, her eyes turned to the glass bottle of blood someone had sent to her rooms. A bottle all the hairstylists, the dressers from Vera Wang, and the make-up artists had struggled to ignore. Struggled, but failed. Ophelia had caught the human workers eyeing the bottle with more than a little trepidation.

"A present in celebration of your nuptials by one of your guests," she'd been told by her private hotel servant who'd delivered it with a flourish hours earlier.

The rich blood she scented through the thin glass—a heady mix of adrenaline-filled terror filled her with disgust.

There was only one person who would think to send such a thing—to anyone.

Lucian.

Her fingers itched to launch it across the room. To paint the room red with it. But that wouldn't solve anything. She should have refused it. If she hadn't been so distracted with thoughts of Deacon, she would have.

Somehow, she'd find a way to kill August—a man who had for not one day in her life been a father to her. And after, if he didn't kill her first then she would seek out the sun.

Her heart ached for Selene, but her sister's love wasn't enough for her to cling to life. It hurt too much.

No. Without Deacon, without his amber eyes like liquid gold, grinning down at her, she had no desire to live in a world without him in it, no matter what he'd said.

Selene would be fine. She had Max. They had each other.

At the soft knock on her presidential suite door, her eyes went to the antique clock on the wall of the lounge. The hotel staff had set the dressing table near the windows overlooking the Strip so there'd be plenty of space for stylists to get her ready. Because apparently it took a small army to get someone ready for their wedding.

It was a gorgeous suite. All antique gold and vintage French furniture. But none of its beauty touched her. She could have been in a pay by the hour motel, and her mood would have been the same.

Nine-thirty.

In thirty minutes, she would leave for the hotel lobby via the private escalator where she'd meet August, and from there she'd make her way to the courtyard for her outdoor wedding. At least that was what August had told her.

None of that would happen, of course.

Although she'd locked the door, someone pushed open, uninvited and through the dressing table mirror, Ophelia met the eyes of the Bladed with the deep indigo eyes.

Seconds passed without a word. And when she did nothing more than stare at him, he stepped into the room and closed the door behind him, never taking his eyes from her.

"Why didn't you save him?" she whispered. "You should've saved him not me. Why didn't you?"

"I couldn't." She hadn't expected him to speak, not when before he'd been so silent. But his voice made her pause for only a second, it was low, husky, and with a trace of an accent. What, she couldn't say.

She stood and turned to face him. "But you could have killed him. August. Couldn't you?" Her voice was hard now, demanding.

The Bladed paused, then he nodded, a jerky action that seemed at odds with the graceful way he'd moved earlier.

"Why didn't you? Why did you save me only for me to watch him die?" Her voice shook with the need to shout, to scream.

"There are things—"

"Give me your sword." Her words silenced him.

Stalking toward him, she thrust her hand out. "I said, give me your sword."

He stared at her, unblinking.

A refusal was in his eyes. She could see it there. But

when she opened her mouth, another order on the tip of her tongue, he surprised her by pulling the sword from his sword belt. "Killing is—"

"I don't care about what comes after. All I care about is killing him."

There was a sadness in his eyes as he handed her the sword.

Taking it, the weight of it surprised her. It was lighter than she was expecting, and her hand curved around the hilt automatically. Strange to be with a weapon, she thought. Her. The vampire princess.

"You're holding it too tight. Looser." The Bladed eyed her critically, waiting until she'd changed her grip before he gave her a firm nod.

The sadness in his eyes made little sense to her. Why should he care what happened to her? He was a stranger.

"It shouldn't be you," he said.

That faint trace of an accent again. It sounded a little like Russian, but she couldn't be sure. She shook her head. What did it matter where he was from? Soon enough nothing would matter. At least not to her.

"It has to be someone." Turning, she walked away without another word.

By the time she returned to sit at the dressing table, placing the sword on the table in front of her, her gaze went to the mirror.

The Bladed was gone.

It was five after ten when she heard a key card at the door. August. No one else had a key to her room but him. And she was late. He'd want to know why she was late.

Rising, she picked up the sword and turned to meet him, at the last minute remembering to hold the sword the way the Bladed had shown her.

August stepped in, took one look at the sword in her hand, and started laughing.

"Oh, I see how it is." He laughed. "Is this you putting that plan you all agreed on in place?"

He must have had someone follow her and Deacon. It was the only way for him to know what they were planning. But there wasn't anything she—or any of them could do about it now. The time for talking was over. Now was the time to act. Tightening her hold around the hilt, she raised the sword between them.

Too tight. You're gripping the sword too tight.

"Yes," she said, her voice clear if a little too loud.

He laughed harder as he crossed toward her. Perfectly dressed in his gray and white wedding finery, with a white rose pinned to his jacket pocket, he seemed not to even see the sword aimed at him.

Swallowing hard, she edged back a step as he approached, the sound of her heart a harsh drumbeat in her head. Forced herself not to retreat another step.

What had Selene said? That she was strong, a fighter, and once she found the thing worth fighting for, no one could stand in her way.

Well, Deacon was that thing. He was worth fighting for. She'd give her life fighting for him, and no one would stand in her way. Not even her father.

"Does my living doll think she can kill me—a Councilor?" he mocked her.

She gritted her teeth at the nickname she'd left behind, a name no one had called her in years, at least not to her face. It was a reminder she was nothing more than a pawn, a pretty pawn with no other purpose than to marry who she was told and produce the next Mortlake heir.

Hearing the reminder, the memory of the taunts she'd spent most of her childhood—most of her time in boarding school trying to pretend didn't hurt, opened up a well of pain inside her. Who was she kidding, the pain was just as sharp now as it'd been then.

Where was her strength? Why was everything inside her screaming for her to run and hide?

Without warning, August wrapped his hand around the naked blade and shoved her, hard. Hard enough to send her stumbling back a step and into the velvet stool she'd been sitting on.

Trying to wrench the sword free, only made him tighten his grip on it and grin down at her as if laughing at her for even thinking she could wrestle it from him. Her eyes burned with unshed tears of frustration. Why was she so weak?

"I can smell your fear you know? And it smells delicious." He shoved her back again. Harder this time, letting go of the sword as she staggered back. Behind her, the stool shifted and thumped against the dressing table.

August's eyes were predatory, burning with anticipation. He wanted her to fight. Was excited by the thought of it. Had she finally driven him to the point where he would forget about his need for a Mortlake heir and just kill her?

She was holding the sword too tight, but she didn't care. Technique wasn't important. Results were.

She tried not to notice how much his eyes were like Selene's.

Don't think of that. This man is nothing like Selene. He's nothing like you. He's a monster, and if you don't find the strength to end him right now, he won't just destroy you, he'll go after Selene and Max.

No. He wouldn't hurt Selene. She would not let him hurt her sister.

Back straightening, she planted her feet and met his gaze. She wasn't afraid of him anymore, and she never would be ever again.

At her look of determination, his lip curled in a sneer.

She thrust the sword at his chest. His heart. Amusement lit his eyes as he batted the sword away with one hand as if an afterthought. He was toying with her. Like this was nothing more than a game to him.

Too slow, Ophelia.

Before she could follow her strike with another, August had grabbed hold of the sword and used his full strength to propel her back. Unable to stop herself, she crashed against the dressing table, the back of her head hitting the mirror.

Crying out in pain as the mirror shattered, something crashed to the floor, and then the air was heavy with the coppery tang of blood. Of terror that was not her own.

The bottle of blood.

August's nostrils twitched as his gaze slid from her—

half lying on top of the dressing table, clutching the sword like a lifeline—to the mess beside her. His eyes glazed over as he inhaled loudly, licking his lips.

Ophelia froze as she stared at August. This was it. She had one chance. Only one, and then it would be over.

She whipped the sword up, slashing at a slight angle. Aiming for August's exposed neck. It was both easier and harder than she thought it would be.

Blood splashed onto her face, her dress. Soaking everything.

Closing her eyes at the dull thud, followed half a second later by a much heavier one, she swallowed. Her eyes burned.

Violently, she shook her head. She wouldn't let herself cry. August didn't deserve her tears. Not after what he'd done.

———

The two Bladed standing guard in front of the courtyard doors stepped aside, neither saying nor doing anything to stop her.

Shoving the double doors open, Ophelia stepped out into the courtyard.

A sea of faces swung around to face her. The sound of an organ abruptly cut off, and silence reigned.

There were so many more people than she'd been expecting. No one had told her how many people there would be, and if she were being honest with herself, she hadn't cared enough to ask.

The wedding planner had dealt with all the details.

Her only role in the wedding was to do what she was told. Go here. Look pretty. Be the pretty doll with no thoughts, or wants, or needs other than to please her father.

She didn't recognize any of them, she thought as she scanned the room.

In the wooden pews draped with white roses and festooned with cream ribbons, every seat was filled with elegantly dressed vampires sparkling with jewels. There must be thousands of people. Everyone who was anyone would be here.

"The wedding is off," she said, her voice ringing out sharply. "There's been a death in the family."

Since August had disinherited Selene, it had left only her and August as the last of the Mortlakes. It wouldn't take the wedding guests long to figure out who was dead, and how. If they hadn't already that is.

"Wait just a…" Byron was staring at her in horror as he started down the aisle toward her. His hair was as immaculate as hers had been. His wedding suit, perfectly pressed. Looking for all the world like a perfect gentleman. The perfect husband. Only she knew better. She knew what kind of man he was, and Deacon was worth a thousand of him. A million.

She remembered his part in what had happened to Deacon, and her eyes narrowed. He had told August about her and Deacon, she was sure of it.

Fear bled into his eyes as he jerked to a stop, his gaze dropping to the sword in her hand. The sword still dripped blood. August Mortlake's blood. It didn't take him long to put two and two together.

"Uh, I—" He backed away.

Ignoring him, she reached for the ring on her finger. It slid off her finger as easily as it always had. The ring had never fitted her properly, not that Byron had cared, just as he'd never cared about her. Dropping it on the floor, she turned and stalked out.

Before she could push the door open, it swung open and the Bladed, their eyes hidden behind dark glasses, though she felt their attention as she strode past them. And then she was crossing the lobby, heading for the exit, conscious people had once again stopped to stare at the Councilor's daughter wearing a wedding dress soaked in blood, carrying a bloody sword.

Outside the hotel, the enormity of what she'd done hit her, and she jerked to a sudden stop.

August was dead. She was free. Free now to be with Deacon. She'd go to Desert Pines and curl up in the white dune where she'd taken a chance on a future with Deacon. There she would wait for sunrise. Alone.

Surprised to find her eyes had filled with tears, she blinked them away.

"Ophelia?"

"No." She was already shaking her head as she retreated from Selene stepping out of the back of a car idling outside the hotel. She caught a flash of bright green and hot pink from inside the car. Max in another of his loud board shorts.

Seeing the look on Selene's face, she took another step

back. "I'm not…" Her eyes filling with more tears, and she shook her head sharply. "No."

Her sister's expression was full of anguish. "Fifi?"

"I can't, Selene. Don't ask me to, it's too hard," she said, her voice breaking.

Selene held a hand out to her. "Please, I—" Her eyes shifted over her shoulder and her expression hardened.

Ophelia turned. Saw Mr. Knight crossing the lobby toward them, his eyes fixed on her with a burning intensity.

"Come with me, sis," Selene said.

She had no choice now, not with Mr. Knight right there. There was no way she could face anyone. Least of all a Councilor. Taking Selene's hand, she slipped into the car, slamming the door shut behind her as Selene ordered the driver to take them home.

Her gaze remained locked on Mr. Knight staring after them. Would he come after them? Kill her for what she'd done? She didn't have it in her heart to care. Not when all she wanted to do was close her eyes and never open them ever again. Pressing her forehead against the window, she fought back tears.

"Princess?"

Her heart stopped. Was that…? No. He was dead.

Shaking her head, her words came out in a whisper, "I don't know what game you're playing Selene, but it's cruel."

"Ophelia." There was a wealth of pain in Selene's voice, but Ophelia didn't dare turn and face her.

Instead, she kept her gaze trained on the window. On the tourists and vampires alike milling about on the Strip, their lives going on as normal in a way hers never could. Or would.

"And here I thought you'd always know me, *tesoro mio.*" Amusement softened the voice of the man who wasn't—who couldn't be Deacon. Even if he did know his nickname for her. It couldn't be him. It was impossible.

She squeezed her eyes closed, tight. So tight strange lights danced behind her eyelids, her body trembling so hard the sword slipped out of her hand and tumbled to the floor.

This was madness. She was losing her mind with grief, she thought, raising her hand to rub at her temple.

She went hot, and then cold at the light touch on her hand as someone—Selene tugged her hand away from her forehead. And then something was being pushed onto her finger. On her wedding finger.

Tearing her hand free, she wrenched her eyes open and stared down at her hand. At the ring on it. She stared at it for a long time before she could make sense of what she was seeing.

Deacon's engagement ring was on her finger. It fit her perfectly, as if he'd measured her finger when she knew he hadn't. As if it'd always been there. A part of her.

Instinctively her other hand reached for her neck, searching for the necklace Deacon had hung there the night before. But her neck was bare. How hadn't she noticed?

"Stanley said he found it. I thought you'd want it back," Deacon said.

Tears slid down her cheeks as she forced herself to lift

her head, to turn to the figure beside her. The figure she'd assumed was Max.

"Deacon?"

He looked weak, his cheeks hollow and pale in a white t-shirt and loud lime green board shorts with hot pink cats printed on them, his hair hanging loose around his face. He was wearing Max's clothes, not in the black-on-black she'd never seen him without. No wonder she'd mistaken him for Max.

He was alive. Or rather he was… "Turned." She clapped a hand over her mouth, to silence her choked cry of despair.

Deacon's face fell at the sound, and he started toward her. Frantically, she backed up against the window, holding a shaking hand between them.

He stopped at once. "Princess?" Hurt laced his voice. He thought she was rejecting him but he couldn't be further from the truth.

"This isn't what you wanted. You didn't want this. Selene…" She turned to her sister who sat watching them in silence, her face bathed in tears.

"What I wanted," Deacon said, drawing her gaze back to him, "what I've always wanted—needed, is you. This…" He glanced down at himself. "This is nothing if I can't have you."

She didn't remember moving.

One second, she was staring at him with the hand clamped over her mouth the only thing holding her cries back. The next she was in his lap, her face pressed against his neck, breathed in the scent that was him and him alone, his arms wrapped tight around her, so tight it was painful.

Desperate.

But it didn't matter how tight he was holding her, because she knew—was certain she was clinging to him even tighter.

CHAPTER TWENTY-TWO

They'd been moving every few days for weeks now, conscious that Mr. Knight couldn't be far behind. They were being followed. Had been, since Selene had taken them to Deacon's car and Ophelia had driven them out of Vegas.

She'd killed a Councilor, and the only punishment for what she'd done was death.

But for the first few days, the first few weeks none of it had mattered. All she cared about was that impossibly she had Deacon back. She had her heart back. And it was all thanks to Stanley who'd managed to keep Deacon alive long enough for Selene and Max to come and turn him.

It'd been close. Closer than her sister wanted to admit, even now. But they'd got to him in time, had exchanged blood with him, and shut down his heart to give the vampire pathogen a chance to heal his mortal wounds.

New vampires needed hours, often days of sleeping to regain their strength depleted by their mortal death, and

Ophelia had shouted at her sister for waking Deacon so soon after his turning.

Selene told her part of the reason he'd been so easy to wake was because she and Max had shared blood with him, giving Deacon the strength of two vampires to draw from. Which also, incidentally, meant neither of them was Deacon's Master. The Master-Childe bond which usually snapped into place after a turning miraculously hadn't happened and Selene guessed it was because no vampire could have two Masters.

"But you had to see him, Fee, you had to know he was alive. I saw how you two looked at each other. I knew what you would have done."

Ophelia had fallen silent. There was nothing she could say to that.

Clutching their newest disposable phone tight in one hand, her eyes went to the man she loved with every fiber of her being who'd woken while she was on the phone with Selene, and who watched her with amber eyes carefully neutral. But there was pain there. Hurt. Knowledge if Selene hadn't got to her in time, she'd be dead.

Then he'd held a hand out to her, and she was hanging up the phone and running to him, pressing her face into his chest. Crying. Again. She did a lot of that those first few nights.

"Shh," he soothed her, his hand stroking down her back. "I'm here. It's okay, I'm right here."

It eased something inside her to hear him say it. Like something tight in her chest was being soothed, relaxed. Like she could breathe.

"Can we go to bed?" she'd whisper.

He lifted her, as he always did, and carried her up to bed, loving her with his hands, his mouth, before he slid inside her, and then she knew. Really knew he was there, with her. That this was real.

And then later it was her turn to touch him, to kiss him, to drive him crazy when she took him in her mouth. She couldn't get enough of him. Would never tire of the silky-hard feel of him. In her hand. Her mouth. The scent of his skin. The feel of his hands combing through her hair as he thrust helplessly into her mouth.

She taught him how to feed, and that was about all she had to teach him. He regained his strength with every feeding. Everything else came so easily to him, it was as if he'd been born to it. And when he wielded a sword now... she'd never seen anything like it.

One of her favorite things to do was sit with her arms wrapped around her raised knees as she watched him practice in their apartment, with the furniture shoved against the wall.

He was so beautiful, with his long golden hair hanging loose, wearing nothing but a pair of sweatpants riding low on his hips. And after, when he was hot and sweaty from practice, and she was hot and sweaty from watching him, he'd scoop her into his arms and carry her to their bed.

———

"Ophelia." The call, when it came, didn't surprise her. A part of her had been waiting for it for hours, days, weeks.

Sitting up, she reached for her robe on the chair beside

their bed. It wasn't the silk she'd known all her life, but a cheap cotton robe they'd picked up in Walmart after they'd left Vegas. It was comfortable and it was hers in a way nothing else ever had been before.

She'd become so attached to this first purchase she'd made with the envelope stuffed with bills Selene had pressed into her hand, she couldn't bring herself to part with it.

Her eyes landed on Deacon lying still in the bed beside her. He wasn't her sun-god any longer, but he was still so beautiful to her, she was tempted to crawl back into bed with him and for them to never leave their tiny one-bedroom apartment.

But at just after sunset, she didn't have long before Deacon would wake. And once he woke, he would never let her face the man waiting for her on her own.

He was waiting for her on the top step of her and Deacon's apartment in the Bronx.

Crossing her arms over her chest, she studied him from the door of the building, wondering why he hadn't forced the lock. He hadn't needed to call her to him. Not Mr. Knight, not a Councilor on the Vampire Council.

"What do you want?"

The sound of a police siren cut through the air, shrill and overly loud in her ears. She winced. But Mr. Knight merely stood and watched her, completely without expression.

"You look different," he said.

She touched her hair, a rough knot at the top of her head she'd thrown up before stuffing her feet into some slippers and rushing down the stairs. Strands of hair hung about her face, and she didn't need a mirror to tell her it was messy. That she was messy.

Refusing to be embarrassed, she shrugged. "Appearances aren't everything."

He continued to study her. "No, that's not what I meant."

It took her a second to work out what he meant. And then it hit her. She was physically blocking the door from Mr. Knight. Treating him as if he were a threat, and one she would face down without hesitation.

But Deacon was sleeping upstairs, and that made him vulnerable. Councilor or no Councilor, she wasn't about to let anyone hurt Deacon. Not again.

His eyes flashed, and though his expression didn't change, she had the sense he was laughing at her. No. Not laughing, but amused by her protectiveness.

"It's been a crazy year," she admitted, her voice dry.

"I can well imagine."

They fell to silence then, him staring at her, and her staring right back, waiting for him to get to the point.

"You've been difficult to pin down," he said, once the siren had faded away. There'd be another one soon, Ophelia thought with a mental sigh, there seemed to always be sirens in the Bronx.

She was used to the quiet of life in the enclave high above Vegas, and it was taking a lot longer than she thought it would to get used to all the noise. But she was getting there—she would get there.

"With all your resources, I highly doubt that." Deacon would wake soon, and if he found her gone, he'd be down in a second. She didn't want to think about Deacon and Mr. Knight fighting, especially with Deacon still so new a vampire. It made her anxious.

"Your actions caught the attention of more than a few interested parties."

Ophelia narrowed her eyes. The Council. Was he talking about the Council?

"I'm not interested in anything you have to say. All Deacon and I want is to be left alone."

Mr. Knight shrugged. "I can understand that given everything August did. But," he paused here to eye her closely, "his… absence has left a… how shall I say it? A void, if you will."

Now it was making sense.

"And you want me—a Mortlake to fill it. Any old Mortlake will do, I take it?"

"That's not the only reason you'd make an ideal candidate, Mistress—"

"Don't call me that," she snapped, her gaze searching the quiet streets. Other than a black car parked up the road, presumably Mr. Knight's driver, no one was around. Which wasn't a surprise.

It was winter and the nights closed in early, but soon enough people would return from work or be heading out for a night in the city, and their conversation wouldn't stay private for long.

"You did something no one else could or would do."

"Selene told me about you." Her face hardened as she met Mr. Knight's eyes. "She told me she went to see you

307

and you didn't care about anything but playing your games."

His small dark eyes turned wily. "Perhaps I realized how things would end. Perhaps I was waiting for the endgame to play out before I made my move."

"You mean you guessed I would… I would do what I did?" Her tone was disbelieving, even as she avoided saying out loud what she'd done. Despite not regretting her actions, the memory of it still haunted her.

"Perhaps I saw something no one else did."

"Perhaps, perhaps, perhaps. Bullshit."

He blinked at her in surprise. It wasn't hard to gauge from his reaction he wasn't used to being spoken to like that. But she was learning to enjoy being blunt.

"Regardless of what you think, I come to you with an offer. From all of us. Well… a majority."

She narrowed her eyes. "No, thanks. Find another Mortlake."

"Why not?" he asked. "You've proven yourself more than capable of doing what needs doing."

"You just want someone to stick in front of the camera. Someone to answer the reporter's questions while the rest of you stay safely tucked away in case the world ever turns on us."

"Now, that arrangement was only ever intended to be a temporary measure. You know—first-hand about the attempts to hunt us. In time it might be safe for us to identify ourselves, but right now it would not be… prudent."

He was telling the truth, at least about this, she thought. There had been more than a few attempts to unearth the identities of the Councilors and wipe them out. Some, she and Selene had learned about when August had been the focus of attack by anti-vampire elements in the city after they'd claimed Vegas.

"So, you *do* intend to step out into the open, then? When?"

Mr. Knight didn't answer, instead, he reached into his pocket and retrieved a small black card. He didn't give her a chance to refuse it. Instead, he held it out toward her with a look on his face that told her he was prepared to wait forever.

Sighing, she took it reluctantly, watching as he turned and started down the stairs, his hands folded behind his back.

"This doesn't mean I'm agreeing to anything," she called after him.

"Think about it. Oh, and Ophelia." He paused, half-turned. "Deacon has nothing to fear from me. He was able to save my life some time ago. In fact, it was I who recommended him to… well, I don't think I need to say who, do I?"

Deacon had saved the life of a Councilor? And he hadn't told her? He had so much explaining to do, it was unreal, she thought as Mr. Knight climbed into the parked car before her eyes dropped to the black card in her hand.

It was thick, heavily embossed and it had no other detail on it but a single cell phone number.

How very cloak and dagger, she thought, turning it over in her hand.

A sudden awareness of being observed had her head

jerking up, her eyes searching in the darkness for a presence she couldn't see but could feel.

Her head told her no one was there. But her instincts were crying out that it was him. The Bladed. The one Deacon was sure hadn't been a Bladed at all. Had it been him watching her? Had he come to reclaim the sword she'd taken but never returned?

Her eyes scored the empty streets, seeing nothing, hearing even less.

"Princess? Where are you?" Three floors up and his voice was as clear to her as if he'd been standing right next to her.

Deacon. He was awake. Turning her back on the eyes that continued to watch her, she climbed the stairs up to their apartment. She'd tell him about meeting Mr. Knight and see what he made of it. And then they'd make love as they did after every rising. The thought was enough to have a smile of anticipation stretching across her face as she hurried up the stairs.

He was still in bed, his head resting on the headboard, one leg cocked.

"Hey," she said, closing the bedroom door behind her and leaning against it.

His eyes raked over her. "You okay?"

There was something in his eyes, some knowledge she hadn't been expecting. "You were awake all along. You were listening."

Shrugging, he ran a hand through his hair. "You've

been tense for a while. I figured it'd happen sometime soon, it was only a matter of time."

Her mouth gaped open in surprise. "And you let me go. Alone?"

A smile teased his lips. "I figured you could take care of yourself. What with you having already taken one Councilor down on your own, so…"

She threw the card at him.

Lightening quick his hand flashed out and caught it. After briefly scanning the card, he dropped it on the bedside table before turning his attention back to her. "So, what do you want to do?"

She could see in his eyes he was leaving it up to her to decide. They'd talk about it. Weigh up the risks, but ultimately it was up to her. But Deacon had made it clear they were a team now. A partnership. And together they would be stronger for it.

They could keep moving around, trying to avoid their kin and the vampire politics, and likely the reporters who would figure out the disappearance of August Mortlake occurred around the same time his daughter had been seen wandering the Wynn hotel with a bloody sword in hand. Or she could say yes to Mr. Knight and return to Vegas. But a full-on disappearance wasn't realistic. Not forever at least.

Ophelia shrugged. "I don't know."

"There's no Mortlake on the Council, and the world hasn't ended yet."

"I wouldn't be so sure about that," she muttered.

Deacon's gaze sharpened. "What is it?"

"Something Selene hinted at a while back, about the Bladed. There are... problems there."

Deacon didn't look surprised.

"You knew about it?"

"Pierce mentioned something wasn't right."

She eyed him in silence but couldn't read him. "You think we should go back. You think things are about to happen, don't you?"

He shrugged. "I think you should do what will make you happy."

"You said you were going to take me somewhere with a beach."

"And I will. I think I've had about enough of New York," he said, wincing as a car roared down the street outside their apartment.

Then her hands went to the belt of her robe, and Deacon sat up straighter in bed, his eyes locked on her hands. "But right now, I was kind of hoping..." She shrugged out of the robe, dropping it on the floor and reaching up, released her hair from her messy updo. "That you'd tell me about how you saved Mr. Knight's life."

Deacon's eyes lifted from her body and moved to her face. He was wearing a dazed look on his face. The same look he always wore when he saw her naked body. Stunned amazement. As if he was seeing her for the first time.

"Huh?"

Placing her knee on the end of the bed, she met his eyes. "Knight. You know, you saving his life."

Without warning, he caught the edge of the cover and whipped it off him. Leaving himself as naked as she was.

It was her turn to pause as her eyes locked on his arousal. He was hard already. His erection making her ache for him to fill her.

And distracted, that was when he pounced, and before she could take a breath, she lay naked beneath Deacon with him grinning down at her.

"You're too easy to distract, you know. One look at my c—"

Clapping her hand against his mouth, she rolled until she sat astride him. His body shook with smothered laughter before he peeled her hand away from his mouth. "I believe that fancy boarding school education has turned you into a prude."

Her face flushed hot. "I am *not*. I just don't want to hear you say…" her voice trailed off as he continued to watch her, his eyes laughing.

"No, please. Finish the sentence, princess, I can wait." Suiting actions to words, he folded his hands behind his head and grinned up at her.

He looked happy. He sounded happy, but what if…

"Deacon?"

"Oh no, I know what that tone means." He had her underneath him in a second, his weight braced on his hands above her head.

"I'm being serious." She gazed up at him, her eyes searching his face for any sign of doubt.

"I'm happy. You know I am, just as I know you are. Believe it."

"But you lost everything because of me. The sun, your job… your family—who no doubt hates me for—"

His kiss, hot and hard silenced her.

When he lifted his head, his eyes were tender. Warm. With the smile, she'd claimed as hers and hers alone. A smile she couldn't live without.

"The sun is overrated, I hated my job, and my family... my family loves you. How could anyone not, *tesoro mio?*"

As always, she melted at his nickname for her, and she shifted beneath him, restless, hungry for him. She looked him right in the eye. "Deacon?"

He bent his head to kiss her. "Mmm."

"Tell me again."

"I love you, *tesoro mio.* More than the sun, my sword. Even more than my c—"

Laughing, she pulled his head down and kissed him.

EPILOGUE

*T*hey watched the couple swaying together on the dancefloor.

But they weren't the only ones transfixed by the sight.

All around them, everyone else at Eros had abandoned their attempts to look uninterested as they stared. Even the older vampires. The ones with little else to excite them were looking a little less bored than usual.

As if they didn't feel the eyes of everyone on them, the blond man with his long hair tied back at the nape of his neck, bent to brush his lips against his partner's in such a soft, lingering kiss that seeing it, Selene sighed and rested her head against Max's shoulder.

"They're so perfect together."

Max's hand curled around her waist and tugged her closer.

"You make it sound like we're not," he grumbled.

She smiled up at him. "I didn't say that. It's just it's Fifi."

Max's eyes were laughing as he bent to press his lips

against her forehead. "You realize you're going to have to stop calling her that now."

"Maybe in public," she agreed with a shrug.

"You're impossible."

"But that's why you love me." Wrapping her arms around him, she nestled her body against his, sighing in contentment.

As always, every night she couldn't believe how good it felt, how perfectly they fit against each other as if they'd been made for each other.

"Is it? And here I thought it was because of those luscious—"

"If you finish that sentence Maxwell Brennan, you will not like what I do to you," she threatened.

He grinned down at her, looking like the quintessential surfer boy, even though she'd managed on this rare occasion to get him out of his board shorts and t-shirt and into a suit. But she knew better. He was more, much more than the shaggy blond-haired, blue-eyed surfer from California. He was her world.

"Mmm, I love it when you say things like that."

Shaking her head, she turned her gaze back to Ophelia.

"This new life will not be a safe one for her. Or easy," Max said.

Ophelia was still young, still with a lot to learn. In the soft ivory gown that draped over her slender form, she looked delicate and vulnerable.

Selene's smile faded. Max was right and it terrified her. Her little sister was standing in the jaws of danger, a sister she'd practically raised.

"She'll change things," she murmured as she watched them. "The Council have only ever cared about looking after their own interests. But Fee won't stand for that. Not any longer."

"Well," Max said, his arms tightening around her. Recognizing her fear and trying to comfort her. "It can't hurt her having the best swordsman in Vegas as her husband, can it?"

Her smile returned as she leaned her head against Max's shoulder. Her sister looked beautiful in a simple, but elegant wedding dress and the tall heavily muscled blond man with a black sword strapped around his waist held her protectively—tenderly.

As a human Bladed, his skill with the sword had been unlike anything anyone had ever seen. He'd been a prodigy. But as a vampire… well. Only a fool would even think they had a chance at silencing the voice of his new wife, and the newest Councilor.

"But she's no pushover either," she murmured.

"And they have us," Max added.

Selene nodded. "Yes."

For a second, her gaze connected with those of a Bladed with shaved hair and unusual pale eyes, a mix of hazel with gray flecks staring at her from across the room, before he turned and slipped through the crowd. Disappearing from view.

Selene turned to grin at her sister before sharing a brief smile with Deacon, who shook his head, as if he couldn't believe what they were talking about in the middle of Eros. But she didn't care. If nothing else, it would serve as a warning.

But tonight belonged to Ophelia. Because today her beloved little sister had married the man she loved.

"They do."

To continue the Bladed series
JULIAN is available to pre-order.
Grab your copy here!

EXCERPT OF COLD-BLOODED ALPHA

*M*y bare knees sink into soil still damp from last night's rain, and the touch of the moon on my back is like a soft kiss. Cool, but welcome. And even though my wolf is strangely silent, I know the moon soothes her as it always has me.

Opening my eyes, I stare down at the space between my hands, my shoulder-length hair forming a shield between me and the sharp gazes that surround me— surround us. My new mate, Dayne and I.

It's over now. Done. Yet I don't move, and neither does he. Instead, he curves the long line of his body over mine, and a hot muscled arm settles between my bare breasts as he buries his face in the joint of my neck and shoulders. His hot breath has tension coiling, anticipation thrumming through me.

But he doesn't do what I'm expecting. He doesn't bite me. Just holds me, as he works to steady his harsh breaths in the aftermath of our joining.

He's not alone in fighting for breath in this midnight

darkness, as smoky-white tendrils of airy lighted breath stir around us like spirits.

I can't quite believe this is real. Any of it.

My first time, with anyone, and it's at my moon-blessing ceremony in front of my pack, and with a virtual stranger.

If uncle had been kind, he'd have let Dayne and I meet before the ceremony so we could get to know each other a little beforehand. Then, I could've told him I'd only ever played with the boys in my pack. I'd certainly never gone any further than that.

But no one could ever accuse Uncle Glynn of being kind, least of all to me.

I shift restlessly, unable to silence the rising tension Dayne has awakened, a fierce need I'm desperate for him to satisfy. Only I can't speak, or rather I don't dare to.

Making demands of anyone has only gotten me a slap, or worse. Usually worse.

So, while Dayne found his release, I don't dare to ask for more.

I have a mate now. That should be enough, and I can finally leave. Wanting more is just being greedy.

When the pack throws their head back in a howl to mark the joining of a newly mated pair, startled, I jerk my head up. For the first time my face is no longer obscured by layers of dark-brown hair.

Dayne takes it as a sign the ceremony is over and jerks to his feet so fast I'm not expecting it, nor am I prepared for his sudden absence. Which is when I realize he was the only thing keeping me upright. Without the strength of his arms around me, the muscles in my arms give out and I slump to the ground, at the last possible second stopping myself from face planting.

Great Talis. In front of the pack. In front of Dayne. Just fucking great.

But Dayne isn't paying the least bit of attention to me or to my watching pack. No. Out of the corner of my eye I observe him stalking away, toward the heavily wooded forests, and the pack's house a couple of minutes walk away. Head proudly tossed back, completely uncaring of his nudity.

"Say your goodbyes. We leave tonight," Dayne announces in his low rumbling voice, just shy of a growl, before the thick forests swallow up his tall muscled figure and he disappears from view.

Struggling to my feet on shaking knees, all I'm conscious of is that I'm naked while all around me my pack have the benefit of their wolf shape to preserve their modesty. With not even a second going by before the hot flush of embarrassment is staining my cheeks.

We shifters aren't usually so embarrassed by sex or nakedness since it's part of who we are. Changing shape means there will always be a time before we shift, and just after when others will see our naked form. Except me. I don't change shape anymore. It's not safe. For anyone, least of all for me.

It takes everything I have to not rush over and snatch up my white silk robe from the ground. Instead, I force myself to appear nonchalant as I casually stride over to the material lying neglected between me and the wolves who stare with eyes that glitter silver in the night.

Former pack, I correct myself. After tonight they will be my pack no longer.

Bending down to retrieve it, a bare foot beats my fingers by a hairbreadth. Disbelieving I stare at it. I would recognize that foot anywhere.

Lifting my head, I meet my uncle's eyes. They glitter with malice.

So, nothing new there then.

"You'll have to do better than that," he smirks, "If you want to keep a hold of your new mate."

I flinch at the stinging lash of my uncle's words, since I can hardly ignore the fact that seconds after our mating ceremony, my new mate is stalking away from me without a single backward glance.

The barbs that hurt the most, the ones I can never shake free are always the ones mired with truth.

"Yes, Uncle," I murmur.

"Alpha!" he snaps, inching forward.

Crossing my arms over my chest, I ease back a step, forcing my eyes from his and to the ground.

The rest of the pack are watching me. They've mostly all changed back to human now. All except the submissives and those lower down in the pack hierarchy since it takes them much longer than the mere seconds it takes my uncle—and Alpha to shift.

Predatory anticipation fills the air as they wait to see what my uncle will do to me this time. How will he punish me for whatever preconceived wrong or slight I've done?

With Dayne's declaration we're leaving tonight—now, he's snatched any opportunity for my uncle to strike out at me one last time. If he wants to do anything to me, it has to be now.

"Yes, Alpha," I tell the foot he still has on my robe.

His hand comes from nowhere, and suddenly I'm choking, my fingers scrabbling at his tight grip around my neck.

I go from standing to balancing on the very tip of my toes in a heartbeat as he forces my heels from the ground. "Is that mockery I hear?"

Since I'm struggling to breathe, there's no way I can answer him. All I can do is hope he either drops me soon, or my new mate comes back. But what he'll do, I don't know. The idea of Dayne Blackshaw saving anyone least of all me is ludicrous.

"Answer me!" Uncle snaps as if I'm able to speak a single word at all.

Desperately, I shake my head no.

The sound that emerges from my throat is barely a gasp, and the edge of my vision is darkening as I sink into unconsciousness. Since this isn't the first time for it to happen, I can read the signs before anyone.

"Is there a problem?"

THANK YOU

Thank you so much for you picking up Deacon.

If you'd like to never miss a new release, and pick up your subscriber exclusive story The Lottery, you can keep updated by joining my mailing list here: www. evebale.com/newsletter

You can also "like" my Facebook page at: www.facebook.com/AuthorEveBale

As a new indie author, reviews mean a lot. So, if you enjoyed Deacon and would like to share that with other readers, it would mean the world to me if you'd leave a review.

XOXO